GW00746304

SOLACE
OF
WAR

To Brenda & Walker
with love

Shirley
x

SOLACE OF WAR

SHIRLEY W DIXON

SHUTLINGSLOE PUBLISHING

Copyright © 2016 – Shirley W Dixon

First published in Great Britain in 2016

Published by
Shutlingsloe Publishing
101 Loxwood Avenue
Worthing
West Sussex
BN14 7RD

shirleywdixon@outlook.com

All rights reserved. No part of this publication may be reproduced, stored
in a retrieval system or transmitted in any form or by any means without
prior written permission, nor be otherwise circulated in any form of
binding or cover other than that in which it is published and without a
similar condition being imposed on the subsequent purchaser.

A catalogue record for this book is available from the British Library

ISBN: 978-0-9927278-1-9

Book design and typesetting by Ashdown Creative
www.ashdowncreative.co.uk

Cover photographs © Fotolia.com

This is a work of fiction. Names and characters are the product of the
author's imagination, and any resemblance to actual persons living or
dead is entirely coincidental.

I dedicate this book to my dear husband Frank –
who sadly did not live to see its completion; my loving
daughter Elizabeth and son-in-law Philip, and precious
grandchildren George and Rebecca.

Grateful thanks to my extended family and friends, who have encouraged me over several years; the Patton Appreciation Society; Andy Ashdown for the book cover and layout and Alexa Tewkesbury for proofreading.

CHAPTER 1

When the war ended in 1945 there was great relief
and rejoicing. But for some, it would be many years before
life-changing repercussions were resolved.

SEPTEMBER 1977

THE COTTAGE SMELT DAMP and there was an air of
mournful loneliness. Katherine stood forlornly in the middle
of the square, oak-beamed sitting room. The warm sunlight
streaming through the lattice windows did nothing to thaw the
chill in her heart. *Why* had her mother died so young? Angry
tears rolled down her pale cheeks. She hadn't been able to cry
until now – not even at the funeral. She'd felt guilty for that and
for not being with her mother at the end. Delayed at the *Argus*,
she'd missed their regular Wednesday evening meal. The knot
tightened in her stomach and she averted her eyes from the
armchair where her mother had suffered a fatal heart attack.

Her death had been completely unexpected. She'd appeared

to be perfectly healthy – apart from the smoking habit that she'd never been able to curb.

Evelyn put a reassuring arm around her niece's slim shoulders. 'I'll make a cup of tea and light the fire before you start sorting out Nancy's clothes,' she said, gently stroking Katherine's tumbling red hair that she'd inherited from her mother. 'I still can't believe she's gone. Fifty-two's no age, is it? So unfair! I expect her to walk into the room at any moment,' she said, as tears rolled down her flushed, apple cheeks.

She pulled a pristine, white handkerchief from the pocket of her hand-knitted lilac cardigan, took off her gold-rimmed spectacles and dabbed at her eyes. 'It's so sad that she'll never see you married now, Kathy. She so wanted you to settle down with Alex,' she added, choking back the tears. 'Nancy really thought he was the man for you. You have so much in common – working together on the paper.'

Katherine threw her arms around her and kissed her tenderly on her damp cheek. They clung together, the silence punctuated by the ticking of the grandfather clock that had marked time for Katherine until she'd left home for university. She shivered involuntarily.

Evelyn released her niece and blew her nose hard. 'I'll get that fire going, make the tea to warm you up… and I'll put a drop of whisky in it. You look so pale, Kathy, I don't want you getting a cold on top of everything else.'

Katherine kicked off her loafers and sank down into the settee's deep, rose-patterned cushions. Stretching out her long, jean-clad legs, she thrust her cold fingers into the pockets of her cream fleece. It wasn't the chill of the room that had made her shiver – the emotions she'd held in check had finally caught up with her. She watched as her aunt put a match to the rolled-up newspaper spills, on top of which the logs nestled in the red brick ingle-nook fireplace.

'Won't be long before the place gets warmed up,' Evelyn said, throwing Katherine a cheery smile as she bustled off to the kitchen across the hall.

Katherine reached out and pulled one of her mother's tapestry cushions to her. Hugging it tightly, she listened to her aunt opening the cupboard to bring out the cups and saucers – and the Jasper Wedgwood biscuit barrel that made her eyes sparkle at the prospect of a treat when she was a child. Dear Aunt Evelyn, she was like a second mother to her and, until his death five years ago, Ted had been the father figure in her life. Her brow furrowed. Much as she'd adored her uncle, all her life she'd fantasized about her real father who, her mother had told her, was a soldier killed in the war in 1944 before she was born.

Katherine pushed the thoughts of her father from her mind and closed her eyes, shutting out the vision of her mother's chair. Should she keep it – a constant reminder of her death? Could she part with it? It had been her mother's favourite chair, where she'd sat for hours knitting, working her patchwork and tapestry, and listening to the radio.

Melancholy descended upon her again with the realisation that there would be no more happy times in this room. She was alone in the world now, apart from Aunt Evelyn.

Katherine had never known her grandparents. They'd been killed in a bombing raid on Stoke-on-Trent in 1940. Her mother had miraculously survived virtually unscathed. Evelyn and Ted had taken sixteen-year-old Nancy into their home in the small village of Lower Peover, in the comparative safety of rural Cheshire.

Evelyn had met Ted at a dance in the King's Hall, Stoke. It had, she'd told Katherine many times, been love at first sight. Ted and his friends had made their first foray into city life on an outing from the village to the dance hall. And he would confirm that Evelyn had caught his eye as soon as he'd set foot in the ballroom. 'Pretty as a picture in her Alice blue gown!' Within the year he'd popped the question and Evelyn had not hesitated to accept his proposal. She'd left the city and her job as a free-hand figurine paintress at the prestigious Doulton Factory to marry Ted, a gardener at Toft Hall. It had been heart-wrenching to leave her parents and Nancy. Although Nancy was ten years younger, they'd had a very close relationship – made closer by the tragic death of their parents.

Nancy, who'd worked as a paintress at a rival pottery manufacturers, once settled in with Evelyn and Ted, took a job at a florist's in nearby Knutsford – the genteel town famed as the setting for Mrs Gaskell's novel, *Cranford*. They'd supported Nancy when she became pregnant, and when Katherine was born in 1945, Evelyn generously gave her own share of their parents' legacy to her, to purchase Apple Tree Cottage –

Katherine's home until she'd gone to university to fulfill her dream of becoming a journalist.

They'd all been overjoyed for Katherine when she secured a job as a cub reporter on the *Manchester Argus* – and pleased she would not be too many miles away, having taken a mortgage on a small flat in trendy Didsbury.

Katherine glanced at the photograph standing on the well-polished Welsh dresser. Taken two years ago on her thirtieth birthday, she was surrounded by her colleagues on the *Argus*, glasses of champagne raised, a beaming Alex – the news editor she'd been dating for a year – presenting her with a mock-up of the front page headlined, KATHERINE'S BIG 'O'.

Her job on the *Argus* was fulfilling – too fulfilling for her to ever contemplate giving it up lightly to get married. She'd had a fling or two at university, but none of her past relationships had been serious enough to sacrifice her career over. Now, however, with Alex, they had so much in common that she might say yes if he deigned to propose!

Her friends, scattered around the country, were all happily married with children. Katherine didn't like to admit it, but there were moments when she did feel envious of their very different lifestyles. She adored their children and was godmother to several. They had given up asking when she was going to settle down – while reminding her from time to time that her childbearing body clock was ticking away! They approved wholeheartedly of Alex, who they thought was dashing and charismatic, a promising candidate for marriage

– and Katherine endorsed their sentiments. Alex was tall and handsome, in a rugged, homely way, and he'd certainly made a big impression when he joined the *Argus*.

He'd arrived, a disillusioned national reporter from the bright lights of London to take on the job of news editor on the busy weekly. His first few weeks had been difficult for him. Some of the staff who thought they were in line for the news editor's chair had given him a rough ride. Others, canny and wary of the ways of a top-notcher from Fleet Street, had gone about their business matter-of-factly, accepting whatever assignments Alex dished out. But, very quickly, his competent, easygoing, jovial nature won their support and respect and – eventually – Katherine's affection.

The break-up of his childless marriage he'd attributed to his hectic, anti-social working hours in the metropolis. Now, at the *Argus*, he was relaxed and enjoying life.

At first, Katherine's mother had not wholly approved of her seeing a divorced man, but Alex's charm had won her over. A feeling of desolation washed over Katherine at the thought that, if she did marry Alex, her mother would not be there to share her happiness. And there would be *no* father to give her away.

As Evelyn returned to the sitting room carrying a tray of tea and biscuits, Katherine's tears surfaced. Evelyn put the tray down on the oak refectory table, hurried across the room and dropped down beside her.

'Let it all out, dear,' she said, taking her into her arms.

Katherine laid her head on her aunt's ample bosom.

'Sorry, I know it's just as difficult for you ... but it suddenly hit me that there's only you and me left of the family.' She raised her head and looked at her aunt's sad expression. 'But if Mother *had* told me who my father was, isn't it possible that I *could* have grandparents – somewhere? I suppose you know that his name isn't on my birth certificate? "A soldier killed in the war!" was all I could get out of her.'

As Katherine had grown older, she'd become aware that Evelyn must be party to the whole story of her mother's out-of-wedlock pregnancy, but she'd never dared raise the matter because of her mother's intransigence. She punched the cushion into shape and swung her legs off the settee. Catching her aunt's eye, she was taken aback by the flicker of alarm she saw there.

'Don't ask me about your father, *please*, Kathy. I *promised* Nancy. I ...'

Katherine interrupted. 'Don't you feel I have the right to know the truth after all these years?' Her voice hardened as Evelyn looked away. 'Can I tell you something, Aunt Evelyn? Something I've *never* spoken about – not even to mother.'

She turned away to compose herself, fixing her eyes on the flames shooting up from the crackling logs.

'When I was growing up, I tried to imagine what my father looked like. I cut out a picture of a soldier from one of Mother's magazines.' A smile lit up her face. 'He had blonde hair, blue eyes, and was *very* handsome. I hid the picture at the bottom of the toy box Uncle Ted made me, and I'd take it out and look at it when I felt sad. Do you *know* just how much I wanted to have a real father – like my school friends? I didn't want to be the odd one out. I *longed* for a dad to hug me; to take me for walks through the fields, read me bedtime stories.'

'Why didn't you *tell* Nancy all this?' Evelyn asked. Her voice quivered.

Katherine looked away from the fire and faced her.

'Because, whenever I tried to talk to her about him she got upset, very upset – and cross. So, eventually I stopped asking about him.'

Katherine looked expectantly at her aunt, waiting for a reaction. But Evelyn turned away, lumbered up from the settee and went over to the table.

Her hands shook as she strained the tea into a blue and white china cup and handed it to Katherine.

'Your mother dealt with the situation in her own way – as best she could,' she said. Picking up her cup of tea, barely able to contain her unease, she faced Katherine and shook her head. 'Let Nancy rest in peace, dear,' she whispered as she headed for the door. 'I'll sort out the kitchen, Kathy, and, when you feel up to it, you could make a start on Nancy's bedroom.'

Katherine watched her amble across the room, cup rattling in the saucer. She hadn't really expected her to open up on the subject of her father. If she'd wanted to, she'd had years in which to do so. Katherine had refrained from telling Evelyn that, as she'd grown older, she'd felt certain her mother *wasn't* telling her the truth about her father's death and that, over the years, she'd nurtured the hope that he was, in fact, still alive.

She took a few sips of tea and put the cup and saucer down on the coffee table. Slipping her feet into her loafers, she stood up and made her way into the hall, climbed the narrow stairs and walked along the creaking landing. It had scared her at night-time when she was a child. Walking past her old bedroom, she stepped through the open door into her mother's room.

A heavy, dark oak wardrobe dominated the space. Standing on the glass-topped, kidney-shaped dressing table with its floral flounced skirt, was a collection of photographs in a variety of frames. One of a happy, smiling baby sitting in the navy Silver Cross carriage pram that Evelyn and Ted had bought and proudly pushed around the Peover lanes; one in her school uniform with a toothless grin and, in pride of place in the middle of the dressing table, wearing her cap and gown at her graduation ceremony. She picked up one of her mother and Evelyn when *they* were children, sitting primly side by side on a horsehair settee between their parents. Smiling, she remembered her mother recounting the tale that the horsehair was very itchy on their bare legs and the photographer had reprimanded them for wriggling about too much.

Placing the photograph back in its allotted place, she wandered disconsolately across the faded pink carpet to the latticed window. Lifting the latch, she pushed hard on the warped frame and swung the window open. She placed her hands carefully between her mother's two Doulton figurines on the red tiled window ledge and gazed out across the fields, through which she, her mother, aunt and uncle had rambled together over the years. Katherine could just spy the stream meandering down to the Peover Eye where she'd spent many happy hours splashing about with her friends on warm summer days throughout the school holidays. Why was it, she pondered, that those carefree weeks seemed to stretch forever when now, her holiday weeks were over in a flash?

As an only child, she'd never felt lonely. She'd been content to amuse herself reading and painting. *Children's Hour* on the radio would see her curled up on the settee, entranced, giving her imagination free-rein to write her poems and little stories.

She had greatly enjoyed her years at the village school, tucked away at the bottom of the famous 'Cobbles', along which you could easily turn over an ankle if hurrying, late for assembly. The school was adjacent to St. Oswald's, a picturesque black and white church, and the well-known hostelry, the Bells of Peover Inn. Many of the pupils were from farming families, and had provided her with friends who included her in the excitement of the harvest – riding atop the hay wagon and helping tend the animals.

Friendships had dwindled for a while at the age of eleven when they'd been separated by the iniquitous lottery that was the divisive eleven-plus examination – when Katherine had classed herself fortunate to gain one of the limited places in a system that failed overall to meet the demand for all able children to enter Grammar School. She remembered the agonizing weeks of waiting after sitting the examination, for a brown envelope to drop through the letterbox stating she had been successful. From then on, she joined the uniformed ranks of the elite, whose academic future was assured, as opposed to the 'rejects' who were dispatched to the secondary modern schools, where the curriculum did not cover such things as languages – or much to stretch the mind! At the tender age of fourteen, those pupils left school to take up jobs in the factories and shops. Others, encouraged by dedicated teachers, enrolled at secretarial colleges and night school classes – at their parents' expense – to secure the all-important 'O' and 'A' level examination grades. Many years later, the Comprehensive system was implemented, enabling pupils to continue their education until the age of eighteen.

Katherine sighed, remembering that bitter-sweet time of her life. She was one of the fortunate ones whose friendships had survived the trauma of educational segregation.

Between the trees, she could just make out the tower of St. Oswald's church, and memories of Uncle Ted driving around the narrow lanes distributing harvest baskets to the elderly and infirm of the parish came flooding back. His death, after a stroke, had been devastating. She'd hoped – as he had hoped – that he would be there to give her away when the time came for her to walk down the aisle.

Turning from the window, she walked over to the wardrobe. Reluctant to begin the daunting task of sorting through her mother's clothes, she stood for a while listening to the blackbird competing with the distant traffic hum from the M6 motorway. Taking a deep breath, Katherine grasped the brass handle and pulled open the wardrobe door.

The mottled mirror fixed to the inside of the door reflected her pale, heart-shaped face, abundance of fiery red hair and wide green eyes – so like her mother's. They'd been, so everyone told her, more like sisters than mother and daughter. Not having a father around, the bond between them was exceptionally strong – splintered only by the enigma surrounding her father.

She fingered through the coats, dresses and cardigans that hung on their wooden and padded hangers, and pulled out the cornflower-blue dress she'd bought her mother to wear at her fiftieth birthday party. Tenderly pressing its silky softness against her cheek, she recalled the happy time they'd had with Evelyn and her mother's friends from the florist's and the village. Tears sprang into her eyes. Her mother's perfume – *Anais Anais* – still lingered on the dress. *How* could she possibly discard it? She hung it back on the rail and braced herself to sort through the rest of the clothes.

One by one, she took them from their hangers, clung to the memories they evoked, before carefully folding and placing them in two piles on top of the rose-patterned duvet. One pile, she decided, would go to the Heart Foundation charity shop, and one to the church good-as-new stall.

Kneeling down to sort through the shoes and handbags neatly stacked in the bottom of the wardrobe, she discovered, beneath a tartan shopping bag, a shoebox crammed tight with letters and postcards. Lifting it out, she stood up and put the box on the bed, intending to take it back to her flat and sort through it at leisure. But a faded blue airmail envelope sticking up above the rest caught her eye and, not recalling her mother speak of friends living abroad, she pulled it free.

The stamp on the envelope was postmarked New Jersey, dated December 1944. Intrigued, she took out the flimsy sheet of notepaper and unfolded it. In the top right hand corner was an address in Asbury Park. Katherine began to read, with some difficulty, the spidery handwriting.

The contents of the letter exploded Katherine's brain. From that moment her life changed – forever.

The letter was from her father – the faceless figure of her childhood dreams whose name she had never known. Now, miraculously, there it was before her eyes: his name was Michael – Michael Donnelly, and he was an American G.I.!

Katherine clutched the letter to her and whispered his name over and over as she sat trembling on the edge of the bed. Recovering from the shock, she read again – eagerly – her father's evocative words:

Darling Nancy

At last I have summoned the courage to reply to your letter, which should have reached me when I was over in France, but only caught up with me back home. There is no easy way to tell you what I must, Nancy, I can only hope and pray that you will understand.

By the time your letter arrived to tell me that you were expecting our child – it was too late. Too late for us, Nancy! I am ashamed to confess that I wasn't wholly truthful when I told you I didn't have a girl back home. There was Ellie, who I grew up with. She was desperate that we get engaged before I was drafted to England.

After I left England for Europe I was wounded at Le Mans. My right leg was badly shattered so for me the war was over and I was shipped back to the States. Ellie is expecting our baby and we are soon to be married. You have to understand, Nancy, that because your letter was delayed for such a long time before reaching me, when I didn't hear from you, I imagined that once I'd gone over to France you'd forgotten about me – that happened to a few of my buddies – and when you didn't reply to the letter I sent from France telling you I'd been wounded, well, I guess that convinced me you had lost interest. Maybe I should have persisted and written again, but apart from my shattered leg, I was shell-shocked. My head was pretty messed up. But I've never forgotten you, Nancy. You have to believe me when I tell you that I really loved you. I guess I always will. You gave me so much happiness, comfort and love when I was a scared stranger far from home. When I was shipped over to the fighting in Europe, thoughts of you helped me through the dark days of battle. I know it was unforgivable of me not to tell you about Ellie, and no excuse, but I honestly thought she and I would break up when I got back after the war ended – and I had to face the fact that I might never return. I count myself lucky to have survived. But there is no excuse for my behaviour other than the madness of war, when precious moments had to be grasped in case they were your last! You were my solace, Nancy – and my sanity. Gee, how I wish I could see you, but it's not possible now.

I have no right to ask you to help me come to terms with what happened to us but I do need you to tell me, when the baby arrives, whether we have a son or a daughter. I took the decision to tell Ellie about us – and I have to say she took the news better than I could have expected. She is aware that I intend to offer you financial support – I want to provide for you both, so please allow me to do this for you. The gallery is doing well and Pop is handing over the reins when I feel up to it.

I'm truly, truly sorry for the mess I've made of both our lives. If only your letter had reached me in France. If only you'd received my letter from France. Maybe it never even left France. It was hell out there. I can only hope that you will understand my position and in time find it in your heart to forgive me? I send my love to you, sweet Nancy. Please, please let me know when the baby is born.

Michael

As Katherine stared at the letter, her overwhelming feeling of elation suddenly gave way to rising anger.

Why had her mother been so cruel, denying her the right to know of Michael's existence? Letting her believe he was dead all these years? Not even telling her that he was American!

Hot, angry tears sprang into her eyes. She folded the letter carefully and put it back in the envelope. Surveying her mother's bedroom, she wondered just where she'd been conceived. In Aunt Evelyn's cottage; some hotel room in

Manchester – a hayfield? And why on earth was it important to know that?

Her mother had never once told her she'd *loved* her father. And it was the one question Katherine had never asked, afraid the answer might be no. It had been important to her to cling to the belief that she *had* been born out of a loving relationship.

She recalled her mother's repetitive words when she'd questioned her about her father. 'It's all in the past. Best forgotten – one of those things that happened in wartime when you didn't know if the next day would be your last… like it was for your grandma and granddad. You have to realise that war changed people, Katherine.'

Now at last, unbelievably, Katherine held in her hands proof that they had loved each other. She fought back the tears. If their letters had not gone astray her life – their lives – might have been so very different.

She felt a sense of sadness that her mother had gone to her grave without ever realising the depth of her need to know *exactly* who her father was. And now, at the age of thirty-two, the letter provided a stepping-stone to that aspiration. But never, in her wildest dreams, had she imagined the search for her father would begin in America.

Was he even alive? Did the wounds he'd received in the war lead to an early death? And if he *was* alive, she surmised her appearance would create conflict within his family.

Katherine sat stiff and upright, still stunned by the revelations in the letter, until the clattering of china in the kitchen below penetrated her numbed brain.

AUNT EVELYN! *She* must have known the truth all along – yet she, too, had kept silent.

Katherine took a deep breath to calm her racing heart, got up from the bed and, with shaking legs, prepared to confront her aunt – the only one alive who could provide answers to the many questions whirling around her throbbing head.

Katherine watched, dispassionately, as her aunt's gentle grey eyes widened with shock while she took stock of her niece's distressed countenance. But before she had a chance to speak, Katherine, eyes flashing, flung her pent-up, angry words at her.

'I presume *you* can tell me everything I want to know, *need* to know, about my father? *Michael Donnelly.*' She spat the words out and thrust the letter into her aunt's podgy hand.

'Read it… read it!' she shouted, eyes glinting, voice hard and accusing. 'But I expect you read it when Mother received it – way, way back in *1944!*' she added bitterly, sinking down onto the sofa beside Evelyn.

Evelyn pressed the letter to her bosom with one hand and took Katherine's trembling hand with the other. Her cheeks had lost their rosy glow and, for what seemed like an eternity, the silence hung between them. Without reading the letter, she placed it on the folds of her tartan, pleated skirt. Raising her hand, she gently stroked Katherine's hair.

Her lip trembled as momentarily she was lost for words: 'I'm sorry… *so* sorry you had to find out like this, Kathy, and you're right, I *don't* need to read the letter. I… I assumed Nancy had destroyed it along with Michael's photographs. She told me she'd thrown them on the fire… She was totally *devastated* when she found out that Michael had a fiancé in America.'

Evelyn gazed helplessly at her niece's dejected expression as she searched again for the right words – words she knew would undoubtedly add to Katherine's distress. She lowered her eyes, avoiding her intense gaze. 'I… I have a terrible confession, Kathy.' Her voice was barely audible. 'Something that's haunted me all these years.' She shook her head sadly. 'The letter that Michael mentions – the one he sent to Nancy after he was wounded in France? Well…' She gave a nervous cough and cleared her throat. 'His letter *did* arrive. Your mother was out… I recognized Michael's handwriting. I… I steamed the envelope open. It was wrong to do that, so very wrong.'

She turned from Katherine, remembering the impulsive moment she'd taken the decision to open the envelope. Forcing herself to meet her niece's hostile eyes, she stumbled on. 'But… I was so cross with Michael; upset for your mother for the months she'd waited, absolutely inconsolable, for a reply to her letter telling him she was expecting his baby. I wanted to know his reaction to the pregnancy – I wanted to spare Nancy further hurt, you see. I wanted to find out if Michael was going to stand by Nancy, or if he would keep out of her life and contribute to your upkeep – which happened to girls in a similar situation once the boys got back home. But, when I read the letter and realised Michael hadn't even received Nancy's letter, was unaware she was going to have his child, well… At first I was overjoyed for her and intended to put the letter back in the envelope and re-seal it. But a different scenario hit me… forcefully. The realisation dawned that I could *lose* Nancy. I imagined her replying, telling Michael he was going to be a father… They would marry and off she would go to America. The thought of her – and you – being so far away from Ted and me was unbearable. I'd already lost Father and Mother – and I stood to lose the rest of my family.' Evelyn threw her arms up in despair, afraid to look at Katherine who had sat in stunned silence as she'd rambled on.

'I don't know what came over me, Kathy,' she continued. 'I suppose I just panicked and did something completely selfish – unforgivable… I threw Michael's letter onto the fire, and when this arrived,' she tapped the letter on her knee, 'Nancy was so distressed that Michael had lied to her – that he had a fiancé – she was adamant she wanted nothing more to do with him. Which eased my conscience, and convinced me that what I'd done was in her best interest to save her further heartache.'

Evelyn grasped Katherine's hands.

'I'm truly ashamed that in the heat of the moment it never crossed my mind to consider *your* best interests – the effect upon *your* life, Kathy. But I am certain your mother decided to put Michael right out of her mind, to enable her to cope. To her he *was* dead, and I suppose that if you'd been made aware of his existence, then the pain of loving the unobtainable would have carried on for your mother. It's difficult, I know, but try to understand what it was like for her. Find it in your heart to forgive her, Kathy – and me if you can. I suppose we'll never know for sure if Michael *would* have been prepared to leave Ellie and *their* child for Nancy…' Evelyn's voice tailed off.

Katherine shook her hands free, her face ashen: 'You *didn't* give him that chance – did you?' she interrupted angrily. 'How *could* you keep the fact that he was wounded from Mother? How *could* you? It *is unforgivable*! How can I forgive *either* of you for this… this deception? Did Uncle Ted know what you did?'

Evelyn shook her head. 'I didn't dare tell him,' she whispered. 'But you might feel happier to know that he did want me to tell you about Michael. He thought Nancy was wrong not doing so, he told her so many times. But *I* had to support your mother's decision. The whole unfortunate episode caused much heartache and soul searching.'

Katherine got up from the sofa, grabbed a log from the basket by the hearth and flung it onto the dying embers. She didn't return to the sofa, but sat down in the rocking chair opposite her aunt, who had her face in her hands sobbing quietly.

'Now you have to tell me *all* you know about my father,' Katherine said firmly.

Evelyn wiped her eyes with the back of her hand. 'Where to begin?' she said sadly, shaking her head. 'Well… firstly, I did keep my promise to Nancy that I would never tell you about Michael – and it's amazing no one in the village ever let the secret slip… something we always worried about. But now that your mother is no longer with us I…' She faltered, again.

Katherine's tight expression loosened as she got up and walked across to her.

'I *understand* you felt you had to keep your promise to Mother,' she said, sitting down beside her, struggling to keep her anger in check. 'But please tell me *everything* you know – *now!*'

Evelyn cleared her throat. 'Well… I mustn't blame Michael. He obviously *wanted* to be in your life, didn't he? That much you know yourself from this,' she said, passing his letter back to Katherine. 'Your mother has to take some of the blame. She could have taken up his offer of financial support – but you wonder how Michael's wife would have reacted if Nancy had allowed him to make that commitment. A lot of friction between them I would imagine. After all, she'd also been deceived. But, if that financial line of contact had been put into place, who knows what the outcome might have been?' Evelyn sighed. 'Nancy was always stubborn. She had a mind of her own, God rest her soul. In many ways you're a lot like her, Kathy. She was so proud of you.'

'*Tell* me about my *father!*' Katherine urged.

For a while, Evelyn seemed lost in thought and Katherine curbed her impatience.

Finally she spoke. 'Your father was a lovely young man. Tall… fair hair… *wonderful* piercing blue eyes.' She smiled. 'He was twenty-one, same as Nancy. His paternal grandparents had emigrated to America from Ireland and his father owned an art gallery in Asbury Park, New Jersey. Michael had been a fine arts student at university before enlisting in the army. He was an only child, like you, and was expected to go into the family business when the war ended – *if* he survived! Those boys were under no illusion they would get back home. He came over with General Patton in 1944. January to June. I think you've always been aware, Kathy, that the General's headquarters were at Peover Hall and the American flag hangs in St. Lawrence Church – well, Michael was billeted down the road in Toft Hall where Ted was working.' A broad smile lit up Evelyn's face. 'We used to see Patton flying around the lanes in his big staff car. He came back in 1945, as he promised he would, for a service of thanksgiving and to present the flag that hangs in the church. That's the reason why Nancy wouldn't go to St. Lawrence Church. She couldn't bear to see the Stars and Stripes hanging on the wall – a reminder of what she'd lost … Anyhow, Ted had invited Michael and a couple of his friends to have tea with us. In the village, we all felt for these young boys so far from their homes and families. And Michael? Well, he took an immediate shine to Nancy. They'd go off to the pictures and to dances – and to the Bells and the Royal George for a drink.' Evelyn pulled a face. 'Your mother wasn't too happy that you'd arranged her fiftieth birthday party at the George, Kathy. She never went into either place after she received Michael's letter. When you were planning the surprise party, I couldn't warn you off the idea without you asking for a reason.'

Evelyn sighed and gazed at the flickering flames casting a soft light over the copper kettle on the stone hearth.

Katherine had listened in awe to her aunt's words; words that had brought to life the man who, until now, had only been a figment of her imagination. She leaned forward. 'Tell me more about my *father*,' she said, savouring the word.

'Well… Michael did show us photos of his home in Asbury Park. Quite a large detached house – wooden, I think. It looked quite impressive. I believe it was very near to the sea.' Evelyn sighed again. 'And to think Michael was torn away from all that. So many of those G.I.s, and Canadians – and our boys too – having to leave their families to face the horrors of war, all because of one man's evil fanaticism!'

She took hold of Katherine's trembling hand. 'You're still so cold,' she said, rubbing it gently. 'Nancy should have been the one to tell you all this, Kathy. For what it's worth now, I *always* thought she was so wrong to keep it from you.'

Aware of how difficult it was for her aunt to condemn her beloved sister, Katherine put her arm around her shoulders. Evelyn flashed a grateful smile and lumbered up from the sofa.

'I'll make us a another cup of tea, warm you up a bit,' she said, grateful for the moment to escape from the unbearable tension in the room.

Katherine tried to clear her muddled thoughts. She acknowledged that her aunt, whatever her personal convictions were, could never have betrayed her sister's trust. But destroying her father's letter? Unforgivable! So unlike the loving aunt she doted on. To make sense of *why* she'd done something so out of character, Katherine endeavoured to put herself into Evelyn's shoes.

Having gone through the trauma of losing her parents in horrific circumstances, the prospect of becoming an aunt to her sister's child must have been like a bright light of hope in the darkness of war – all the more important to her because she and Ted were childless. Her fear that they would leave England for a life in America at a time when air travel was not commonplace or affordable, must have been unbearable.

Gradually Katherine's anger toward both her mother and her aunt lessened. Evelyn was right when she'd said that she was stubborn like her mother; her mother had taught her to be self-sufficient, beholden to no one. In truth, and with the benefit of hindsight, was it the trauma of losing Michael and rearing her alone that had made her mother strong, determined as a single parent to do her best to raise her daughter to be the confident woman she now was?

Katherine picked up her father's letter from the table. She would read it yet again – but this time through her mother's eyes; try to take on board her anger and anguish when she'd found out that the man she loved had another love in his life; try to come to terms with her mother's reasons for concealing her father's existence.

A sudden ray of sunshine slanted in through the sitting room window, illuminating the photograph in the gilt oval frame that hung above the fireplace; Evelyn, in a slinky, white satin and lace bridal gown; her mother in her voluminous, powder-blue taffeta bridesmaid's dress. Looking at their happy, carefree expressions, a feeling of warmth evaporated the anger she'd felt toward them on discovering her father's letter. Its contents had paralysed her emotions, blocked out memories of the blissful years with the most important people in her life. Her mother had provided the strength and judgment of an absent father-figure. Katherine had to acknowledge that she'd been brave at a time when to have a child out of wedlock was frowned upon; she had to give her credit for not going to some back-street abortionist. She had given Katherine life – against all the odds – and she'd obviously reasoned they would be better off without the complications that contact with Michael and his wife would inevitably bring.

Her mother had never taken another lover and, importantly, Katherine now believed that she'd died still loving her father. The tears began to trickle down her cheeks. Intuitively, she knew her mother had intended her to find the letter – when there was no prospect of her having to expose her broken heart.

Katherine rose from the sofa and went into the kitchen to Evelyn.

'Don't bother with more tea,' she said softly. 'I'd like to get back to Didsbury. Let all this sink in, you know.'

Evelyn stared at Katherine with a hurt expression. She switched off the kettle, threw her arms around her and kissed her damp cheek.

'Of course, dear… I understand! We'll come back and finish off on Sunday… You could have lunch with me first? Maybe Alex would like to come too?'

Katherine pursed her lips. 'He's off to London for the weekend.'

'And you're not going with him? A change of scene would do you good, Kathy.'

'I've not been asked,' Katherine replied, not meaning to sound so disapproving. 'He's meeting up with his Fleet Street cronies and I wouldn't want to be stuck inside a watering hole for the weekend… I'll let you know about Sunday. There's no rush, is there?' she added, walking into the hall to collect her coat, anxious to make her exit and wallow alone with her scattered thoughts.

Evelyn followed her to the front door, returned Katherine's peck on the cheek and watched her drive away down the lane. When Katherine's Mini was out of sight, she closed the door and stood weeping, uncontrollably, behind it.

Katherine put her foot down on the few straight stretches of road that would take her not to Didsbury, but to St. Lawrence Church in Over Peover where, Evelyn had told her, her father had worshipped alongside General Patton.

Turning off the main road, she drove carefully down the narrow, tree-lined lane that led to the church, passing through a farmyard and down another narrower stretch to the church gates. In the small car park, she swung into a space opposite to a large white Volkswagen – the only other vehicle there.

Getting out of the car, Katherine wondered if the church would be open. She'd covered several stories of theft and vandalism resulting in some churches keeping their doors firmly locked.

Pushing through the small gate, she saw a comely, grey-haired woman in a floral dress and bright blue cardigan walking toward her down the path from the old Norman church, sweeping brush in one hand and black plastic bucket in the other. Fortunately, Katherine didn't know her. The collective Peover villages were close-knit communities, but today, Katherine was not in the mood to explain why she was visiting St. Lawrence.

The woman stopped and smiled as they came face to face. She placed the bucket, full of dead flowers and foliage, on the path and rested her arm on the broomhead.

'Good afternoon,' she said, pleasantly, beaming Katherine another friendly smile. 'If you're wanting to see the church, I'm afraid it's locked. But if you're not going to be too long, I'll unlock it for you,' she added quickly, noting Katherine's look of disappointment. 'I'll be back in twenty minutes or so.'

Katherine's heart began to race. 'Thank you, I'd really appreciate that. I won't be long and I'll wait until you return to lock up again – mustn't leave it prey to vandals.'

'No indeed! I heard the other week that an offertory box was wrenched off the wall. You wonder how desperate people are to stoop so low?'

The woman propped the broom against a bush and fished a large key out of her sagging cardigan pocket. Together they strolled, companionably, down the path between the ancient gravestones, exchanging comments about the warm September weather. To Katherine's relief, the woman didn't question the reason for her visit.

'See you later then,' the woman said, unlocking the heavy door. 'Do be careful of the step around the font – a few folk have tripped there.'

Katherine assured her she would take care, and stepped into the coolness of the church.

When her eyes had adjusted to the dim light, they were drawn immediately to the Stars and Stripes hanging on the wall to the left of the centre aisle. She walked down the aisle and slid along the pew nearest to the flag. It felt unreal, sitting in a place where her father had sat thirty odd years ago – maybe in the very same pew! Choking back the tears that threatened, she reached up and touched the hem of the flag.

Gazing around the empty church, she tried to visualize the rows of young American servicemen sitting behind General Patton – fearful for their lives; praying for deliverance from the battlefields lying in wait. Closing her eyes, she prayed that her father *had* survived and that she *would* find him. And if he *was* alive, it was a long shot that he would still be living in Asbury Park – but at least it gave her a starting point. Wherever Michael Donnelly was – despite the complications of encountering his wife and family – she had to try to find him. Katherine had to lay the ghost that had haunted her for thirty-two years!

CHAPTER 2

AS SOON AS SHE ARRIVED BACK at the flat, Katherine called Directory Enquiries, and was ecstatic when informed that there was a Michael Donnelly listed in Asbury Park – albeit on a different street from the one on the letter. Surely this must be her father? She was so excited; so tempted to telephone immediately to confirm that it *was* him. But, calming herself, she decided a tentative letter would be more appropriate. If this Michael Donnelly was her father, it would be less of a shock than having a disembodied voice on the phone telling him she was his daughter! She speculated whether the baby he'd written about was a boy or a girl – and maybe by now he had more children? Who knows, she could have several half brothers and sisters in Asbury Park – a thrilling prospect!

After tearing up the first two attempts, she eventually penned a short letter stating that she hoped he was the father she was searching for and, on that basis, explained that she had not been aware of his existence until the death of her mother and the discovery of his letter. She included a photograph of herself, sealed the envelope with an unsteady hand, and addressed it to the man who could be her father. Totally elated, she walked on air to the local post office and handed it over to the counter clerk. She watched her weigh it and attach the blue airmail sticker, restraining herself from blurting out its importance as the clerk dropped it into the mailbag.

Only when she got back to the flat did she think about telephoning Alex.

She made herself a cup of tea, settled in the armchair, picked up the telephone from the coffee table and dialled the *Argus*.

Alex listened intently as she relayed the morning's events, only interjecting a few 'wows' as Katherine told him about the life-changing letter she'd found at the cottage, and of the one that Evelyn had destroyed. Alex had been aware, from the moment he and Katherine had become an item, of the mystery surrounding her father. He had, in fact, suggested that she dig around to see what would come to light, but Katherine had not wanted to upset her mother. Now, fate had taken a hand. His immediate reaction to her discovery was, '*Terrific story!*' and Katherine had to read the riot act to stop him getting it into print immediately. She placated him by agreeing that he could run the story *if* her father made contact, and *if* he gave *his* consent. She was fully aware that publication would affect not only herself, but also Aunt Evelyn, setting the whole village agog. It would definitely be a learning curve for her to be on the other side of a news story!

Apart from seizing upon the newsworthiness, Alex's reaction surprised and disappointed Katherine. Having suggested in the past that she try to find her father, he now expressed strong concerns about the wisdom of contacting him.

'You should think carefully before opening an unknown chapter of your life – and your father's life. It could result in heartache all round,' he warned.

'But, hopefully, it will result in happiness all round,' Katherine responded, wondering why he was now dampening her enthusiasm.

'Well, only time will tell… I suppose this calls for a glass or two. I'll bring a bottle round when I've finished here. I miss you when you have a day off.'

Katherine smiled. 'Miss you too. See you soon, then. Get a good red, will you?' she added, before putting the receiver down and settling back in the armchair.

Theirs was a comfortable, compatible relationship. They slid along, going out for a quiet drink, sharing meals in their respective flats; eating out occasionally in one of the many hostelries in Cheshire and Manchester, and taking up the cinema, theatre and Halle press seats.

But, to date, Alex hadn't raised the topic of commitment, reticent, she surmised, with one failed marriage on the spike.

Two weeks went by after Katherine had posted the letter to her father – two unbearable weeks during which she contemplated the worst scenarios. Her father wanted nothing to do with his past; his wife had opened and destroyed her letter, in the same way that her aunt had destroyed her father's letter – or, he was no longer alive. She strived to push the negative thoughts to the back of her mind as she waited anxiously for his reply.

She went about her daily routine on the Women's Page, endeavouring to keep her mind on the job in hand – but thoughts of her father and the suspense of awaiting a reply chipped away at her concentration. Everyone in the newsroom – including Alex – skirted around the subject, not wanting to raise Katherine's hopes with unrealistic predictions as the days passed with no word.

Over the bottle of Cote du Rhone that Alex had brought to the flat the night she'd discovered the letter, Katherine's bubble of heightened excitement had been well and truly burst. She'd been disheartened by Alex's scepticism. Although his nose for a good story had kicked in initially, several scenarios he'd played over in his mind had given him cause for concern. He enjoyed the predictable, uncomplicated relationship he and Katherine shared. The thought of her crossing the Atlantic and plunging herself into a whole new, and possibly more exciting lifestyle, made him feel uneasy – jealous even. He'd laboured the point again that Katherine should think twice about raking over old wounds. But she'd been resolute in her decision to carry on with her quest to find her father.

And the momentous day finally arrived.

Katherine came home from the *Argus* and, on opening the door to the flat, saw the blue airmail envelope lying on the black and white tiled hall floor.

Closing the door behind her, she dropped her bag and newspaper, bent down and picked up the envelope.

A sudden chill of uncertainty made her shiver. The writing was spidery – the same as the writing on her father's letter to her mother in 1944, indicating that he *was* alive! With trembling fingers she tore open the envelope, withdrew the one sheet of white notepaper and sank down onto the bottom step of the stairs. Her mouth was dry as she braced herself to read the most important letter of her life. The words on the page danced in her shaking hands as she tried to focus through the tears welling in her eyes:

My dearest Katherine (would her father ever realise how much those three words meant to her?),

I'm sure there is no need for me to tell you that your letter came as an enormous shock. When I'd gotten over it, I was truly overjoyed. After all these years of wondering, it was real swell to find that I have a daughter. From the photograph you sent, you certainly are beautiful – and the image of your mom. Darling Nancy. It broke my heart to hear that she died so young. The truth is, Katherine, you've been in my heart, even though I never knew if I had a son or a daughter – or even if you were alive. But I'm sure glad that you found my letter, and I guess Nancy intended for you to do so one day and know the truth about us. But you have to know that it was Nancy's decision to keep me out of your lives. I understood her reasons and had to respect her wishes – but it was mighty hard for me to accept that she didn't want any contact or financial help from me.

Now, I hope I can try to help you understand how things were during those terrible uncertain war years. Everyone lived for the day – as did your mother and I. But be certain of one thing, Katherine – we loved each other deeply. I don't regret a moment of the short time we had together, and I pray Nancy didn't either. You are the wonderful outcome of our love. My deep regret is the way things turned out – all because of an unfortunate set of circumstances – and that I caused you and your mother so much heartache. Believe me when I tell you that I've thought and wondered about you all these years.

A glow of happiness seeped through Katherine's body knowing her father had fantasized about her, as she'd fantasized about him. Eagerly she turned the letter over and read on:

You know, Katherine, I always had the feeling that one day we would meet. And I'm delighted that you are a girl. I have my son, Patrick – your half-brother. He has a ten-year-old daughter, Meredith. Sadly my daughter-in-law, Barbara, died two years ago from breast cancer and Patrick and Meredith came to live with Ellie and me. It was difficult breaking the news of your letter to Patrick. He was shocked, of course, but we had a long talk about my relationship with your mother. He knows all about the pressures of war having served in Vietnam. And now he's gotten his head around it, he's looking forward to meeting you. As you know, from my letter to your mother, Ellie was already aware of Nancy. However, it's difficult for her after all this time – as I guess you can appreciate. But I've made it clear to Ellie that I intend to see you, Katherine. So – when are you crossing the pond? Much as I'd like to see the old country again, my health is not great. It's best you come over here. I hope I'm not being too presumptuous to say I'll pay for your flight. Come to New York – see the sights. Let's not delay this important meeting any longer. Let me have your flight details and I'll meet you at the airport. I haven't sent a photo – haven't got a decent up-to-date one and I don't want to scare you off! I'll wear an English rose in my lapel!

I was sorry to hear that Ted died. He was a swell guy – he introduced me to your mom. I'm sure Evelyn and Ted were very supportive when you were growing up. Please give Evelyn condolences and good wishes.

Until we meet, God bless you, Katherine.

Michael

Katherine folded the letter, put it back in the envelope and hugged it to her chest, her heart thudding ten to the dozen. Overcome by the emotions she'd kept in check awaiting a reply, she wept silent tears of relief. At long last she was going to meet her father. She had no choice but to make the journey to him – but it would be difficult meeting his wife. Of his request to give her aunt his good wishes, she had to decide whether, eventually, to make her father aware of the disastrous part Evelyn had played in keeping him and her mother apart. An unwelcome feeling of bitterness toward her resurfaced. But, she told herself firmly, she shouldn't let anything cloud this joyous moment. The past could not be altered. She had to look forward, optimistically, to her future!

In view of Alex's lack of enthusiasm in her search for her father, Katherine did not show him her father's reply, merely related the basic content. She arranged for her assistant, Josie, to hold the fort on the Women's Page for a week, and booked a week's holiday – with Alex's lukewarm agreement – and her flight to New York. Resisting the temptation to telephone, apprehensive that Michael's wife might answer, she posted her itinerary to her father.

On a bright, sunny Sunday afternoon, Katherine took her camera to Lower Peover and photographed the church, the Bells of Peover Inn and Aunt Evelyn's cottage, reassuring her aunt that she would deal sensitively with the problem of the letter she'd destroyed.

She went on to her mother's cottage, selected several photographs, and took them out of their frames to take with her. At Over Peover, she was pleased to find St. Lawrence Church open, and photographed the American flag. Now she felt ready for the trip of her lifetime!

Alex had been silent on the drive from Didsbury to Manchester Airport for Katherine's shuttle flight to Heathrow. The knuckles of his tanned fingers were white as he gripped the steering wheel of the BMW – still resolute in his belief that she was making an error opening up this lost chapter of her life.

At the entrance to the departure lounge, he gave her a cursory peck on the cheek.

'It's not too late to change your mind,' he said impassively, as though she'd selected an unsuitable outfit to wear.

Katherine longed for a reassuring embrace from him; a reality to cling to; a reminder of the ordered lifestyle she was leaving behind before plunging into the unknown. She looked dispiritedly at him.

'You know I *have* to do this Alex… It's only for a week,' she added, trying to hold back the exasperation she was feeling, not wanting their parting to be acrimonious. She tightened her grip on the handle of her black leather shoulder bag containing the photographs and her father's letters. Her voice seemed to be disconnected from her brain – everything suddenly unreal, and she felt an overwhelming rush of panic.

'I'd better go,' she said softly. 'I'll phone as soon as I can.' And she walked away. Before turning the corner out of Alex's field of vision, she stopped and looked back, hoping for a last minute sign of encouragement – a smile or a friendly wave. But she was disappointed.

Alex stood motionless, hands dug deep in the pockets of his expensive grey slacks, his full, sensitive mouth set hard in condemnation that she had disregarded his advice.

The departure lounge was crowded and noisy. Katherine walked between the rows of occupied seats, avoiding the hand baggage that littered the floor, eventually sinking down gratefully onto the seat from which a harassed mother had yanked her unwilling toddler. She smiled, thanked the woman and, hugging her bag, closed her eyes. She felt deflated – wearied by the weeks she'd clashed with Alex in an effort to persuade him to accompany her to New Jersey.

Without warning, hot tears erupted and rolled down her cheeks. She opened her eyes self-consciously. But no one gave her a second glance – sad farewells were part and parcel of airport life. Rummaging in the pocket of her new, black leather jacket, she extracted a handkerchief and dabbed her eyes. She had to pull herself together; nothing should mar the significance of the moment when she would come face to face with her father.

After the short flight to Heathrow, Katherine felt calmer, happier and, with a sense of mounting excitement, boarded the New York flight. Taking off her jacket, she stowed it in the overhead luggage compartment and settled into her window seat, as a young couple stacked their rucksacks in the locker and sat down alongside her. The engines revved on take-off, and she smiled encouragingly at the girl, whose face became tense as she gripped the boy's hands.

'First flight,' the boy explained, raising his eyebrows.

Once the roar of the ascent was completed and the plane had levelled out to a cruising speed, the girl giggled and settled down with her head on the boy's shoulder. Katherine, too, began to relax with a refreshing gin and tonic from the steward's drinks' trolley. But it wasn't long before Alex invaded her thoughts.

She pictured him driving furiously back to the *Argus* – and Josie!

Her brow furrowed... Josie?

Since Josie had arrived in the Reporters' Room as her assistant some months ago, Katherine had been beset by a nagging suspicion that she had ambitions to step into her shoes as Women's Page editor.

She pictured Josie at her neat and tidy desk, holding her brightly decorated, art-deco mug – which no one dared touch – between long, red fingernails; flicking her sleek blonde hair over her shoulders, and flashing a perfect set of teeth in the direction of Alex, lounging in his swivel chair behind the news desk.

Katherine poured more tonic into the plastic glass and wondered about the wisdom of giving Josie free rein for a whole week.

Her head began to throb from the constant drone of the engines and the babble of conversations between her fellow passengers. Reaching up, she pulled on the air cooler, directing the flow to her flushed face. The young couple – who'd told her they were taking a gap year after university before getting jobs, excited at the prospect of backpacking across America – were entwined in each other's arms, oblivious to what was going on around them.

Katherine closed her eyes, hoping to catch some sleep and take her mind off the nagging doubts that were emerging. But thoughts of her mother, Alex and the *Argus* whirled around in her head. Would her trip to America prompt Alex to propose and, if so, what would her answer be?

She glanced at the couple again and wondered whether, if she could turn the clock back, would she do things differently? Several of her university friends had taken gap years to travel to far-flung places in the world to – as they'd said – widen their horizons after the cloistered university lifestyle. Had she shied away from serious relationships because she was afraid of commitment or because she'd been subconsciously influenced by her mother's mistrust of men?

Suddenly she felt confused and unhappy, despite the fact that the dream she'd held on to for so long was only hours away. Her eyes swam; she felt clammy and faint; she was tense with expectation and fatigued by the flight.

Time passed slowly after the debris of the meal had been collected by the pert, smiling stewardess. Having read her newspaper and scanned through her magazine, Katherine clamped on the headphones to watch the in-flight movie. But her seat was uncomfortably close to the one in front, forcing her to constantly shift position so that her long, slender legs didn't press against the back of it. Finally she gave up trying to concentrate on the film, and gazed out of the window at the snowy, cotton wool clouds spread beneath her.

The sun, brilliant and blinding, bounced off the wings of the plane. She sighed. If there *was* a heaven then, she reckoned, this was the closest she would get to it in her lifetime.

She experienced a sudden glow of contentment – an

overwhelming feeling that her mother was with her in spirit to face whatever trauma lay ahead. Closing her eyes she drifted away at last into a dreamless sleep.

Hours later, she was awakened by the stewardess announcing that seat belts should be fastened. They were about to land at Kennedy Airport.

CHAPTER 3

KATHERINE FELT A SURGE OF EXCITEMENT peppered with apprehension as the plane touched down on American soil. Her mind raced ahead in the slow-moving queue that snaked between the sectioned aisles toward passport control. After collecting her luggage, she only had to clear customs, walk out into the Arrivals concourse, and her father would be waiting for her!

She smiled happily in response to the cheery, 'Have a nice day, m'am!' as she trundled her trolley carrying her suitcase and hand luggage past the security guard and out into Arrivals.

She walked past the crush of people lining the barriers, some holding placards above their heads bearing the names of their expected passengers.

Her eager eyes scanned the crowd. Where was her father? He'd told her he would be there – wearing a rose in his lapel.

Patrick picked Katherine out immediately from the abundance of red hair framing her pale, oval face. She was, he thought, even more attractive than the photograph she'd sent his father. He was apprehensive. Katherine was expecting his father to greet her. *Her* father – *their* father! He'd recovered from the initial shock of finding he had a half-sister in England.

It was an intriguing situation, to say the least. But how would *she* react toward him? As his eyes followed her through the crowds, he was surprised by the feeling of warmth this beautiful stranger generated within him.

Katherine's legs felt in imminent danger of giving way. Bewildered and fighting to hold back her tears, she spotted a tall, handsome young man who was smiling broadly as he strode purposefully toward her. Casually dressed in smart blue jeans and white polo-neck sweater, he sported a red rose in the lapel of his expensively cut black jacket.

'Katherine – Patrick!' he announced confidently on reaching her side, grasping her hand and shaking it vigorously. His warm, brown eyes gazed directly into hers.

'There's no mistaking you from the photo you sent Pop!' he grinned. 'I'm afraid Pop's not feeling too good – he's sure sorry he couldn't make it to the airport, but I'm mighty pleased to be here to greet my *sister*.'

Katherine smiled and tried to hide her disappointment that her father was not there to meet her. And she was somewhat surprised by Patrick's appearance. She'd imagined he would have the same fair hair and blue eyes that Aunt Evelyn said her father had. But he had a shock of thick, black hair.

'Welcome to the U.S. of A. – and the Donnelly family,' Patrick said. Folding his arms around her, he planted a kiss on her flushed cheek.

Locked in his arms, Katherine experienced a tingle that sped down to her toes. She pulled back and searched for her voice. When she found it, it came out thin and shaky.

'Thank you, Patrick,' she said tearfully. 'Sorry...' she murmured. 'It's all so...'

'Don't be sorry. I understand... truly,' Patrick said soothingly. 'Let's get away from here. I've had instructions from Pop to take you into town for a meal to catch your breath before you meet him – and Mom,' he added, raising an eyebrow. 'We have plenty of time before we take the train from Penn to Asbury.'

Twining one arm through Katherine's, he propelled her and the trolley toward a long line of yellow taxis.

Settled in the back of the cab, Katherine tried to get her head round the fact that she was actually here, in America – and the extremely attractive man sitting beside her was her *brother*. She tried hard to concentrate on his running commentary as the taxi crawled, bumper to bumper, toward Manhattan.

'This area is Queens,' Patrick announced, as they passed through a built-up area of shops, apartment blocks, and roads dotted with trees sporting their autumn colours. 'Do you see *Cagney and Lacey* on English T.V.? This is where most of it is shot – right here in Queens.'

'We do get the programme at home. It's very popular – very slick and well made. The format's similar to *Starsky and Hutch*, which I prefer – they're a cute duo,' Katherine laughed.

Patrick pulled away from her, feigning shock. 'You *like* *Starsky and Hutch*? You Brits have time for them when you have all those great Shakespearian guys?'

'Now you're teasing me!'

'And you're beginning to relax, Katherine!' Patrick grinned.

She eyed his smooth, tanned hands resting on his thighs and stifled an inexplicable urge to reach out and touch him. Turning away, she looked through the window and gave a cry of delight as she caught her first glimpse of the unmistakable Manhattan skyline looming ahead.

'That is breathtakingly impressive!' she enthused, craning her neck for a better view. 'I've seen that panorama many times at the cinema and on television… But for real – wow! As skylines go, this takes some beating,' she said excitedly.

Patrick laughed. 'Well, hopefully it will become a commonplace skyline – Pop sure will want to get you over here as often as he can persuade you.'

Katherine turned and faced him. 'And your mother?' she queried tentatively.

'Ah… Mom?' Patrick's smooth, high brow furrowed. 'How's about we talk about Mom later?'

Katherine's heart sank. What kind of reception *would* she get from her father's wife? She'd deliberately pushed all thoughts of Ellie and the probable hostility to the back of her mind. But it was a dilemma she would soon have to face.

As the taxi crossed the East River, still moving at a snail's pace, Katherine craned her neck, pressed her nose against the window and looked up in wonder at the towering skyscrapers of concrete, glass and steel that tickled the clouds.

She sank back into her seat, the thrill of being in New York abruptly eclipsed by the anxiety of what problems lay ahead.

How *would* her sudden intrusion into the Donnelly family affect their lives?

She stole a glance at Patrick's profile. He was staring straight ahead, he, too, seemingly lost in thought. She tried to picture *his* reaction when her father received her letter – as shocked as she had been on finding her father's! And *he* had the added complication of dealing with his mother's reaction to the news that her husband had fathered another child. And how on earth had he explained the delicate situation to his young daughter? Her heart raced. She struggled to quell her rapidly growing unease. Doubts were creeping into her head. Was her father *really* too ill to make the journey to the airport or had Ellie dissuaded him? A renewed sense of foreboding sent a shiver down her spine.

Then, as though aware of her apprehension, Patrick turned toward her, a look of concern in his eyes.

'Don't worry, Katherine – it's gonna be difficult for all of us,' he conceded. 'But we *will* get there… We have to, don't we?' He took hold of her hand and squeezed it tenderly. 'We'll have a swell meal at Charlie's Steak House – it's a great diner. Always go into battle on a full stomach – that's one of Pop's favourite sayings,' he added with a laugh.

Katherine let her hand rest in his and began to relax.

The taxi turned into Broadway and pulled up across from the famous Radio City.

As Patrick dug into his jacket pocket, pulled out a leather wallet and sorted out the fare, the Italian driver looked over his shoulder and beamed a wide smile at Katherine.

'You from England, lady?' he queried.

She nodded, returning his smile.

'I gotta cousin in Ber…ming…ham. Umberto! Been there ten years now. He's got a diner – Umberto's Pizza Place,' he said with pride. 'You know it, lady?'

Katherine smiled again. 'I'm afraid not. But, if I go to Birmingham I'll certainly look him up.'

'You tell Umberto, Luigi sent you, lady,' he said, taking the dollar bills from Patrick.

Patrick opened the taxi door and climbed out onto the pavement. Katherine slid along the seat, took his outstretched hand and stepped out into the cacophony of sound that was this vibrant city. She stood alongside Patrick and breathed in the warm, but fume-laden air, as he hauled her suitcase from the front passenger seat.

Luigi switched on the ignition, saluted them, and with one hand on the steering wheel, deftly forced his way back into the convoy of honking traffic.

Katherine savoured the scene. The yellow taxis expertly jostling with stretch limousines; pedestrians dicing with death, weaving through the traffic lanes.

The pavements were overflowing. People in business attire

hurried along as though late for important appointments; tourists ambled by, window shopping, and – to her amazement – a policeman on a small brown horse was galloping confidently down the road through the thick of the traffic flow.

Patrick laughed at the look of astonishment on Katherine's face.

'These mounted cops sure are brave guys – aspiring cowboys at heart, I suspect,' he said, picking up her suitcase and taking her arm. 'Let's get off the sidewalk and get us some of Charlie's famous steaks.'

After depositing the case with the manager, they were ushered to a table by the window overlooking the busy scene beyond. Katherine felt extremely hungry. Picking up the menu propped on the table, she scrutinized it with enthusiasm, and was relieved to see that – apart from steaks of varying weights – slices of roast chicken breast were on offer. She glanced up at Patrick. Now she had to tell him that she didn't eat red meat and that she wasn't about to partake of the recommended Charlie's 'famous steak'.

'We've got a lot to learn about each other, haven't we?' Patrick grinned, as she made her confession.

A chirpy waitress appeared at their table, bade them good day and deposited a complimentary carafe of red wine between them.

'Just what's required,' Patrick said, pouring the wine evenly into two large glass goblets and handing one over to Katherine.

'To us!' He picked up his glass and clinked it against hers.

'To discovering everything there is to know about each other – and our families.'

'I'll second that,' Katherine smiled, beginning to feel calmer.

The 'famous steak' filled Patrick's dustbin-lid-sized plate, and Katherine's plate was similarly loaded with succulent slices of chicken breast. Having been warned by several of her colleagues on the *Argus* that portions of American food were not for the faint-hearted, she picked up her knife and fork, fully intending to do justice to her first meal on American soil.

England – and Alex – seemed a lifetime away.

The restaurant was crowded. Snippets of conversation in a variety of American and foreign accents buzzed around them, and varying aromas floated on the air. Katherine felt like pinching herself. Here she was on Broadway with her half-brother, for whom she'd felt an *immediate* attraction. Was it sibling affection? But Patrick was a virtual stranger – a very attractive guy. If they'd grown up together, she would have had something to qualify her feelings with. She looked up from her plate. Patrick was gazing at her quizzically.

'Hey, lady – come back to me,' he grinned.

Katherine could not contain the blush that rose from her neck to her cheeks.

'I guess you're getting a little nervous about moving on from here to meet the folks,' Patrick said, sawing away at his mammoth steak. 'Ask any questions you want – if it will help.'

She placed her knife and fork at the side of her plate and leaned back against the chair, meeting Patrick's expectant gaze.

'Well, if I'm honest, my main concern is your mother's reaction to all this. I am, naturally, apprehensive about meeting my father, but feel sure things will work out for us... I'm not sure that will be the case with your mother, though?'

Patrick was silent for several seconds. Looking thoughtful he picked up the carafe of wine and topped up their glasses.

'I'll be honest with you, too, Katherine. I think we have to acknowledge it's going to be difficult for Mom – as I'm sure you can appreciate.' He took a gulp of wine. 'But, I'm also sure that, given time, the two of you will get on just fine.'

'I'd like to think so.' Katherine picked up her glass and took a sip. 'Do you mind me asking how she reacted to the news that your father had been unfaithful?'

Patrick's face hardened somewhat as he studied Katherine's expression.

'Well... according to Pop, Mom went ballistic at first then, strangely, she never mentioned it again. Pop said he'd tried to get her to open up about it later... but all she said was that the past couldn't be undone and they had to live with the consequences.'

'And her reaction when she found out that I was coming over?' Katherine persisted.

Patrick sighed, reached across the table and touched her hand – again sending a tingle down her spine.

'It's kinda strange, you know, Katherine. Mom seems to be worrying more about the effect a sister will have on me – how *I* will react to you.'

Katherine's eyes widened. 'She's more concerned about my relationship with *you* than with her husband?'

'It appears so. But you need to know that Mom's real possessive, and quite jealous by nature. She enjoys being the centre of attention – she was desperate to come with me today, but I stood my ground and said *no*! I intend to be firm with her as far as you are concerned, Katherine.'

Katherine pulled a face. 'Now I feel even more apprehensive… What about your daughter? How's she taken to the idea of having an aunt descend upon her out of the blue?'

'Meredith?' Patrick laughed. 'At ten she's at an age when it's difficult to find out exactly what she feels about *anything*. But I do know she's been impressing her friends with the fact that she now has an English aunt. She's a great girl, Katherine. It's been difficult for her since Barbara died.'

'Tell me about Barbara,' Katherine said softly. 'Your father didn't say too much in his letter.'

Patrick twirled the stem of his glass and cleared his throat.

'We met when I was studying at Massachusetts Institute of Technology. Barbara worked in the library there. We got married pretty quickly. That didn't go down well with Mom, I can tell you. When I graduated I got a job with a big steel company in Worcester, where we set up house. Meredith was born in 1967.' His face lit up. He smiled broadly. 'Life was pretty dandy for us.' He paused and the smile faded. 'Pretty dandy that is until Vietnam and Barbara's cancer. She died just over two years ago, practically a year to the day after she found the lump in her breast. She had the operation pretty quick and then… then came the secondaries. Mom and Pop were very supportive and I was fortunate to get back from Vietnam just before Barbara died. I managed to get out on one of the last 'copters to pull out of Saigon. Until I could get released from the army, Meredith stayed with Mom and Pop and they persuaded me that it would be easier for both of us to live permanently with them. So, I decided to give up engineering; sold the house in Worcester and here we all are in Asbury Park. It works real swell. I've taken over most of the work at the gallery – buying the paintings and ceramics, trying to gauge which new artists will become famous and make me a fortune one day,' he laughed. 'Pop helps out with the paperwork, and Mom in the gallery when needed. But Pop's never been a hundred percent fit since he was wounded. He makes light of his condition, but since the war he's had several operations on his leg. A vein had to be removed resulting in circulatory problems that affect his heart.'

'He didn't tell me *anything* of this in his letter. Is his heart condition very bad?' Katherine asked, with concern.

'If he takes life in the slow lane he'll be just fine,' Patrick said reassuringly, picking up the menu. 'Now, how's about a pudding?' he asked, as the waitress arrived and started to clear their plates from the table.

Katherine felt that she'd already eaten far too much, but wasn't ready to leave the intimacy of the restaurant – anxious to hear more about her father. She surveyed the menu and decided on a slice of homemade apple pie which, when it arrived, was several inches high and looked big enough for a family of four!

'Oh my!' She smiled at the waitress and groaned. 'If all the meals are going to be like this, I'll be paying excess baggage when I fly home!'

'Please don't talk about going home when you've only just got here, Katherine. Besides, we may decide to keep you,' Patrick grinned, as he watched her pick up her spoon and attack the pie.

She savoured a mouthful before replying.

'A lovely thought, Patrick, but I doubt Alex would go along with that idea.' She frowned. 'I wanted him to come over with me, but pressure of work,' she said, not wanting to divulge how sceptical and unsupportive he'd been about her trip.

'Alex is your guy – right? I recall Pop mentioning that you two work together on a newspaper? I guess that's a real interesting job – no two days the same? Are you and he planning to marry?'

Taken aback by the directness of the question, Katherine took a sip of wine and met his eyes. 'We haven't got that far… I… I really ought to have phoned him to let him know I've arrived OK,' she said quickly, changing the subject. Taking another spoonful of pie, she made a mental note to phone Alex as soon as she got to Asbury Park.

She glanced at her watch and pictured him at his desk in the newsroom, perusing the diary and holding forth on what stories had to be covered the next day. She also visualized Josie fluttering her eyelashes, hanging on to his every word. Would she be making capital of her absence? Why *did* the pairing of Alex and Josie in her mind invoke such feelings of unease, she questioned, toying with the pie?

'You've gone away from me again,' Patrick murmured.

'Jet lag catching up with me,' she said emphatically. 'And the wine hasn't helped,' she laughed.

'Helped you relax, though – you'll be able to rest on the train. It's about a one-hour forty journey and I promise *not* to talk. I had an idea to take a cab drive around town for a little sightseeing, but if you're tired? And, anyway, I'll be coming back with you when you fly home. As you have an early flight, Pop suggested we stay in town overnight. That'll give us a chance to take in a Broadway show; go down to Battery Park to see Lady Liberty and stroll around Central Park.'

Katherine saw the enthusiasm in Patrick's eyes, pushed the pleasurable thought of the two of them returning to New York out of her mind, and focused on the reason for her visit: her need to get to her father without further delay.

'That sounds a great idea – all the places I want to see,' she replied. 'But for now, I think I'd better put the sightseeing on hold and get down to Pennsylvania Station.'

CHAPTER 4

FROM HIS POSITION at the news desk – from where he could survey the whole of the large, square newsroom – Alex glanced up at the big wall clock and pursed his lips. Surely Katherine had landed by now. So why hadn't she phoned, as promised?

He loosened his tie and slouched back in his swivel chair. His irrational annoyance with her decision to go to America resurfaced.

Katherine was a competent journalist; practical, thorough and dependable. He smiled inwardly. They made a good team – and he didn't want to share her with a new family who might come between them from many aspects.

He scanned around the room. Several reporters were beavering away on their typewriters, cigarettes dangling from their lips. Others were in earnest dialogue on the phones, and then there were the empty desks of those reporters out on assignments.

Alex's eyes finally alighted on the shapely figure of Josie, bending over Beryl the copy-typist, her long, blonde hair swinging between her and Beryl's broad shoulders.

Josie's arrival had caused quite a stir in the newsroom. She was a definite distraction, and her stunning looks worked wonders eliciting information from uncooperative sources. Alex was surprised that Katherine was tolerant of Josie's ebullient personality. She showed no apparent signs of jealousy. But Josie? Alex was well aware that she had her eye firmly fixed on editorship the Women's Page.

Flicking through the desk diary, Alex found the Asbury address and telephone number Katherine had given him – stressing he only call her if there was an emergency.

He frowned, undecided as to whether to wait until *she* called him. Then – What the hell, he thought! It would lessen his irritability if he could speak to her right now. He sat up, grabbed the phone, dialled the Asbury number and lay back in his chair again. After several rings and before he could utter a word, a high-pitched, female voice said: 'Patrick?'

Taken aback by the abrasive tone, Alex replied that he wasn't Patrick and asked warily if he was speaking to Mrs. Michael Donnelly.

'Who wants to know?' was the curt response.

Alex frowned. 'This is Katherine's fiancé – Alex,' he stated, making a quick decision to use fiancé instead of friend to set out his stall with the Donnelly family. 'Is it convenient to speak to her?' he asked.

There was silence on the line for several seconds.

'She's not here!'

Alex's frown deepened. This conversation was worse than trying to get information from government departments. He adopted his well-practised cajoling voice.

'*Am* I speaking to Mrs. Donnelly?'

'Yeh – you are,' the woman said irritably.

'Good. Then I'm very pleased to be talking with you, Mrs. Donnelly, and I know Katherine's looking forward to meeting you,' he lied, knowing perfectly well that she was petrified at the prospect of meeting her father's wife. 'I assumed Katherine would be with you by now,' he continued, undaunted.

'As did I… I expected them hours ago! I guess *she* persuaded my son to show her around town.'

'I thought Katherine's father was to meet her at the airport?' Alex queried, envisaging Katherine's disappointment.

'I didn't let my husband go to the airport… He's not a well guy… All *this* has gotten to him, you know,' she said accusingly.

Alex took a deep breath. 'I appreciate your position, Mrs. Donnelly, I really do. But it has been a big shock for *all* of us,' he added, struggling to contain his mounting resentment toward the strident, disembodied voice in his ear. 'I wonder, Mrs. Donnelly, would you be good enough – when Katherine does arrive – to let her know that I phoned? Nice talking with you,' he added, tongue-in-cheek, before replacing the receiver.

Lolling back in his chair, he mulled over the conversation. It was blatantly obvious that Katherine was in for a rough ride from Mrs. Donnelly. He felt guilty for not being there to lend his support, and fervently hoped Katherine's father and Patrick would make up for her animosity.

Patrick… Alex turned the name over in his head, and wondered what kind of man he was and how Katherine would react to her newly acquired brother. Irrationally, he experienced a pang of jealousy. He wanted her here – in the newsroom! Tomorrow she was supposed to accompany him to a reception in the Lord Mayor's parlour, not be, seemingly, gadding around God knows where with her half-brother.

His eyes roved the newsroom and came to rest on Josie as she turned away from the copy-typist's booth. She flashed him a wide smile. With no Katherine to accompany him, why not take Josie to the reception? Returning the smile, Alex beckoned her over to his desk.

Ellie was aggravated by the telephone call from England. She'd pounced on the phone expecting the caller to be her beloved Patrick. Her lips tightened. Where on earth was he? She'd specifically instructed him to come straight back home. She was certain the delay was entirely of Katherine's doing – taking in the city sights. Ellie gave no thought or consideration to the possibility that Katherine's flight might have been delayed.

Sitting on the elegant, gilt chair beside the green, marble-topped telephone table, Ellie tapped the pointed toe of her expensive pink satin slippers on the black and white tiled hall floor. Somehow, she told herself firmly, she had to get control of her feelings. She'd promised Michael that she would extend some of the famous American hospitality to his daughter – but it was a promise she doubted she could keep. Her dark eyes narrowed, hardening the expression on her perfectly made-up, well-preserved, elfin-like face. She was keenly aware that she had to be careful how she handled the situation that had been thrust upon her. To be openly hostile toward Michael's daughter would be counter-productive.

She looked through the archway to the sitting room where Michael was slumped in his favourite red leather armchair in front of the T.V. He'd fallen asleep – as he often did – almost as soon as the ball game began. The years of pain he'd suffered from his leg wound were deeply etched on his still handsome face.

From the moment Michael had got back from the war, her life had been dominated by his disability. The constant hospital visits; operations needed to save his leg; and, in the last year, his added heart problems, had further curtailed their social activities. Her only consolation in life was Patrick and her granddaughter, Meredith.

After her daughter-in-law's death, when she'd finally managed to persuade Patrick that it would be better for them to live with her and Michael, she'd been much happier. There was no way, now, that she would allow Michael's daughter – a total stranger – to muscle in on her family's affections. Her heart began to thump as the colour rose to her cheeks. What *right* had this woman from Michael's past to invade their lives and cause such turmoil? Her mouth tightened again as the black cloud of jealousy descended.

Rising from the chair, she tiptoed across the wide hallway and lifted her snug, cream jacket from the wrought-iron coat stand. Discarding her slippers, she pulled on the comfy tan sneakers she wore for her solitary strolls along the boardwalk.

Closing the door gently behind her, she stood on the wooden veranda that hugged three sides of the house. A strong breeze blowing in from the ocean hit her face. Shivering, she pulled the hood over her head, and ran down the wide flight of steps to the front yard and sidewalk, her mind full of dark thoughts.

It was unbearable that another woman was coming into her home. It had been difficult when Patrick had married Barbara, but Michael's own flesh and blood? She hurried along, her resentment mounting. If Patrick arrived while she was away, then they'd have to wait for their meal until *she* felt like returning, she decided – giving no thought to Meredith's imminent return from school.

Meredith strolled down the sidewalk, a multi-coloured, fringed, woven bag full of schoolbooks hanging heavily from one shoulder. Her wind-blown, blonde hair straggled across her lightly tanned face; her bright blue eyes, wide with disbelief, roved over her companion's earnest expression.

'You're kidding, Cassie – right? *You* think Katherine – Pop's sister…'

'Correction – half-sister,' her friend butted in breathlessly, as she lumbered along beside Meredith, sagging under her own weight and a plastic carrier bag full of books.

'OK, OK, half-sister,' Meredith conceded. 'You think Aunt Katherine could be some sort of con-artist after Gramps' money?'

'Sure – could be!' Cassie replied smugly, eager to burst Meredith's bubble of joy at the prospect of having someone from England come to visit her house. 'I saw this movie on T.V. once, about these G.I. brides who came over from England after the war... with *babies*!' Cassie stopped to catch her breath. 'And they could never be really sure the babies *belonged* to the G.I. guys!'

'Well, who did they belong to?' Meredith asked, wide-eyed again.

'English guys, I suppose.'

Cassie's mother had expressed the opinion that Meredith should never have been told about what her grandfather had got up to in England; it wasn't right – she maintained – for a ten-year-old to be exposed to such things.

But Cassie knew that Meredith was far from worried about 'such things'. On the contrary, she was very excited. She felt important at school. She'd become a sort of celebrity entertaining someone from England. Well, Cassie thought, it might not be as exciting as she imagined if what Meredith had told her about her grandmother's feelings on the matter were true!

Meredith gave Cassie an unenthusiastic, 'Bye' as they parted company to go their separate ways.

Pop and Gramps had very gently explained things to her

after the big row between Gram and Gramps when Katherine's letter arrived. But, secretly, *she* rather liked the idea of having an aunt around, even if Gram had raged against it.

Since her mother had died, Meredith's life with her grandparents had been very different from her life in Worcester, where there was plenty of stuff going on. She'd missed her friends – desperately. Life in Asbury Park was slow, less exciting – just school and the beach. An English relative, she reasoned, would liven up her daily life considerably. Despite what Gram had told her – that Katherine's visit had to be 'tolerated' and they might never see her again – Meredith had eagerly listed in her 'My Thoughts' notebook, all the places in Asbury Park that she and Pop could show her English aunt. And, more importantly, all the places in *England* that she would like Katherine show to *her*. Top of the list, underlined in red, were London and Buckingham Palace.

Meredith climbed the steps to the veranda and opened the front door, feeling sick with excitement at the prospect of meeting Katherine who, Gramps had assured her, would be there when she got back from school.

The house was quiet. She'd expected a babble of voices, but all she could hear was the T.V. commentary of the ball game. Placing her bag in the hall cupboard, she took off her sneakers, put on her fluffy white slippers and wandered through to the sitting room.

Michael stirred in front of the television and rubbed his eyes as Meredith knelt at his side, resting her elbows on the arm of his chair.

'Where *are* they, Gramps? I thought Pop and Katherine would be here – has Gram taken Katherine down to see the ocean?' Meredith gabbled on without waiting for a reply.

Michael looked at his granddaughter's flushed, eager face and glanced across at the antique wall clock. Five thirty. Patrick and Katherine should have arrived hours ago.

'I don't know where they are, honey,' he said, taking her hand. 'Maybe the flight was delayed.' His daughter should be here – would be here shortly. His *daughter*! He let the word roll around his head.

Before he'd opened the envelope bearing an English stamp and Cheshire postmark, he'd wrongly assumed – had hoped – that the letter was from Nancy. And when Ellie handed the envelope to him he knew, from her expression, that she thought so too.

Nancy! She was always there between them – even though Ellie seemed to accept the situation when Nancy's letter, telling Michael she was pregnant, had arrived in 1945.

For thirty-two years Nancy, and the child he'd known nothing about, had been constantly in his thoughts – a secret place he retreated to from a marriage he found bearable only because of the unconditional love he received from Patrick and Meredith.

He'd opened Katherine's letter with trembling fingers and read it as Ellie stood scowling beside him. When he told her that Nancy was dead, she'd registered no emotion other than a gleam of satisfaction in her eyes – which quickly disappeared when he informed her that the photograph he held in his hand was of Nancy's daughter – his daughter. Katherine.

Ellie had snatched the photograph from him. 'Is she like *her*?' she'd spat out.

'She's exactly like her *mother*,' Michael had murmured, through tears he was desperately trying to hold back, unable to freely express the joy and exhilaration he was experiencing.

'Where *is* Gram?' Meredith's voice cut into his bitter-sweet memories.

'Isn't she in the house, honey? She *should* be preparing the meal,' he replied, struggling to drag his mind back from the past.

'I don't think so, Gramps,' Meredith said, picking up on the apprehension in her grandfather's voice.

Young as she was, Meredith understood the difficulties her newly acquired aunt would encounter from her grandmother when she entered the Donnelly household. She gazed solemnly at her grandfather.

'Are *you* happy to see Katherine, Gramps? I know you can't get as excited as me… because of Gram… But, gee, Gramps, you must be *exploding* inside?'

Michael's face relaxed. He smiled tenderly at Meredith and pulled her down into his arms, nuzzling his face in her hair, which smelled of the ocean.

'You know, Merry, you're right on the button. I sure *do* feel like exploding! Couldn't have put it better myself. But I'd better *not* explode – don't want to muzzy up your grandmother's new white hearth-rug,' he added with a chuckle.

How was it, he wondered, that kids were so wise these days? His treasured granddaughter had lightened his anxiety, and he fervently hoped she would ease the tension that would surely affect the house when Patrick brought Katherine home.

Home? Who was he kidding, it wasn't Katherine's home. Her home had been with Nancy in England – a home *he'd* not been a part of. He felt a dull pain in his heart at the thought of what might have been – should have been. He was certain they would have been blissfully happy sharing a life together.

His marriage to Ellie was without the passion and tenderness he'd experienced with Nancy. He'd tried to conceal his unhappiness in order to provide a stable home environment for Patrick, but he regretted sacrificing his and Nancy's happiness by settling for the easy option to stand by Ellie in 1945.

Now, the prospect of seeing his and Nancy's child was a miracle he felt certain that Nancy – somewhere along the line – had had a hand in!

CHAPTER 5

ON THE TRAIN JOURNEY to Asbury Park, with her head resting on Patrick's broad shoulder, Katherine managed to catch up on some long overdue sleep.

Her dreams were muddled: Alex and Josie locked in each other's arms, dancing around the office desks – Alex in a sparkly dinner jacket and Josie in a white meringue wedding dress. Then, suddenly, she was back on the plane, the passengers screaming as it spiralled out of control toward the grey Atlantic. She cried out in terror, and awoke with a shudder.

Patrick was gazing at her in alarm. 'Hey, take it easy there – you OK, Katherine?'

'I am now I'm awake and not in a plane about to crash… I don't usually have nightmares – specially not during the day!'

'I guess you're all keyed up. The long flight and everything.'

'"Everything" meaning the imminent meeting with my father and the rest of the Donnelly clan?'

'Well, you've ticked *me* off the list, so the worst is over,' Patrick laughed in response to Katherine's wry smile.

'Where are we?' she enquired, as the train hurtled through countryside which, she thought, was remarkably similar to Cheshire.

'We're nearly home. Next stop Asbury Park.'

There was no platform at Asbury Park. Patrick lifted Katherine down from the steps of the train, stood her beside the track and reached up for her suitcase. In the fading light, she could just make out clapboard houses on a tree-lined avenue fronted by a wide, grassy, open space, where a group of children were gathered.

'Those are some of Meredith's friends. She's told them all about her English aunt coming to visit. I guess they're hanging around to catch a peek of you.'

Katherine laughed and relaxed a little. 'No turning back now, then.'

Patrick took her arm. 'Come on. We're much later than I expected. Pop will be anxious and Mom, well – we'll see...' he said, pursing his lips.

As they walked across the green, the children gave Katherine wide smiles and followed them onto a bridge over a watercourse. On the other side, Katherine could see a large, detached house with a verandah at ground floor level supported by orange and white wooden columns. Several broad steps led up to the bright turquoise front door, and in the doorway was a pretty young girl looking eagerly across at them.

'That's my daughter,' Patrick said proudly, giving Meredith a wave.

Meredith ran down the steps, raced across to them and flung herself at Patrick, squeezing him tightly around his waist. Looking up, she flashed a beaming smile at Katherine.

'Hi,' she said shyly.

Katherine stepped toward her and held out her hand.

'Hi,' she responded warmly. 'I'm so pleased to meet you, Meredith. Your father and grandfather have told me a lot about you.'

Meredith shot a smile of satisfaction to her friends who were standing, open-mouthed, behind Patrick and Katherine.

'Sure pleased to meet you too… I just *love* England. I haven't been there, but I've seen it lots of times on T.V. and at the movies,' Meredith said excitedly, and grasped Katherine's hand. 'Come on up to the house – Gramps has been waiting a long time for you.'

Led by Meredith, Katherine entered the house and stood in the hall. She stared up at the wide, sweeping staircase, the white wrought iron balustrade leading to a long, galleried landing. Dominating the hall was an enormous crystal chandelier. Through an arch to the right, Katherine could see a big rectangular room with cream walls, on which hung many oil and water-colour paintings that she presumed were from the gallery. A very large, red leather settee and several cream leather armchairs stood on the silver grey carpet. Heavy, red velvet drapes hung each side of a patio window that ran the length of one wall.

A log fire crackled and spat in the Adam-style fireplace, either side of which were matching crystal wall lights. Slouched in a red leather armchair, facing a big console television, was her father – *the man she'd fantasized about all her life*!

Katherine's heart began to race; her feet frozen to the floor, beads of perspiration forming on her pale brow. How to greet him? Should she address him as 'Father' immediately? She'd gone over this scenario many times in her mind, but now that he was actually there, in front of her…?

As she took control of her legs and approached him, Michael turned and struggled to stand up.

'Please… don't get up,' she murmured. Taking his arm, she lowered him back into the chair and knelt beside him.

They faced each other, Katherine's eyes brimming with tears, her father's full of wonderment. Reaching out, he gently stroked her hair.

'You're… so like your mother, Katherine… so like Nancy,' he said, shaking his head sadly. Katherine struggled to find her voice and failed. She felt as though she was in a dream – afraid that she would awake at any moment.

Michael pulled her to him and, locked in their embrace, they wept.

Standing in the hall, Patrick and Meredith hugged each other in awed silence, listening to their gentle sobs.

Then, shattering the moment, the front door was flung open, letting in a blast of cold air and the smell of the ocean.

Patrick turned and faced his mother. He put a finger to his lips and shook his head, alarmed at the expression on her face. As she swept past him, he touched her shoulder. But Ellie did not look at him nor register the anxiety on her granddaughter's face.

Katherine felt her legs weaken again as she stood up and met Ellie's steely gaze. She offered a shaky hand. 'I'm very pleased to meet you … so grateful … I appreciate how difficult this must be for you …' she managed to blurt before her voice petered out.

Ellie briefly touched Katherine's outstretched hand, her collection of gold bangles clinking on her slim wrist. 'It's my duty to support my husband!' She shrugged her shoulders. 'All *this* … well, it's difficult for him too, you know. He's not at all well.' She turned to Michael and rested a hand on his shoulder. 'But we'll get through it – together – won't we, honey? Now, if you'll excuse me, I'll see if I can rescue the meal I'd prepared,' she said, throwing Patrick a withering look. 'I expected you home hours ago.'

Patrick's face tightened. 'I took Katherine into town for a meal … I thought I'd told you that's what I planned. I guess we got carried away getting to know each other. Sorry.'

Ellie, without responding, turned to Meredith. 'Come along, Merry – you can set the table.'

Katherine noted Meredith's look of disappointment.

'Can I help?' she asked, as cheerily as she could.

'Patrick can assist,' Ellie said sharply, as she strode out of the room.

Patrick gave Katherine a meaningful, supportive wink.

'You and Pop have a lot of catching up to do,' he said. 'I'll leave you and…'

'Katherine must be tired after her long flight,' Michael interrupted. 'I'm sure you're ready for a rest and a soak in the tub before we eat? Tomorrow we can go down to the boardwalk, sit by the ocean and have a heart-to-heart – without any interruptions.' Lowering his voice, he took Katherine's hand. 'I must apologize for Ellie, Katherine.'

'There's no need, really… I do understand,' Katherine replied, saddened by her father's drained expression. She hesitated before turning away. Should she kiss him? She desperately wanted to. *Why* was she hesitating?

As though sensing her thoughts, Michael gazed at her affectionately, pulled her down to him and kissed her on the cheek.

'I should have persisted with Nancy… I should have kept in touch… I have no acceptable excuse to offer you, Katherine,' he said dejectedly.

Katherine fought to keep her tears at bay.

'I doubt you'd have changed Mother's mind – she was one stubborn lady! Once she'd made her mind up about *anything* there was no turning back. And that applies to me too – which created just a little friction between us from time to time,' Katherine grinned, pleased to see a smile light up her father's face. 'Now, I think I'd better go and change for dinner. I don't want to…'

Before she could finish the sentence, Meredith rushed in from the kitchen, face flushed. 'Gram says to tell you there won't be time to go in the tub. We have to eat in fifteen minutes, or *everything* will be spoiled,' she announced breathlessly. 'Please sit by me, Aunt Katherine… I *can* call you Aunt, can't I? She can sit by me, can't she?' Meredith implored Patrick, who had followed her in from the kitchen.

'I guess there's no problem there, Merry. What say you, Katherine?' Patrick said, taking her arm and guiding her toward the staircase.

'I'd love to sit by you, Meredith – but on one condition. Can I rely on you to nudge me when you think I'm about to fall asleep? I'm afraid the jet lag will creep up on me and I don't want to appear rude,' she laughed.

'Deal!' Meredith said happily. '*I'll* take you up to your room – come on,' she added excitedly, grabbing Katherine's hand.

'And I'll be right up with your suitcase,' Patrick called after them, returning to his father's side.

Michael's eyes were closed. He looked older than his fifty-three years, Patrick thought as he touched him lightly on the shoulder.

'You OK, Pop?'

Michael brushed a hand wearily across his eyes. 'I'll be fine, Patrick, I've a lot on my mind – nothing to worry you, son.'

'Well, it can't be Katherine, Pop – she's just lovely, isn't she?'

'It's not Katherine – it's your mother.'

'What's new there? Don't let her get to you. Katherine needs you to be strong for her. *Don't* let Mom spoil things for you now. Is she… is Katherine everything you expected?'

'More than I expected. She's the image of her mom. Katherine could *be* Nancy. I could see that from the photograph she sent, but in the flesh – it's quite a shock,' he said, patting his heart.

'But a happy and rewarding shock, I hope?' Patrick bent down and kissed Michael on the forehead. 'Would you like me to get you into your room before I take Katherine's baggage up?'

'You know, son – just for once I'm going to skip the changing for dinner routine,' Michael said, with a sigh. 'I just want to sit here quietly… I hope to God Ellie will be more civil and welcoming to Katherine. We've talked this through over and over… I thought we'd gotten *everything* sorted. I appreciate it's difficult for her – for you too.'

'It's not difficult for me, Pop. I'm delighted with Katherine – truly. And it's obvious Merry's entranced by her. I'm sure Katherine will win Mom over.'

Michael laid a hand on Patrick's arm. 'I wish I had your confidence!'

After the fastest shower she'd ever taken, Katherine descended the staircase feeling like a schoolgirl afraid of being late for class. She'd selected the emerald green silk dress she'd worn at her mother's fiftieth birthday party; the colour heightened the green of her eyes, and the draped skirt emphasized her tiny waist.

She'd had a good cry in the privacy of the fairy-tale bedroom, which Meredith had told her was kept for special houseguests – and she was never allowed to play in there.

After Patrick had handed over her case and ushered Meredith out of the room, she shied away from the colonial-style four-poster bed, with its white voile drapes and white cotton bedspread. Instead, she knelt on the blue and yellow floral sofa that filled the square bay window, and looked out. Between the tall trees in the garden, she could see the moon's silver path streaking across the surface of the distant ocean.

When her tears finally subsided, she felt less tense; the worst was over, she told herself. She was *here* with her father at last and, although she had every sympathy for Ellie's position, she would *not* allow her to spoil the precious time she was to share with him. As for Patrick and Meredith – what more could she have asked of their warm reception?

At the bottom of the stairs, she could hear the murmur of voices emanating from the dining room and felt her confidence waver. She desperately wished that Alex were at her side for support. She hadn't phoned him, as she'd promised. She didn't dare delay Ellie's dinner plans by asking to use the telephone. Alex would have to wait until afterwards.

She approached the white, louvred dining room doors to the right of the stairs, took a deep breath, grasped the crystal doorknob and slid the door across. All eyes turned toward her; Michael's full of pride as he sat at the head of the large, rectangular table, his wheelchair beside him; Patrick's full of admiration, and Meredith's twinkling in anticipation. Ellie, sitting next to Michael, fixed her with an immobile expression.

'Come sit by me,' Meredith said, patting the seat between her and Patrick.

Katherine covered her disappointment at not being placed next to her father – speculating it was by Ellie's design – and flashed a smile around the table.

Patrick stood up and pulled out her chair. He gave her shoulder a reassuring squeeze as she sat down on the pink velvet seat.

Another huge crystal chandelier sparkled above, reflecting in the highly polished rosewood table. Silver tureens rested upon black, wrought iron trivets; heavy silver cutlery with ornate handles and crystal glasses were set out on silver and gold place mats. Katherine struggled to contain the emotions she was feeling to be sharing her first meal with her father. A white, linen napkin, impeccably folded into the shape of fan, stood upright on her white, gilt-edged china side plate.

Michael gave Katherine a broad smile. 'I think I should serve our guest first,' he said, removing the lid of a tureen to reveal somewhat over-cooked, man-sized steaks.

Katherine's heart sank at the sight of them. A hot flush rose to her cheeks. 'I… um…'

Patrick came swiftly to her rescue.

'Sorry, Mom, 'fraid I forgot to mention that Katherine doesn't eat red meat – I found that out when I took her to Charlie's steak house,' he laughed, hoping to lighten the situation.

Ellie glared across the table at Katherine.

'Well, think yourself lucky! These steaks have been hanging around too long,' she said, stabbing a serving fork into the offending meat. 'There's cold chicken and salmon in the ice box – if *either is* acceptable to you?'

'Chicken will be just fine – thank you, Ellie.'

'May *I* have chicken too?' Meredith piped up, anxious to support her newly acquired aunt.

'Give her the steak, Michael… the small one,' Ellie said, ignoring Meredith's request as she pushed her chair back, stood up and flounced off to the kitchen.

Michael sighed. 'Sorry, Katherine.'

Meredith looked as though she were about to burst into tears. Patrick, with a face like thunder, rose from the table and headed after his mother.

Katherine felt the room spin. She looked at her father's crestfallen face. She struggled to find the right words, but felt totally drained and inept. Had Alex been right after all, warning her not to open up this lost chapter of her life? Had she selfishly not fully appreciated the impact her appearance would have on this family? Could it *ever* be *her* family?

The sound of a phone ringing in the kitchen penetrated Katherine's thoughts. She heard Patrick speak her name: 'Yes, she's here. I'll get her to take your call in the sitting room. Hang on… Yes, yes, I'm Patrick. Nice to speak with you too, Alex.'

Before Patrick came in from the kitchen, Katherine was already making her way to the sitting room, grateful to escape the heavy atmosphere in the dining room.

The red telephone stood on a glass-topped magazine table next to her father's chair. Katherine sank onto the chair and picked up the receiver.

'Hello,' she said softly.

'You OK ... ? You sound ...'

'I'm fine,' Katherine replied, without conviction. 'I'm sorry I didn't get a chance to phone you earlier.'

'I was worried, that's why I rang,' said Alex. 'I spoke with your father's wife earlier. Didn't she tell you I called?'

'No... no, she didn't ... Look, Alex, it's a bit difficult at the moment.'

'Michael's wife was more than difficult with me. What a dragon! I tell you, Katherine ...'

'I really can't talk now, Alex,' Katherine interrupted. 'I've just sat down to dinner... Are you at the office?'

'Yes. I've got a few things to tidy up before I can get away.'

'I'll phone you as soon as I've eaten – you'll still be there?'

'I'll hang on.'

'Thanks... Everything OK at the *Argus*?'

'Couldn't be better – Josie's on top of things.'

'I *bet* she is,' she said, regretting immediately her sharp retort.

'What's that supposed to mean?' Alex responded.

'Nothing... I really do have to go... Speak to you later, then.'

'Missing you, Katherine.'

'Missing you, too,' Katherine said, replacing the receiver and bracing herself to return to the dining room.

This should have been the happiest day of her life – sitting down for a meal with her father – but the thought uppermost in her mind was how soon she could make her escape to the sanctity of the bedroom. She took a deep breath. She had to force herself to look beyond the enormous strain of this first evening. Bizarrely, the words of Scarlett O'Hara came to mind: 'Tomorrow is another day!' She consoled herself with the thought that tomorrow she would have her father all to herself.

CHAPTER 6

THE NEXT DAY, Katherine awoke briefly disorientated, before remembering she was in her father's house. Stretching out her arms, she smiled broadly and snuggled down again under the white coverlet.

Pale sunlight filtered into the room through the heavy, cream lace curtains. She could smell the sea air, and she could hear the swell of the ocean breaking on the shore. She took a deep breath – magical.

But it hadn't been magical last night. Her brow furrowed. The tension throughout the meal had been lightened, to some degree, by Meredith's enthusiastic chattering and eager questions about Katherine's life in England. As soon as the meal was over, Katherine had used the legitimate excuse of her jet lag to retire to her room. She'd been elated to receive tender kisses from her father and Meredith, but Ellie had whisked Patrick away to the kitchen. Wriggling her toes under the covers, she speculated about the kiss she might have had from her handsome brother.

She turned her thoughts to Alex and the phone conversation they'd had when she'd finally escaped to her room. She'd confessed to the hostility she was encountering from Ellie – and waited for Alex to say, 'I told you so.' But, to her surprise, he'd made no comment. He'd seemed, she thought, somewhat offhand – not giving her his full attention. Then she'd heard Josie's tinkling laughter in the background.

There was a momentary silence before Alex asked if she would like to speak to Josie. 'Check if she has any queries on the Women's Page?'

Katherine gritted her teeth. 'I'm sure she'll manage *very* well… I'm spending tomorrow morning with my father,' she said, changing the subject. 'Just the two of us. I'll phone when I can – let you know how it goes.' She felt a rush of uncertainty. 'I wish you were here, Alex. It would be so much easier.'

'You know it's difficult for the two of us to be away from the office at the same time, Katherine.'

'I'm sure you could have worked something out – if you'd *wanted* to,' she said wearily.

Alex sighed. 'Let's not go over all that again. Get a good night's sleep. You'll feel heaps better in the morning… I'll have to go… Bye. Love you,' he said hurriedly.

Katherine felt more ill at ease after speaking to Alex, and didn't expect to get much sleep. But, despite the trauma of the day, once her head had touched the pillow, she'd gone out like a light. She did feel heaps better when she awoke; refreshed and energized by the smell of the ocean wafting through the room.

And a broad smile lit up her face at the prospect of spending quality time with her father.

Katherine checked her watch: eight thirty. Her father had told her that Patrick would take her to lunch and then on to see the gallery. Ellie – Michael had insisted – was to have coffee with a friend, leaving the field clear for him to devote the morning exclusively to her.

Sliding out of bed, Katherine padded across the deep pile, cream carpet to the bathroom. She gazed at her reflection in the huge, bevelled mirror, fixed to the sparkling white tiles by gilt cherub corners. Running a hand through her tousled hair, pushing it off her face, she surveyed the long glass shelf above the vanity unit that held an array of bath oils. Between the two bowls of the vanity unit stood a gilt basket full of differing shapes and sizes of toilet soaps. Katherine selected a mimosa bath oil, turned on the gilt taps and poured the oil under the gushing water.

After a leisurely bath, immersed up to her chin in the expensive bubbles, she applied a little moisturiser, green eye shadow, and brown mascara to her long lashes. Dressed casually in cream trousers and white shirt blouse, she brushed her hair, smoothed it back and tied it with a white chiffon scarf.

Descending the stairs, the only sound was the ticking of the clock. When she reached the bottom, through the open dining room door, she saw her father sitting alone at the table. Aware of her presence, he smiled affectionately.

'Good morning, Katherine. You sleep well? I wouldn't allow them to wake you earlier – much to Merry's disappointment,' he laughed. 'Patrick had a hard time persuading her to go to school. She wanted to stay home and breakfast with you… There's orange juice, cereals, scrambled egg, tomato and toast on the hot tray on the side table… and grapefruit and yoghurt in the ice box.'

'Quite a selection – thank you. But I'll be fine with the toast and orange juice. That's my usual before I rush off to work,' Katherine smiled.

Michael raised his eyebrows. 'Are you telling me you *don't* have those great British fry-ups Evelyn used to cook for my buddies and me? She was fortunate to be living in the country where she could sometimes get a hold of pork and eggs to eek out those meagre rations you Brits were existing on during the war.' Michael gazed lovingly at her. 'How is Evelyn, Katherine? She must miss Ted. He was a great guy… They were a great couple.'

'Evelyn's fine. They never had children of their own and spoiled me rotten.' Katherine lowered her gaze. Now, she felt, was not the time to tell him of her aunt's intervention in his and her mother's lives, when she'd seen fit to destroy his letter.

She took a couple of slices of toast from the silver toast rack, poured a glass of fresh orange juice into a cut-glass tumbler and sat down beside her father.

'I can't tell you how much it means to have you here with me, Katherine.' Michael's voice broke and his expression hardened. 'And I can't apologise enough for the way *Ellie* behaved yesterday. She has a lot to answer for!'

Katherine was taken aback by the unexpected bitterness in her father's voice.

'Please… don't upset yourself.' She took his hand. 'I understand, truly.'

Michael shook his head. 'No… you *don't* understand, Katherine. She's a law unto herself. But let's forget about Ellie today. We've got so much to say to each other.' His face relaxed. 'So, when you've finished your breakfast, we'll go down to the diner on the boardwalk by the ocean and get on with it, shall we?' he said, raising a smile.

Katherine found it distressing watching her father struggle from his chair into the wheelchair, but he kindly refused her offer of assistance. He was independent – like her mother. A knot formed in her stomach and a wave of sadness washed over her, thinking of the life they might have shared – the three of them.

Once in the wheelchair, rather than propel himself into the hall, Michael did allow Katherine to push the chair, sensing her need to assist him. She took a warm, suede jacket from the hall cloaks cupboard; helped him into it; wrapped a check scarf around his neck and handed him a pull-on, navy, woollen hat and matching gloves.

'All set for what the weather will throw at us,' Michael laughed. 'But you'd better get a jacket for yourself, Katherine – always a breeze down by the ocean.'

Katherine ran quickly up the stairs and collected her leather jacket from the wardrobe.

Back in the hall, she assured her father that she'd like to push the wheelchair. He directed her through an arch beneath the staircase that led to a small, square hall, where a collection of shoes and wellingtons were lined up neatly. Katherine opened the half-glazed door, and Michael indicated that she should open it wide, and insert the wooden wedge he'd taken out of his pocket and handed to her.

With not too much trouble, she pushed the wheelchair over the low step and onto a small, open sided porch. A chill wind stung her face and ruffled her hair.

A long, wooden ramp sloped gradually down to a concrete path edging a large, rectangular lawn, surrounded by shrubbery with yellow and russet leaves. Green wrought-iron chairs and tables sat beneath one of the tall fir trees. At the rear of the garden was a circular pond, in the middle of which, standing on their tails, were three large, metal, sculptured fish.

Michael reached out and depressed a switch on the door frame, and nodded toward the pond. Cascades of water shot several feet into the air from the fishes' mouths, the wind bending them from the perpendicular.

'Wonderful! You have a beautiful, natural garden – I do love trees,' Katherine said, breathing in the crisp sea air.

'And you have many beautiful trees in Cheshire.' Michael smiled up at her and pulled his hat down over his ears. 'I remember your mother and I strolling down a narrow lane behind the church and the old inn in Lower Peover.' He laughed. 'It took me a while to get the pronunciation right –

P-e-ver! There were so many Peovers. I liked the sound of Peover Superior! You know I attended Over Peover church with the General – is it St. Lawrence? Anyway, your mom and I liked the lane near the church in Lower Peover…'

'St. Oswald's,' Katherine prompted.

'Ah, yes… and just down the lane was a little bridge over a stream. It was *so* peaceful there, pretty secluded too,' he chuckled. 'Your mom and I just loved that spot. Our special place, you could say. The fighting over in Europe seemed so far from that idyllic haven.'

'I know it well. Mother used to take me there often when I was a child. I'd throw leaves and twigs into the stream and watch them sail out the other side of the bridge.'

'And she never mentioned that we'd been there?'

'I didn't know you existed, did I?' Katherine murmured.

Michael looked up at her and caught hold of her arm. 'Of course you didn't… Sorry… I wish *I* could have seen you as a little girl,' he said sadly.

'And so you will. I've brought lots of photographs with me.' Katherine patted the sizeable handbag dangling from her shoulder.

'Great – can't wait.'

When she'd pushed the wheelchair slowly down the ramp and manoeuvred it through the wooden gate cut into the hedge, Michael insisted he take over propelling it along. He pointed toward the bottom of the narrow road. A steel-grey ocean met a sky dotted with darkening clouds, through which the sun briefly emerged. 'See the parking lot – the diner's just beyond on the left, right next to the ocean. You can eat a *proper* breakfast there,' he told her, enthusiastically.

Katherine felt overwhelmingly happy as she walked alongside her father, past the clapboard houses painted white and pastel shades. Several residents – out on their porches – smiled and nodded as they passed by.

'Do they *know* about me?' Katherine queried.

'You bet they do, Katherine. Ellie's circle of friends have a circle of friends – who have a circle of friends!' he laughed. 'I suspect the whole of Asbury Park knows you're here. But I don't care… I'm proud, not ashamed, to have you with me at last!'

As they turned into the parking lot, the sun disappeared behind the clouds. A strong, chilly breeze was blowing in from the ocean, and beyond the parked cars, Katherine could see a handful of people walking along the boardwalk away from a single-storey wooden construction, which she assumed was the diner.

'We'd better get inside out of this wind. We'll get onto the boardwalk later if it drops,' Michael called back to her, as she stopped to brush strands of hair from of her eyes.

Struggling against the breeze, they reached the diner and, with difficulty, Katherine held back the heavy, red wooden door for her father to wheel himself through.

There were no customers at the yellow formica-topped tables and no one behind the counter, laden with an assortment of cakes under clear plastic domes. Michael expertly weaved his way towards a table by a window that faced an angry, turbulent sea.

'Sure is working up for a mighty rough one,' he said, lumbering himself onto a blue lacquered, bentwood chair.

When Katherine was seated facing him and had smoothed out her hair, he reached out and took her cold hands in his. For several seconds they looked at each other without speaking, savouring the moment, until the poignant silence that hung between them was shattered by a cry from the direction of the counter: 'Hey, Mikey – you ought'a have given me a shout out back. Didn't hear you come in.'

Katherine turned to see a small, well-rounded woman who looked to be in her forties, standing behind the counter. She wore a blue and white check dress with a white sailor hat clipped at a jaunty angle on top of a mass of strawberry-blonde curls. Her heavily made-up face broke into a broad smile as she lifted the counter flap and sashayed over to their table.

Michael released Katherine's hands and grabbed the woman's arm.

'Angelina – *this* is Katherine… who I've spoken about,' he said proudly.

Angelina beamed at Katherine.

'He sure has, lady! Pleased to make your acquaintance… Welcome to Asbury Park!' She grasped Katherine's hand. 'You sure are cold – but a nice hot drink will soon warm her up,' she said, turning to Michael. 'Ellie not with you, then?'

Michael shook his head and pulled a face.

'Not so good, huh?' Angelina gently squeezed Katherine's hand before releasing it.

'You'll be OK, honey. Ellie's a little fiery, but I'm sure she'll calm down.'

'I do appreciate it's difficult for Ellie,' Katherine responded, wondering just how much Angelina knew about Michael and her mother.

Angelina smiled. 'I'm going to leave you two alone after I've served up some hot drinks – and how's about pancakes with maple syrup and ice cream? They're yummy… Mikey's favourites. On the house?'

'Not for me, but thank you. I've already had breakfast, Angelina… Coffee will suffice,' Katherine said, giving her a grateful smile.

'Gee – you speak so pretty. But I thought you all drank tea over in England,' Angelina chortled. She turned to Michael. 'How's about you – usual pancakes and hot chocolate?'

'Well, today… I think I'll join my beautiful daughter with a cup of coffee and – maybe just *one* pancake.'

'Two coffees, one pancake coming right up.'

'What a friendly, cheery lady,' Katherine said, as Angelina bustled away.

'Never any different. She has a smile and a kind word for all her customers. Angelina's cheered me up over the years. I come here mostly with Patrick and Merry. Ellie not that often. For some reason, she's not keen on Angelina.'

Within minutes Angelina returned, put the tray of coffee

on the table and handed Michael his pancake. 'Enjoy. You two sure look swell together. But, I have to say, you don't look much like Mikey, Katherine – much better looking!' she laughed.

'Thanks for that, Angelina – I can hang out some place else, you know,' Michael joked. 'But you're right. Katherine's the image of her mother, and she was a beautiful English rose,' he added, stroking Katherine's hand.

'Then I sure can see why you lost your heart over there,' Angelina said, turning away as a couple, wet and windblown, swept in, letting in a blast of cold air.

Katherine looked out through the rain-lashed window at the waves and spume crashing onto the shore. 'I think we'll be here for a while,' she speculated.

'No hassle, Katherine – we have all morning. Patrick is coming back to the house around one to take you to lunch,' Michael said, picking up his spoon and digging into the pancake. 'Poor Merry, she was pretty piqued about missing out today.'

Katherine took a sip of coffee. 'You definitely won't be coming to lunch with us?' she asked, a note of disappointment in her voice.

'No, sorry. I have to pace myself through the day, and it's best I stay home… Try to keep Ellie sweet for this evening,' he said, giving Katherine a wry smile. 'But I'll be fine,' he added quickly, noting Katherine's look of concern.

'Are you sure?'

'Sure! Now, where are those photographs you promised to show me?'

Katherine picked her handbag up from under her chair, took out a bulky brown envelope and placed it on the table.

'My past, starting at the very beginning, right up to the present.'

Michael pushed the pancake to one side and picked up the envelope. His fingers trembled as he pulled out the photographs of differing sizes. Spreading them out on the table, he selected a black and white photo of Nancy gazing lovingly at Katherine, nestling in the crook of her arm, dressed in a long, lacy christening robe.

Michael's eyes filled with tears. Unable to speak, he fished a handkerchief out of his jacket pocket and dabbed at his eyes.

Katherine reached out and gently stroked his hand.

'Goddammit, Katherine, what did I *do* to her…? What did I *do* to the both of you!'

'It wasn't *all* your fault. Mother could have let you keep in touch – as *you* wanted to.' She looked at her father's woeful expression. 'But to be fair to Mother, according to Aunt Evelyn, she was absolutely distraught when she found out you were engaged to Ellie,' Katherine added, feeling the need to make that point in her mother's defence. 'And now, you and I have to move forward, don't we? Put it all behind us,' she said softly. 'Mother would want that, I'm certain of it – just as certain as that she intended me to find your letter!'

'You're just… just amazing, Katherine,' Michael murmured.

'And you're not so bad yourself,' Katherine laughed, breaking the tension. 'Now, let's lighten up and have a laugh at my school photographs – please take note of the ludicrous hairstyles.'

She selected photos from the pile and passed them over one by one.

'Me with the pudding basin haircut; with pigtails; ponytail, and – the sophisticated French pleat, all grown up at eighteen.' She paused. 'And this one – this is me and Mother on the occasion of her fiftieth birthday party.'

Michael's eyes moistened again as he looked at Nancy and Katherine, smiling happily, raising their champagne flutes. 'You look like sisters,' he said at last. 'Nancy, still so beautiful, so lovely. Just like the young woman I remember in 1944.' He shook his head. 'You said she hadn't been ill before the heart attack?'

'No. At least, she never complained of feeling unwell. Not to me – or Aunt Evelyn.' Katherine's stomach lurched at the mention of Evelyn. She still didn't feel ready to tell her father it was she who had destroyed the letter he'd sent to her mother telling her he'd been wounded. 'She *was* a heavy smoker,' she continued. 'Aunt Evelyn and I tried our best to get her to kick the habit, but we never succeeded. Smoking *was* a contributory factor in her death.'

'I guess you can attribute *some* blame to me for that, then! I was the one who gave Nancy her first cigarette – a packet of Lucky Strikes. There was a lot of smoking during the war, calming the nerves, I guess... I haven't managed to give up myself. But I have cut down. The doc keeps giving me warnings – bad for the circulation in the old leg; bad for the heart etcetera.'

'Then you should *listen* to him,' Katherine said ardently.

'Yes, m'am.' Michael gave her a military salute and picked up another photograph. 'Who's this good-looking guy – the boyfriend?'

'Yes, that's Alex. I told you about him in my letter.'

'You work together, right? On the newspaper, the ... ?'

'The *Argus*,' Katherine prompted, and took the photograph from him. Alex's handsome face smiled back at her. She'd taken the photo at a National Union of Journalists' conference where they'd spent their first weekend – and night – together.

Michael studied his daughter's face. 'You going to marry Alex, Katherine?'

Taken aback by the directness of the question, Katherine did not immediately reply. If anyone had posed it to her a few months ago, she felt certain her answer would have been, 'Very likely'. But now, here in America with her father, distanced from Alex? Why the uncertainty, she wondered?

'You're having to think about that?' Michael queried.

Katherine felt flustered. 'Let's ... let's talk about *you* and Mother,' she said hastily.

A look of melancholy took hold of Michael's expression, and Katherine became aware of Angelina looking poignantly across at them. She waited patiently as her father gazed absently through the window at the still turbulent sea.

When he turned to face her, his eyes were filled with tears:

'We had such a short time together, Katherine, but I loved Nancy so much – from the moment I set eyes on her – and I know she felt the same about me. Nothing to do with the war and the uncertain circumstances we were in. It was as though there was an invisible thread of deep longing connecting us. The depth of my feelings for her took my breath away – literally. I *loved* your mother more than I've loved *anyone* in my whole life. You have to believe that, Katherine,' he said, his voice choking with emotion. 'And I hope… I hope that *you* will accept my love now?'

Katherine studied his troubled expression.

'I've *wanted* to love you… have loved you ever since I was a child. I understand the feeling of being joined by an invisible thread. I felt it… felt that you were alive and, somehow, I knew that one day I would find you – or you would find me. And now,' she smiled broadly, 'there's no getting rid of me.'

'Despite Ellie?'

'Despite *anyone* !'

She leaned across the table and kissed her father on his cheek. Time seemed to stand still as they relaxed into easy conversation.

Michael spoke about his sadness and fears when he left Nancy and England to fight in France. He touched, briefly, on the harrowing experience of being shot. Anxious to discover the full extent of her father's disability, Katherine pressed him gently to elaborate.

'Well, as you can see, I have difficulty using my right leg –

which took the bullet – from the thigh to the calf. I was lucky the guys at the field hospital took the decision to save the leg. Though sometimes, I think I'd have been better without it – all the operations and constant pain.' Michael paused. 'I used to be a hot shot at baseball,' he said regretfully. 'But I shouldn't gripe. At least I'm still around to watch the game at the stadium and on T.V., which is more than the buddies I lost can do. After all these years, I still get nightmares. I was stupid enough to believe that World War II would be the end of all wars. But then came Korea… and Vietnam. Ellie was inconsolable when Patrick was drafted to Vietnam.'

'That must have been horrifying for you – after your own experience,' Katherine said. A chill ran down her spine as she recalled the graphic newsreel footage from Vietnam that dominated the T.V. screens.

'It sure was. Patrick was there right up until the U.S. pulled out of Saigon. He was lucky to get out before the Viet Cong took over – quite a hair-raising story. But Patrick can tell you that one, *if* you can get him to talk about it! But enough of war. How's about you and me sharing this traditional – now *cold* – American pancake? It will only be half the calories and I won't take no for an answer,' he said, with relish.

Bidding farewell to Angelina as she held the door open for them, reluctantly they left the warmth of the diner.

Katherine helped push the wheelchair back to the house, battling against the ever-increasing gale. As she turned it through the gate, she saw Patrick standing on the back porch and felt a tingle of pleasure as he ran down the ramp to meet them.

'Let's get you two inside out of this wind. I was about to get the car round to the diner to pick you up – you should've hung on there, Pop,' he said, giving Katherine a peck on the cheek. Relieving her of the chair, he wheeled it into the house.

'You and Pop have a good heart to heart, Katherine?' he asked, as he took off Michael's coat and settled him into his armchair.

'The first of many, I hope,' Katherine said, glowing with contentment.

Patrick smiled. 'Good! That means you'll be coming back to us, eh, Pop?' he said, putting a hand on Michael's shoulder. 'Where's Mom? I take it she didn't join you at the diner?'

'Nope. I insisted Katherine and I spend time on our own. Ellie arranged to have brunch with one of her coterie. We had a lot of catching up to get through at Angelina's. You'll have to get Katherine to show you the photographs over lunch – she was a pretty cute kid,' Michael laughed.

'She's pretty cute now!' Patrick said, looking across at Katherine and holding her gaze a fraction too long.

Katherine felt the colour rise to her cheeks and averted her eyes.

'We can certainly look at the photos but, as for lunch – maybe not, after breakfast *and* half a huge pancake that your father insisted I ate!' she said, wondering why she had said *your* father and not just – Father.

'Pop! You *knew* I was planning to take Katherine out to

lunch,' Patrick remonstrated and turned to Katherine. 'I'm sure you'll be able to manage a bite of something, I'm absolutely starving. So – let's hit the highway.'

'Do I have time to freshen up?' Katherine said, indicating the tangled state of her hair.

'You look swell to me, but if you must,' Patrick replied agreeably.

Katherine ran up to her room, changed quickly into her warm black trousers and white polo-neck sweater. She applied fresh lipstick and brushed her hair. Elated at the prospect of lunch with Patrick, she checked her appearance in the gilt-edged cheval mirror and smiled contentedly. She'd had a truly memorable morning with her father, exceeding all expectations. She crinkled her nose. The only dark cloud on her horizon was Ellie, and the prospect of sitting through another strained evening meal.

CHAPTER 7

PATRICK DROVE KATHERINE down the coast to the Ocean Grove Auditorium in his pale blue Packard, and by the time they'd arrived at the impressive Victorian building, the gale had almost blown itself out.

Patrick seated them at a quiet corner table and handed Katherine the menu. Still feeling full from the delicious maple syrup pancake her father had encouraged her to try, Katherine managed to convince Patrick that a chicken sandwich would suffice which, when it arrived, turned out to be a massive three-tier affair with an abundance of salad garnishing.

She sighed and Patrick laughed. 'This is one of my favourite places – apart from good food, they have great Saturday concerts,' Patrick said, as he tucked into his king-size burger and chips. 'If you like, Katherine, I'll find out who's performing. There are usually top-name popular and classical artists,' he added, squirting a liberal amount of tomato ketchup onto his burger. 'I saw Frankie Valli the last time I was here. But if concerts don't appeal, on Sundays they have some of the finest preachers and evangelists. There's a lot of history in Monmouth County and I'd like to show you some of it this week, if I can get Mom to cover for me at the gallery.'

Katherine instinctively doubted that Ellie would look favourably on her taking up more of Patrick's time.

'Maybe we should check with Father?' she queried, her heart skipping a beat. It felt good – but unreal – saying 'Father'.

'*Father* actually made the suggestion, Katherine. Pop's disappointed he's not able to ferry you around himself, but he doesn't like driving. He finds it painful and… he's been really bushed of late.' He took a bite out of the burger and wiped the ketchup from the corner of his mouth with his napkin.

Katherine frowned. 'Pain is so debilitating. I'm grateful that Mother didn't suffer any pain in her lifetime – not *physical* anyhow!'

Patrick chose to ignore the comment and gazed earnestly into her eyes. 'How did you and Pop get on this morning?' he asked. 'Difficult for both of you, I imagine?' He lifted the jug of water. 'Would you like some?'

Katherine nodded. He poured half measures into two tumblers and handed one to her.

'Was there any… acrimony?'

'Not at all! After all these years it's too late to attribute blame, isn't it? Unless you blame Hitler for throwing the world into turmoil; the insanity of war and the inescapable position Mother and Father – along with millions of people – found themselves in. They were both casualties of the war,' Katherine said fiercely. 'They…'

'They and *you*!' Patrick interrupted. 'You don't class yourself a casualty?'

Katherine sighed. 'I *suppose* I am, growing up without a father. Being deprived of my grandparents by a German bomb. Did Father ever talk to *you* about the war? And, while we're on the subject, I believe you've had *your* share of warfare in Vietnam?'

Patrick wiped his mouth and fingers with his napkin and pursed his lips.

'I'm trying to forget all that; the boot camp where I was trained to be a robotic killing machine; the bloodshed and total mayhem – and for what? At least Pop believed in what *he* was fighting for – the destruction of a mad fascist whose ideology was for a so-called superior race of blue-eyed blonds! Hitler's rhetoric whipped Germany into a frenzy with the horrific consequence of consigning millions of Jews, blacks, gypsies and the mentally impaired to the extermination camps – not forgetting the armed forces and civilians who lost their lives.' Patrick shook his head. 'I don't understand how he managed to con the intelligent German nation. But Vietnam? A whole different ball game. I think we lost our way there – and I lost two of my best buddies in Nam,' he said sadly. 'My time out there put an added strain on Pop and Mom. Pop only spoke about *his* time in Europe after he received your letter, Katherine. That was the first I knew of his affair with your mother.'

Katherine looked at Patrick in astonishment. Her eyes flashed. 'It wasn't an *affair*,' she said hotly. 'Father wasn't *married* to Ellie, was he? And Mother wasn't even aware of her existence,' she added defensively and, for the first time, she experienced a tinge of resentment toward her father. She averted her eyes from Patrick's crestfallen expression. Did he, did Ellie – did the whole of Asbury Park – perceive her mother as a seductress?

'Sorry, Katherine, forgive me… I'm afraid that came out all wrong,' Patrick said softly. 'I know Pop loved your mom, he told me so, and I guess I can put myself in his shoes after the trauma of Vietnam. I missed Barbara and Merry like hell. The war zone is a lonely, frightening place.'

'That we *can* agree on… Let's move on, shall we?' Katherine said, noting Patrick's strained expression. 'Tell me… tell me about Father's parents… my grandparents – a potted insight into the Donnelly family tree.' She smiled, anxious to defuse the awkward moment that had sprung up between them.

Patrick looked relieved.

'Well, I'll try. It's pretty complicated. Obviously, with a name like Donnelly we have a connection with Ireland. If I remember correctly, from what Pop told me, my great great grandfather Sean and his wife Maeve emigrated to the States in 1847, along with many thousands after the infamous potato famine. They landed in Boston, but because of the animosity toward immigrants at that time, they moved on up to New York where they had twins – a girl who died at birth, and a boy they

106

named Sean. He married an American girl, Annie, and they had one child – Patrick – my great grandfather, hence my name. Patrick married and had a son – another Sean, traditionally! In 1921, *he* married Greta and moved to Asbury Park. The two of them produced our father, who married Ellie. Her family were Norwegian immigrants!' Patrick took a deep breath. 'I hope you're keeping up with all this, Katherine?'

'Fascinating! Do carry on,' Katherine laughed. 'It's good to confirm Father's connection to Ireland – I had assumed there was one. I'm afraid I don't have such a chequered ancestry. Mother's immediate family lived in North Staffordshire all their lives. Her sister, Evelyn, broke the mould when she moved to Cheshire – and Mother joined her in Lower Peover after their parents were killed in the air raid.'

'True English thoroughbreds, then?' Patrick said with a wry smile.

'Not quite – a great great grandfather came from Wales. I should point out that visiting holidaymakers from abroad generally say they are "going to England" – lumping Wales and Scotland under the England umbrella! But Wales has its own language – although the majority do speak English.' Katherine picked out a slice of tomato from the salad garnish. 'Do carry on, Patrick,' she said, before popping it into her mouth.

Patrick held her smile. 'Okay… Where was I…? Pop's parents – my grandparents who set up the gallery. When Grandfather died some years ago, Grandmother left New Jersey and moved to California for the warmer climate. She's a very independent lady and enjoys life on a retirement complex that caters for her every need. She doesn't travel to Asbury now – but I take Merry to visit in her school holidays.'

'Does your grandmother know about me?'

'No, not yet – Pop wanted to wait until you'd been over, so he could give her the up-to-date picture,' Patrick said, offering Katherine the plate of cookies he'd ordered.

'No thanks.' Katherine patted her stomach and took a sip of water. 'So… to recap… I'm from good Irish stock? Coincidentally, I studied Irish history at school – the potato famine and the terrible consequences of it. Had I known then that I had Irish ancestors, the "troubles" would have had an even bigger impact on me.' She pursed her lips. 'But we won't go *there*.'

'Let's *not*,' Patrick said emphatically.

'And what about Ellie's parents. Do you see them?'

'Nope, not since I was a kid. Mom fell out with them – and her sister. Never found out why. They're all up in Tacoma, Washington State.' Patrick smiled. 'Now, I think that's enough of the family tree. Let's get to the gallery – it's well past our opening time.'

They drove back along the coast under scudding white clouds in a bright blue sky, arriving late afternoon at the gallery, tucked away in a side street behind the railway station.

Katherine stood on the pavement looking through the large plate glass window. Framed oil and watercolour paintings were displayed on easels, and a variety of modern ceramics stood on plinths of varying heights. She looked up and gazed with pride at the gold lettering on the green sign above the window: 'Donnelly & Son – Fine Arts' – and smiled at the four-leaf clover on the right hand corner above the name.

'Pop put me up there when I got back from Nam,' Patrick beamed.

Katherine turned to him. 'I really *would* like to hear about your time in Vietnam.'

Patrick shook his head. 'Your reporter's nose kicking in? Well, please don't rely on getting an exclusive from me,' he laughed, turning the key in the impressive, shiny, dark green door.

Ushering Katherine into the gallery, he switched on the lights.

As she stood on the varnished wooden floorboards, Katherine looked around and gasped. The gallery was a veritable Aladdin's cave. Colourful ornaments sat on illuminated glass shelves; framed paintings of every size, lit by over-frame or ceiling spotlights, hung on the stark, whitewashed brick walls.

Patrick, arms folded, stood looking at her expectantly.

'What do you think of the family business?'

'V-e-r-y tasteful. I've dabbled a little with oils myself, but I couldn't get along with watercolours. Mistakes are more easily rectified with oils,' she grinned.

Patrick raised his eyebrows. 'You're an artist as well as a

writer? I'm impressed… Any other talents I should know about?'

Katherine laughed. 'If pressed, I could knit a sweater… Mother taught me to knit – and sew a button on in my formative years. *Her* real forte was gardening and floral arrangements – but I couldn't get enthusiastic about those either. I much preferred to stick my nose in a book or listen to plays on the radio,' she said, scanning the walls of the gallery.

Her eyes were drawn to a monochrome painting in tones of brown and ochre, depicting an open window, with flimsy lace curtains blowing into an unrevealed room. She walked over to observe it more closely. Beyond the window, way below, was a cart track heading to the sea. Despite the fluttering curtains suggesting a strong breeze, the artist had captured the feeling of oppressive heat within the room, leading the viewer to imagine someone had flung open the window to enable them to breathe. Just looking into the painting, Katherine experienced the sensation of intense heat.

'Wow!' she murmured, and took a few steps back from it.

'Amazing, isn't it?' Patrick responded, coming over to stand behind her. 'It's entitled "Wind from the Sea"; a very popular print by Andrew Wyeth – my favourite artist. He painted it in 1947 when…'

Patrick's words were muffled to Katherine's ears, his closeness provoking a peculiar effect upon her. A rush of heat ran through her body, fusing the feeling of overwhelming heat captured by the artist. The painting swam before her eyes; she felt faint and clammy. Reaching out, she caught hold of the corner of a display unit.

Patrick grabbed her arm. 'You okay? You're very pale.'

Embarrassed, she steadied herself and faced him, tears springing into her eyes. Patrick grasped her shoulders and pulled her to him. 'What is it, what's wrong, Katherine?' he asked.

She had no answer. She didn't know what was wrong; she was confused by the chemistry she felt between them. She only knew that she felt secure – at peace. She looked up helplessly and saw the concern in Patrick's eyes.

'I guess we've underestimated the trauma this trip has had on you, Katherine,' he whispered into her hair. 'The long flight – being out of your comfort zone. I sure feel guilty rushing you down the coast today. I should have brought you straight to the gallery and…'

'Please… you've nothing to feel guilty for,' Katherine interrupted, and backed slowly out of Patrick's arms. 'I… I don't know what came over me… Jet lag, I suppose.'

'Well, whatever the cause, I think I should get you back to the house for rest and recuperation!'

Katherine composed herself. Her legs felt less like jelly and the muzzy feeling in her head was receding.

'I think that's best. The gallery is *wonderful,* there's so much to take in. Maybe I can come back another day?' She looked at her watch. 'I don't want to upset your mother by being late for dinner again.'

Patrick frowned. 'You've really got to stop tip-toeing around Mom. She'll come round soon, I'm certain.'

'I do hope so,' Katherine replied, thinking she wouldn't place any bets on it.

When they got back to the house, Meredith – who had obviously been waiting for them – was standing on the verandah, wrapped warmly in a blue coat with fur-trimmed hood. Spotting the car, she waved frantically and skipped down the steps to greet them.

'Have you had a swell day? I wish Pop had let me stay out of school and come with you,' she said, grasping Katherine's hand to help her out of the car.

'Keep you out of school and risk the wrath of Miss Doheiser – I don't think so,' Patrick laughed. 'But, as there's no school tomorrow, tonight, after dinner, we'll plan what we're going to do with Katherine. How's that sound?'

'Tomorrow, Gram says you and Gramps have to stay home,' Meredith said with gusto. 'Gram's taking me and Katherine shopping in the mall … and then we're to have lunch with Aunt Yolande and Gram's friends.' She flashed a smile at Katherine. 'Aunt Yolande's not my *real* aunt,' she explained as she went ahead into the house.

Katherine felt less than enthusiastic at the prospect of being scrutinized by Ellie's friends as she followed Meredith into the hall.

'They're back!' Meredith called out excitedly.

There was no sign of Katherine's father. A baseball game was in silent progress on the television, his chair beside the dying embers of the log fire empty.

Ellie approached from the kitchen, a frilly organza apron tied tightly around the waist of her pale blue linen dress; not a stray hair, or a hint of shine on her carefully made-up face – looking the epitome of a Stepford wife! She wore an expression of wariness.

'Where's Gramps?' Meredith asked.

'Your grandfather is lying down. I told him to take a rest before dinner – and *you* can hang up your coat and tidy your room, missy,' she said curtly.

Meredith pulled a face. 'But I wanted to talk to Aunt Katherine,' she pleaded.

'I'm sure Katherine will want to go to her room until dinner!'

Standing firm, Katherine flashed a conspiratorial glance at Patrick. 'I was hoping to see Father *before* going up… But if he's resting, I won't disturb him. Maybe I can help with the meal?' she asked, in the faint hope she could thaw Ellie within the environs of the kitchen.

'No, thank you. You're a guest in the house.' Ellie turned on her heel. 'There was a phone call from England an hour back – a Josie?' she called over her shoulder.

'Josie?' Katherine's heart sank. She looked at her watch. Five o'clock – twelve o'clock at home. Josie normally lunched around noon.

'I *should* call her – but if it's an expensive time, I could…'

'Go ahead, call her now,' Patrick said. 'Make as many calls as you like, you don't have to ask, Katherine.'

'Thanks. There's probably a problem with the Women's Page – and I really ought to catch up with Alex,' who she hadn't given much thought to over the past few hours.

'Try and rest after your call,' Patrick said softly as they stood facing each other.

She nodded, turned away and headed for the stairs.

Closing the bedroom door behind her, she sighed. Why was *Josie* phoning and not Alex?

She walked over to the white and gilt walk-in wardrobe, took off her coat and hung it on one of the silk padded hangers. Kicking off her shoes, she stretched out on top of the bed, picked up the telephone from the bedside table and dialled the *Argus*. The line was engaged. She tried again without success. Anxious to get the call out of the way in time to take a relaxing bath before dinner, she dialled the operator to check it out and lay back, cushioning her head on the frilly pillow.

A few minutes later the operator rang back. 'Sorry, m'am. Your party's busy right now,' she informed her. 'Would ya want me to call when the line is free, m'am?'

'I would, thank you.' Katherine lay back again and closed her eyes, her thoughts drifting over the events of the day; the wonderful morning she'd spent with her father – she still wanted to pinch herself to believe she was actually with him. Those first short hours they'd spent together at the diner had been so precious, so perfect – everything and more than she'd ever dreamt of.

Her thoughts turned to her mother and the short time she and her father had had together. A time when he was young and his handsome face was not creased with pain. Katherine had been disappointed that her father wasn't around when she'd returned from the gallery. Ellie had said that she'd *told* him – not asked him – to take a rest. And, if what Meredith had said was true, Ellie had tomorrow all mapped out, which meant no more time alone with her father. She felt certain Ellie was doing her utmost to keep them apart. And there was little she could do about it.

Reflecting on the afternoon with Patrick, she felt uneasy about the feelings he aroused in her.

The telephone rang, breaking into her thoughts. Sitting up, she picked up the receiver.

'I'm connecting you to your party, m'am,' the voice drawled into her ear.

She could hear the clattering of typewriters and the murmur of voices down the line.

'Hello?' she said tentatively.

Josie's languorous, sexy voice replied.

'Hi, Katherine. Can you hear me okay? There's crackling on the line.'

'It's fine this end… What is it you want, Josie? I don't want to be on the phone for long, it's an expensive time and I'm about to get ready for dinner.'

'Oh. Would you like me to phone back then – reverse the charge? I'm sure the *Argus* can stand the cost of *one* international call,' she said waspishly.

Katherine felt her hackles rising. 'No, no… What's the problem?'

'Well, I thought I ought to let you know that we're carrying the story of you and your father etcetera, this week. News actually, not the Women's Page!' Josie said, with relish.

Shocked, but determined to keep calm, Katherine asked to speak to Alex.

'No can do, Katherine – he's off for the day.'

'*Very* convenient. He *promised* not to run the story until I got back with the *full* picture,' Katherine said heatedly, finally losing her cool. 'There'll be repercussions in the village if it's not handled sensitively – and I'm the only one to ensure that doesn't happen,' she added angrily.

'That's the way the cookie crumbles, I'm afraid – you know the score.'

Katherine took a deep breath and, despite her racing heart, managed to take control of her voice.

'If Alex *should* get in touch with you, please tell him to phone me – immediately.'

'Will do.' There was silence for a few seconds. 'I will be seeing him tonight. He's taking me to the Lord Mayor's reception as you're not around. *You* enjoying yourself over there?' Josie asked chirpily.

'Just ask Alex to call me,' Katherine said as civilly as she could, before replacing the receiver.

She sat for a while taking on board the disturbing news that Alex was running the story early – and that he was spending the evening with Josie. That he was going ahead with the story distressed her more than his dalliance with Josie.

Picking up the receiver again, she dialled Evelyn to prepare her for the impact on her – and the village – when the story broke.

Luckily she was fortunate to get through without delay, and Evelyn was elated to hear from her.

'You sound as though you're in the next room,' she said excitedly. 'How wonderful to talk to you, Kathy. Is it going well? How is Michael?' she asked, without drawing breath.

'He's… he's – everything I'd dreamt of, Aunt Evelyn. But… he isn't well – I don't think he's been fully fit since he was wounded.'

'I'm sorry to hear that. Did you… have you talked a lot about Nancy?'

'Yes, we have. We spent this morning together. I can't tell you how wonderful that was. Just the two of us, sitting in a café overlooking the ocean – albeit a very rough ocean. I showed Father' – she still felt such pleasure to use the word – 'lots of photographs of me and Mother… He asked about you and…'

'Did you tell him… what I did?' Evelyn interrupted. 'That I destroyed his letter?' she asked nervously.

'No, I didn't feel the time was right.'

'But you *will* tell him? I really think he *should* know.' Evelyn's voice broke.

'I *want* him to know, Kathy. I want him to *forgive* me. It's important that Michael forgives me!' she said tearfully.

'If you're certain that's what you really want, then I'll tell him before I leave.'

'Promise?'

'I promise. But the reason I'm phoning is to let you know that the *Argus* – *Alex* to be precise – will be running the story about Father and me *this* week. I thought I ought to prepare you for the gossip there's bound to be in the village. I'm absolutely *furious* with Alex, Aunt Evelyn. He *promised me* he'd wait until I got back to write the story myself!'

'Oh dear! But don't upset yourself, Kathy, I can cope with any gossip. People are more open minded than we give them credit for, you know. But I am surprised – and disappointed – with Alex. What did you say to him?'

'Nothing as yet. I haven't been able to get hold of him. He's conveniently out of the office today,' Katherine said angrily.

'Then… how did you find out about the story?'

'Josie! She phoned me. Alex is taking her to the Lord Mayor's reception – tonight.'

'Josie? Isn't she the one who's always batting her eyelashes at Alex?'

'She's the one!'

Evelyn sighed. 'I'd have thought *she* was too flighty for him. I wouldn't read too much into it, Kathy,' she added reassuringly.

'You know what, Aunt Evelyn, strangely, I don't feel at all bothered!'

'Oh dear – well, I don't know what to say to that.' She paused. 'Tell me, how are you getting on with Michael's family… his wife? How did she react to your arrival?'

'Much as you'd expect any woman to react when her husband's love child lands on her doorstep. Ellie's very offhand, to say the least… I wasn't expecting open arms. But, unlike me, who's only just found out I have a father, she's had the past thirty odd years to get used to the fact that I *could* exist!'

'And what about Michael's son? What kind of reception have you had from him?'

Katherine's voice softened. 'Patrick has been a rock. We got on really well from the moment we met at the airport. You know, Aunt Evelyn, it feels like we've known each other for years. He's so kind and considerate. I have a *very* handsome half-brother – and his daughter, Meredith, is so sweet. She's so excited by me being here… and I'm an aunt myself now,' Katherine laughed. 'So, if it's only Ellie that can't accept me, I'll have to learn to live with it. Although I've now realised *my* dream of meeting Father, it's really brought home to me the pain Mother must have suffered losing him!'

'Oh dear, Kathy. I'm never going to get rid of the guilt I feel destroying Michael's letter,' Evelyn said, her voice breaking again.

'Please don't cry. I've given that some thought too. If Mother *had* read the letter, it wouldn't have altered the fact that Father made love to her when he was engaged to Ellie! He would have had to confess at some stage and, when he did, that surely would have altered her opinion of him; shattered love's young dream. Would their relationship have survived?'

'Maybe not – but we'll never know for sure, and it doesn't excuse what I did.' Evelyn sniffed. 'Anyway, you mustn't let those thoughts affect your time with Michael. In wartime, survival was paramount – the uncertainty of not knowing if you would live or die changed people's attitudes to life. The comfort of a loving relationship was high on the agenda for survival. Don't dwell on the unknown. Enjoy being with your father. Promise me?'

'Promise,' Katherine said affectionately. 'And don't *you* worry anymore – new start for all of us. It's been good to talk with you, but I have to go now. Mustn't be late for dinner. I don't want to incur Ellie's wrath … I'll call you again after I've spoken to Alex. I'd like to strangle him,' she said bitterly, before replacing the receiver.

Feeling less tense after a soak in copious scented bubbles, Katherine put on her emerald silk dress. As she fixed her silver loop earrings, there was an urgent knocking on the bedroom door.

'Gram says to come down right away. Everyone's in the dining room waiting,' Meredith said, breathlessly, after bounding up the stairs at top speed.

Katherine opened the door.

Meredith's face had a rosy glow that matched the pink dress she was wearing.

'You look real swell,' she said admiringly.

Katherine gave her a wide smile. It was *great* being an aunt. 'And you, young lady, look pretty swell yourself,' she responded.

Meredith blushed and took hold of Katherine's hand. 'Will you sit by me, *please*? Gram's put you at the end of the table – opposite Gramps. But please tell her you want to sit next to Gramps and me – *please?*'

Katherine looked at her eager, upturned face. 'I'll give it my best shot – promise!' she said, bracing herself at the prospect of tackling 'Gram'.

When they entered the dining room hand in hand, her father's expression of pleasure was matched by Patrick's – looking stunning in a crisp white shirt and maroon bow tie. His eyes roved appreciatively over her.

Ellie, in a figure-hugging black lace dress, did not look up as she placed a dish of steaming vegetables onto the table.

'You look beautiful, Katherine,' Michael told her, wanting to add, but refraining from doing so – just like your mother.

'I'll second that, Pop,' Patrick grinned.

Meredith tugged Katherine's hand. 'Go on,' she whispered.

'*What* are you cooking up, Merry?' Ellie said sharply.

'She'd like me to sit between her and Father,' Katherine said, giving Ellie a disarming smile.

'It's okay by *me*,' Michael said. 'I want to hear what you thought of the gallery. I'd hoped you'd come in to see me when you got back.'

'I thought you were sleeping,' Katherine replied, wishing she'd ignored Ellie's request not to disturb him.

Michael flashed a quizzical look at Ellie as she dished out salmon steaks onto white china plates.

Patrick pulled the chair next to her father away from the table: 'Please be seated, m'am,' he told Katherine... 'And, does *this* seat meet with your approval, Miss Meredith?' he laughed, patting the chair next to Katherine.

'For goodness' sake – the food's going cold!' Ellie said, sitting down and shaking out her napkin.

Michael placed his hand on top of Katherine's and gave it a gentle squeeze. 'What did you think of the gallery? You like it?'

'Oh yes! V-e-r-y tasteful, the way everything is displayed – and the subtle lighting. You have a wonderful collection of paintings. My favourite was Andrew Wyeth's "The Wind from the Sea" – so evocative, I felt the oppressive heat he'd captured in that room.'

Patrick laughed. 'I can vouch for that, Pop. Katherine was so overcome by the painting, she literally swooned into my arms.'

Ellie threw Katherine a frosty look.

'I... I just felt a little faint,' Katherine said, blushing.

'You sure you're okay now?' Michael asked anxiously. 'Maybe you should...'

'Oh, don't fuss, Michael,' Ellie interrupted.

'I'm fine, really,' Katherine said, wishing she was at the end of the meal and not at the beginning; her resolve to stand up to Ellie ebbing.

As they ate, Katherine's mind wandered. What would her mother think of her being here in the heart of the Donnelly family? She felt a desperate need to bring her into the conversation – but thought better of doing so! Why did she feel disloyal to her mother sitting at this dinner table? *Had* she been wrong to come to this house? She caught her father's eye; he smiled, his eyes full of love, dispelling her reservations. No, she *hadn't* been wrong; she must enjoy the short time they could spend together, she told herself decisively.

Ellie's shrill voice chiding Meredith for having her elbows on the table, brought her back to reality.

Patrick was glaring at his mother.

Ellie was glaring back. 'Don't give me that look, Patrick – it's your place to see she watches her manners at the table.'

'We should *all* watch our manners when we have a guest at the table,' Michael said, and winked at Meredith.

Ellie's face tightened. She stood up, clattered the plates together and retreated to the kitchen.

Patrick sighed. 'I'd better go see…'

'*No*, Patrick,' Michael said firmly. 'Leave your mother… please.' He grasped Katherine's hand. 'Sorry!' he said, shaking his head.

'Don't worry – I understand,' she replied.

Meredith grasped Katherine's other hand. 'It'll be okay tomorrow, Aunt Katherine – promise. Gram just *loves* to shop!' Meredith said reassuringly.

CHAPTER 8

THE NEXT DAY DAWNED, warm and sunny, the sunlight filtering through the gap in the curtains throwing a beam across the bed. Katherine stretched lazily and looked at her wristwatch. Seven a.m.

Patrick, Meredith and Ellie's muffled voices rose from below, but Katherine was unable to make out what was being said. She surmised Patrick was gearing up to go to the gallery; Meredith getting excited at the prospect of the shopping trip and lunch with Ellie's friends.

In truth, Katherine wasn't enthusiastic about either venture. She would have preferred more one-to-one time with her father; there'd been no opportunity after dinner. With the exception of Ellie – who never reappeared – they'd played Scrabble until bedtime, the American spelling putting Katherine at some disadvantage!

She wrinkled her nose and told herself not to be so negative. Today she might be able to build bridges with Ellie, and it would be interesting to see what kind of reception she'd get from Ellie's friends.

After a leisurely shower, she applied a little make-up and selected her smart black jeans and cream cashmere sweater. Checking her appearance in the mirror, she fastened her hair back in a black ruched band and went down for breakfast.

She was disappointed not to see her father at the dining table.

Meredith rushed in from the kitchen to greet her, wearing pink and white pyjamas and fluffy bedroom slippers.

'Mornin', Aunt Katherine,' she said cheerily, taking her hand and leading her to the table. 'I had my breakfast with Pop, but Gram says *I* can make scrambled eggs for you – if you like?' she asked, eyes full of anticipation.

Katherine stroked her hair and smiled down at her. 'I'd love that – just with two eggs and one slice of toast, thank you, Meredith.'

'And orange juice – I've squeezed it special?'

'Yes, please, that would be nice.'

Meredith hurried back to the kitchen, full of enthusiasm.

Sitting down at the dining table, set only for one, Katherine hoped her father's absence was not due to him being unwell. She listened to the clattering of utensils emanating from the kitchen. If Ellie was in there with Meredith, there was no conversation between them.

Meredith pushed through the swing doors, face flushed, carrying a plate of scrambled egg, triangles of toast, slices of tomato and twists of cucumber, which she ceremoniously placed before Katherine.

'That looks magnificent – thank you!' Katherine picked up the silver knife and fork laid out on top of a peach linen napkin. 'I'm really going to enjoy this,' she said, tucking in heartily.

Meredith's smile was radiant. 'Swell – see you in a bit, then... after I get dressed.'

The kitchen doors swung open. Ellie entered the room carrying a tray on which was a crystal tumbler half-full of orange juice.

'We need to get to the mall as soon as possible. Yolande wants us at her apartment at twelve – and I don't want to be late,' Ellie said, before Katherine had time to say good morning. Not meeting Katherine's eyes, she placed the tray on the table.

Katherine forced a smile and swallowed a mouthful of egg. 'I won't be long – one of my failings is eating too quickly. Mother used to tell me it was bad for...' Her voice tailed off as she was momentarily thrown to have mentioned her mother to Ellie.

'How's Father?' she asked.

'Totally exhausted... I've taken breakfast to his room.'

Katherine bit into a slice of toast – registering the fact that Ellie had said 'his room' not 'our room'.

'I'm sorry to hear that... I'll look in on him if there's time?'

Ellie turned on her heel. 'I don't want him disturbed... and I want to leave in a ten minutes.'

Alone in the dining room, Katherine's appetite waned. No

Father to start her day – and the ordeal of lunching with Ellie's friends ahead of her.

It was a short, brisk walk to the mall, crossing the railway line that had transported Katherine from New York into her new world. Was it really only two days ago?

Ellie led the way, and Meredith tugged Katherine in and out of assorted shops on the heels of her grandmother: a jeweller where Ellie purchased a pair of pearl drop earrings; a boutique where Ellie bought a brilliant-pink T-shirt spattered with rhinestones – and Katherine bought Meredith the Yogi Bear nightdress she'd enthused over.

Making her escape from Ellie to browse in a quaint second-hand bookshop, Katherine discovered an illustrated book on Andrew Wyeth. Leafing through, she was delighted to find a colour plate of 'Wind from the Sea'. She ran her fingers over the page and decided she had to buy it; a lasting reminder of the moment she'd stood, enthralled, in front of the painting – with Patrick at her side.

As she was handing her new, crisp dollar bills over to the young sales boy – a dead ringer for Woody Allen – and answering his questions: where in England did she live? Had she been to a Manchester United match? – Meredith rushed in clutching a small, black and gold cardboard box.

'For you,' she said proudly, thrusting the box at Katherine. 'Open it now, please.'

'Oh, you shouldn't have, Meredith,' Katherine said kindly, and opened the lid. Inside, nestling on black tissue paper, was a green crystal replica of the Statue of Liberty.

'Oh my… she's beautiful! Thank you,' Katherine said, genuinely touched by Meredith's gesture. 'It's very kind of you, dear – but you ought not to spend your pocket money on me. I'm sure it cost quite a lot, and you must be saving it up to buy something special for yourself?' she smiled.

Meredith's happy expression suddenly faded.

'I *am* saving, Aunt Katherine. I'm going to buy a little marble vase to put on Mom's grave, beside the big one. Pop wanted to do it, but I want to buy it all by myself, for my *own* flowers!' She looked up at Katherine, her smile returning. 'But… if Mom was here and not in Heaven, I know she'd want me to give you this to remind you of America – and us – when you are back home in England.'

Tears rose to Katherine's eyes. She bent down and kissed Meredith on her forehead. 'I won't need reminding, I won't ever forget you, Meredith – any of you. You'll be here,' she said, taking hold of Meredith's hand and placing it over her heart. 'And I'm truly sorry I never got to meet your mother. I'm sure we would have got on famously.'

'Mom would have liked *you*. She was kind and beautiful. Like you.' Meredith's eyes lit up. 'Pop said you *would* have been friends. He says you're like Mom in lots of ways – though she didn't have your red hair. She was blonde, like me!' she said, flicking her locks.

Katherine swallowed the lump in her throat and pulled Meredith into her arms.

'Hurry up, you two – we're gonna be late for lunch,' Ellie's strident voice called from the doorway, shattering the magic of the moment.

Taking Meredith's hand, Katherine headed for the door, struggling to hang on to Andrew Wyeth and the Statue of Liberty.

'You have a nice day, m'am!' Woody Allen said.

'Will do,' Katherine called back, hoping that lunch with Ellie's friends would constitute a 'nice day'.

Following Ellie, who had more up-market carrier bags dangling from each arm, they didn't have far to walk to Yolande's high-rise apartment block.

Ellie keyed in the security code at the main door and they entered the foyer and crossed the grey marble floor to the lift. Meredith pressed the sixth floor button and opened the lift door when it arrived, Katherine's apprehension accelerating as the lift ascended. Stepping out, she heard the clicking of heels coming toward them along the wide hallway.

Yolande, the same shape and size as Ellie, was wearing expensive black crepe trousers, topped by a frilly, cream lace blouse. Her bouffant, blue-black hair framed a pale, flat, oriental face. Her dark, almond-shaped eyes roved over Katherine.

'Hi, honey,' she said, giving Meredith a hug. Turning to Katherine, she extended a slim hand overloaded with sparkling rings and jangling gold bangles.

'Pleased to meet you,' she drawled, in a heavy southern accent.

Katherine noted the cautious glance she threw to Ellie, and her heart sank.

'Come on in and meet the girls,' Yolande continued, indicating the open door and standing back to allow Katherine to pass between her and Ellie.

Crossing the threshold of the apartment, Katherine tried to dismiss the thought that she was entering a gladiatorial arena!

They walked through a hall, passing a black lacquered chair and an ornate Chinese table bearing a vase embellished with green and gold dragons, and entered a large square room. One wall had a glass door leading to a balcony laden with plants and potted palms. Three 'Stepford wives' with identical winged hairstyles sat primly on a huge black leather sofa; three pairs of eyes stared impassively at Katherine.

Her mouth went dry. She took a deep breath and told herself she was able to deal with this, having weathered countless mentally taxing interviews in her journalistic career.

Meredith took hold of Katherine's hand.

'This is my Aunt Katherine... from England,' she said proudly, beaming a smile up to Katherine.

'Hi!' the three voices said in unison.

'Hello, nice to meet you,' Katherine responded. None of the trio rose from the sofa to shake the hand she offered.

Standing apprehensively on the palest of blue shag-pile carpet surveying the scene, she smiled inwardly. It was a surreal, and somewhat comical moment, and the thought crossed her mind that one day she might find herself writing about the encounter. She allowed Meredith to draw her towards a black leather armchair and sat down, Meredith perching contentedly beside her on the wide arm.

'Don't *crowd* Katherine. Come sit over here, Merry,' Ellie said, patting the seat of a striped blue and white tub chair next to her.

'She's fine – really,' Katherine countered.

Ellie glowered at her.

'*Here*, Meredith,' she said, resolutely.

Meredith's lip quivered, but she slid off the arm of the chair and crossed the pale blue divide to sit alongside her grandmother.

Yolande glanced at the Stepford wives and, to Katherine's surprise, shook her head disapprovingly at Ellie. 'Meredith can help *me* hand round the sandwiches and cookies – can't you, honey?' she said soothingly, beckoning Meredith to her.

Sandwiches! Katherine latched on to the word and felt relieved that she wouldn't have the ordeal of sitting formally in close contact around a dining table to face the inevitable cross-examination.

Meredith threw her a smile before following Yolande through the double glass doors and across the hall to the kitchen.

There were a few moments of awkward silence before Ellie spoke. 'Let me introduce you to my *darling* friends,' she said into thin air, waving her arm expansively at the Stepford wives: 'Jane, Roberta – but we call her Bobbie – and Lois.'

'We've been friends from high school – there's not much we don't know about each other,' Lois volunteered.

'But we've learnt a few things we *didn't* know about Michael,' Bobbie giggled girlishly.

'Sure have, hun,' Jane chipped in. 'Ellie's been… Well, you have to admire her. It's been difficult,' she said, fixing Katherine with an icy stare.

Katherine took a deep breath. 'It's been difficult for everyone,' she said calmly, despite her rising hackles.

'Your mom… I believe she died recently?' Jane persisted, fingering the lacquer-stiffened wing tips of her silver-streaked hair.

Katherine was in no doubt that all Ellie's acquaintances would be aware of exactly when her mother had died, and also of *everything* about her mother and Michael's relationship – or as much as her father had disclosed.

'Yes, she did,' Katherine confirmed and, not expecting sympathy, prepared herself for the next round.

'We do have G.I. brides in Asbury Park – I think I'm right in saying about 30,000 or so came to the States from England,' Jane said, glancing at Bobbie for support.

'Boat loads arrived in '46 – they called it the *diaper run*,' Bobbie laughed. '*I* don't think any of our poor boys should have been sent to fight in that war. I really do not,' she said emphatically.

Katherine felt her face flush as she held Bobbie's expectant gaze.

'I can sympathize with that sentiment – being so far removed from all the bloodshed and misery in Europe. But I can reassure you that when you came to our aid after Pearl Harbour – it altered the course of the war. Without your help there's no doubt we'd have lost the fight against the Nazis!'

There was silence for several seconds. Lois shot an apprehensive glance at Ellie before giving Katherine a look bordering on admiration.

'Well… we *did* see the terrible newsreels at the movies – of London being bombed… I guess we did the right thing,' Lois acknowledged, giving Katherine the first smile she'd encountered since entering the lions' den. '*We* were lucky that our beaus didn't get killed… or wounded like poor Michael… But, I've never been able to get my Artie to talk about his time out in the Pacific.'

'Huh! A lot of brides and their bambinos arrived from the Pacific,' Ellie said testily.

Bobbie and Jane raised their eyebrows and stared hard at Lois, whose neck had gone bright pink.

'Well, *I* had no doubts about trusting Artie,' Lois challenged, eyes flashing.

To Katherine's relief, Meredith came in from the kitchen, smiling happily, and carrying a silver platter on which a variety

133

of triangular sandwiches were artistically arranged.

Ellie, tight-lipped, jumped up and took the tray from Meredith, whose smile vanished.

'Ellie, hun... I promised Merry she could be our little hostess and hand them around,' Yolande said. Passing the tray she was carrying over to Bobbie, she took the platter from Ellie. 'And I always keep my promises!' she added, handing it back to Meredith. 'Now, somebody tell me what I've missed when I was out back.'

No one spoke, then Lois chipped into the silence.

'Oh... we just talked about the war – and things,' she said hesitantly.

Yolande turned to Katherine. 'Well, I guess *you* know more about that subject than any of us?'

Bobbie and Jane exchanged glances.

'Hardly.' Katherine felt a flush rise to her cheeks. 'As I'm sure you know, I wasn't born until the end of the war. But I learnt a lot at school, the cinema, and through what I've read and written about.'

'Can we *please* talk about something else?' Lois appealed. 'Meredith doesn't want to hear about silly old wars, do you, honey?'

Meredith looked uncertainly from Lois to Yolande and then to her grandmother.

'You know what, Merry,' Yolande said, taking back the platter, 'I'm so stupid. How are we going to hand out the sandwiches and cookies when I haven't given anyone a plate to put them on?' she laughed, lightening the tension in the room. She stroked Meredith's hair affectionately. 'Be a darling and fetch them from the kitchen.'

'The white plates or the ones with the pretty blue flowers?' Meredith queried.

'*You* choose – surprise us, honey.'

Meredith hurried away.

'I don't think we should burden the child with all this,' Yolande said sternly, when Meredith was out of earshot.

Ellie glared at her. She picked up a glossy magazine from the white marble and gilt table that divided the sofa from the armchairs, and proceeded to flick through the pages, absenting herself from further comment.

Meredith returned and handed out the chosen plates, patterned with the pretty blue flowers, and with Yolande's help, offered round the sandwiches and cookies.

Bobbie was first to re-open the conversation. 'I was in Europe last year – in Innsbruck at the Winter Olympics. They should've been in Denver, you know, but they didn't want to spend money on the event.' She tutted. 'It would've been cheaper to go to Denver, but I'm sure glad we got to see Innsbruck – it's *so* picturesque. I just loved being there; I just *loved* the ice skating; such pretty dresses.' She babbled on in fine flow, despite the somewhat bored expressions on the faces of her friends who, Katherine surmised, had been regaled many times with the Innsbruck saga. 'And it was *so* exciting when our own Colleen O'Connor and Jim Millns won the bronze medal in the ice dancing – wasn't it, girls?' Everyone nodded, with the exception of Ellie.

Katherine seized upon the chance to engage in the conversation.

'And it was exciting for me when John Curry won Gold in the men's singles!' she said, and, feeling more relaxed, went on to commiserate about Elvis Presley's untimely death, only weeks before her arrival in Asbury Park.

The general opinion – apart from Ellie who carried on leafing through the magazine – was that Katherine should take the opportunity to make the pilgrimage to Elvis's home, Graceland, while she was in America.

'I'm sure it would be worthwhile; I'd love to write a piece about the experience,' Katherine said. 'Elvis has so many ardent fans in the U.K., me included. But unfortunately, I won't have the time.' She smiled, feeling she just might be winning over Ellie's friends.

Meredith chipped in, stating that she and her father were going to visit England next year.

At this pronouncement, Ellie put down the magazine, raised her eyebrows and looked at Katherine. 'Is there something I should know?' she questioned.

'Oh, Aunt Katherine doesn't know *anything* about it yet, Gram,' Meredith said. 'I asked Pop if he'd ask Aunt Katherine if we *could* go. But he thinks it's a great idea. It would be so exciting… a big, big adventure!' She looked appealingly at Katherine.

Ellie's expression darkened. 'And am I to be included in this – *adventure*, missy?'

Meredith shook her head from side to side and swallowed a mouthful of cookie. 'No, Gram… *You'll* have to stay and look after Gramps, won't you? Pop says it would be swell if Gramps *could* go back to England when there isn't a war or fighting and stuff – but he isn't well enough to go all that way now, is he?'

Katherine felt a warm glow spread through her body. Patrick was considering visiting her in England!

'Gramps certainly isn't well enough, but I wouldn't be happy about you and your pop being so far away from us,' Ellie said firmly.

Meredith looked crestfallen. 'But, Gram, we'll be…'

'We *won't* talk about it *now*!' Ellie interrupted.

'It *would* be a great experience for the child, Ellie,' Yolande said. '*I* sure wouldn't pass up an opportunity to go to England… I'd just love to go,' she drawled, smiling at Katherine.

Katherine did not respond, deducing it would be untimely to extend an invitation to Ellie's 'best' friend, although she could get a few column inches for the Women's Page from her visit – an insight into Ellie and the Donnelly family from a different viewpoint.

Her thoughts strayed to the *Argus* and the story that was shortly to appear about her and her father. Resentment toward Alex rose again. She had to try to speak to him, even though it was probably too late to pull it now.

Ellie's strident voice cut across her thoughts.

'I'd be grateful, Yolande, if you *don't* put such notions into Merry's head. It's for *me* to sort out with Patrick,' she said, ignoring Meredith's protestations.

Feeling decidedly ill-at-ease, Katherine managed to survive the next hour of tittle-tattle, and was relieved when Ellie said they would have to leave.

Everyone said their goodbyes and Yolande went as far as to extend another invitation to Katherine, if she had the time. On the way back, Meredith chattered away, clutching Katherine's hand, Ellie ahead, teetering on her high heels.

When they entered the house, Michael was asleep in his armchair.

'Don't disturb him,' Ellie said, kicking off her shoes and slipping her feet into pink leather loafers, lined up at the ready in the hall.

Michael stirred and turned toward them.

'I *want* to be disturbed, Ellie!' he called out, his face wreathed in smiles as he winked at Katherine.

'But...' Ellie began.

'*No* buts! I wasn't asleep, just resting my eyes... I'm gonna talk with Katherine for a while before we eat.'

'I'm sure Katherine will want to soak in the tub before dinner,' Ellie persisted.

'Not now, Ellie. I'll grab a quick shower later,' Katherine responded.

Ellie turned and faced Meredith, who'd been standing

alongside Katherine biting her bottom lip. 'Take your shoes off and put on your slippers!' she told her.

'No, leave them on,' Michael said. 'Cassie called in when you were out. I told her that if there was time when you got back from Yolande's, you could go visit her... She wanted to know if you'd like to go to the movies tomorrow.'

Meredith glanced apprehensively at her grandmother.

'Well – if Gramps told Cassie you'd go visit, I guess you'd better go visit!' Ellie agreed reluctantly. 'But don't be late for dinner!'

Meredith beamed. 'Can I tell her I *can* go to the movies tomorrow? It's Elvis *Presley*,' she said excitedly. 'A *special* showing of *Love Me Tender* – 'cos of him dying and stuff.'

'You'd better check with your father,' Ellie told her.

'No need... Patrick came home to lunch with me. He's planning on taking Meredith, Cassie – and Katherine too, if you wanna go,' Michael said, taking hold of Katherine's hand.

'Super! Please come... *please*, Aunt Katherine,' Meredith implored.

'How could I pass up a chance to see Elvis – sad though it will be under the circumstances?' Katherine replied, happy to be included in the outing.

'Don't worry, Aunt Katherine. There sure will be a lot of blubbing,' Meredith said, as she rushed to the door.

'Do *not* be late,' Ellie reiterated, before turning on her heel and retreating to the kitchen.

Katherine glanced at her father. He shook his head wearily.

'Throw another log on the fire, Katherine, and tell me how you got on in the inner circle,' Michael chuckled. 'And we've a lot more to talk about; we haven't gotten around to dear Evelyn yet.'

Katherine's heart quickened. Was now the moment to tell him that Aunt Evelyn had destroyed his letter? She'd promised Evelyn she *would* tell him.

Selecting a large log from the wrought iron basket standing beside the hearth, she placed it carefully on top of the smouldering embers and watched, pensively, as it ignited and began to crackle and spit.

'Better put the mesh fire screen up front,' Michael said. 'Can't risk a hole in the rug – I managed to do that last fall… Ellie wasn't too happy, but calmed down at the prospect of shopping for a replacement!'

Katherine positioned the ornate brass screen around the fire; pulled up the red leather pouffe and sat down beside her father.

Michael took her hand and squeezed it. 'How was it at Yolande's – truthfully?' he said gently. 'Sure as hell couldn't have been *easy*?'

Katherine studied his concerned expression. He looked so tired; grey and drawn. Was this the way he always looked, or was she responsible… causing him added stress? Alex, for *whatever* motive, had warned her about muscling in on his family.

She wrinkled her nose. 'I think I managed to win over a couple of Ellie's friends,' she told him. 'But it couldn't have been an easy situation for them either, could it?'

'I guess not. That's why I tried – unsuccessfully – to dissuade Ellie from taking you to meet them. They're quite a decent bunch normally. They just adore Merry and rallied round when our darling Barbara died. Poor Merry,' Michael said sadly. 'We do our best, but she misses her mom so.'

'She spoke to me about her mother today. I can relate to how she is feeling.' Katherine's voice dropped. '*I* miss Mum so much… But for a child? I can't begin to imagine what it was like for her when Barbara died.'

'She was very brave… and I'm so pleased to hear that she talked to you about her. You know, Katherine, Merry's really taken to you. And so has Patrick, I'm mighty relieved to say. You've lit up this house. Believe me.'

A lump rose in Katherine's throat. 'That means a lot… I've been so worried about the stress my visit has put upon everyone.'

Michael cupped her face in his hands. 'Don't ever feel that way. I *needed* to know about you and Nancy… You know how guilty I feel for not making more of an effort to find out what happened to you both?' Michael's expression tightened. 'The blame rests with Ellie,' he said vehemently. 'It could have been so, so… *different*, Katherine.'

Katherine frowned, baffled by his outburst.

'You surely can't blame Ellie,' she said softly.

'Oh, I think I can… And if only Nancy had replied to the letter I sent, it could have made the world of difference to our lives – the three of us would have been together!'

Katherine took his hands from her face, the tears welling in her eyes.

This was the right moment to tell him of Evelyn's part in the events that had affected their lives.

'I… I have something important to tell you. I…' she faltered, her heart thumping. 'The letter… the letter you sent to Mother after you were wounded – she… she never received it!'

Michael's eyes widened. 'Nancy never received it?' He stared at her, perplexed. 'But how would you know that, Katherine? It was before you were born.'

Katherine was silent, unsure how to proceed.

Michael raised his eyebrows. '*How*?'

Katherine shook her head and held his questioning gaze.

'Because Aunt Evelyn confessed to me – after Mother died – that your letter *was* delivered!'

Michael looked at her in disbelief. 'Nancy received it?'

'No. I'm afraid not… Mother was out when it arrived. Evelyn opened it. She read it and destroyed it. Mother never even knew that you'd sent it!'

Michael, looking totally bewildered, rubbed his forehead. 'But in God's name why? Why would Evelyn *do* that?'

'For very selfish reasons, I'm afraid, which she freely admits to and, with hindsight, bitterly regrets.' Katherine touched Michael's arm. 'You remember Mother was living with Evelyn because they'd lost their parents in the blitz? Evelyn's explanation for her actions was that she couldn't face the possibility of losing Nancy, speculating that Mother would have joined you in America when the war ended and taken me with her.'

Katherine watched the anger rise in her father's eyes.

'She is full of remorse,' she said softly. 'I, as you can imagine, was *very* angry – distraught when she confessed. I literally went ballistic. It *was* unforgivable and, I have to admit, quite out of character for her.' Katherine paused. Seeing the disbelief on her father's face, she searched for the right words to further reveal what she knew would be even more upsetting for him. But it was necessary to give a full account so they could all start again with a clean slate.

'Evelyn also told me she'd salved her conscience somewhat, when another letter from you arrived – your reply to the one Mother wrote telling you she was pregnant; the one that chased you around Europe but didn't reach you until you were back in America? Fortunately Mother kept it and I found it – or we wouldn't be sitting here together. That letter, informing her you had a fiancé who, ironically, was also pregnant, so incensed Mother, she told Evelyn she wanted no help from you and would erase you from her life! She was adamant about that apparently.'

'And *you* from *my* life!' Michael said bitterly. 'I didn't *mention* Ellie to Nancy when I was over in England because I honestly expected Ellie and I would go our separate ways – *if* I survived the war. And, believe me, it was a very big *if*! I count myself lucky I didn't arrive home in a flag-draped coffin!'

Katherine looked at her father's strained expression. 'I've read enough about the war to understand the uncertainties…

that living for the moment seemed the best option for many. *But,*' she said firmly, 'we can't alter the past, can we? We agreed yesterday to put the past behind us. The future's about you and me now. I'm telling you this because Aunt Evelyn begged me to do so. She could have kept her silence, but she wanted us to know the truth. She wanted *my* forgiveness as well as yours… Can we forgive her? We can *try* to understand her motives for destroying the letter. She's lived with this secret eating away at her conscience all these years.'

Michael sighed. 'There's a lot of forgiving to be done all round, Katherine, but I don't think I can speak with Evelyn right now.'

'There's no need – we have time on our side, haven't we?' Katherine stressed. But looking at her father's grey face, etched with pain, she felt a moment of alarm.

He did not respond, and closed his eyes.

She sat in silence for a while in the warm glow of the fire. She could hear Ellie in the distance moving around the kitchen, and wondered if she should offer to lend a hand. But she still felt uneasy in her presence – and it was obvious that Ellie felt the same. She was surprised that her father apportioned blame to Ellie. After all she, too, had been deceived by him. *Could* he have been certain that their engagement would end when he got back home? Some long-term relationships, especially ones that started during teenage years, inevitably burned themselves out. But then, wasn't first love supposed to be something special? So far, she hadn't witnessed a close, loving relationship between Ellie and her father – separate bedrooms? Patrick appeared to be the cornerstone of their marriage; certainly he was the main focus of Ellie's displays of affection. Katherine's heart quickened at the thought of Patrick and the prospect of seeing him again at dinner.

Michael stirred but didn't open his eyes. He appeared to be asleep.

Deciding not to rouse him or to intrude upon Ellie's culinary activities, Katherine quietly left her father's side and headed for the staircase. She'd take a quick shower and put in a phone call to Evelyn and, maybe, Alex, even though she was annoyed that *he* hadn't seen fit to contact *her*. She looked at her watch. Ten o'clock at home. He could be having a late night drink with the boys – or was he with Josie?

She pictured her aunt fretting about the outcome of the unfolding events in Asbury Park – and the *Argus* that was about to drop through the letterboxes of the Peover residents.

Katherine was still furious with Alex. Why the urgency to get the story into print? Josie's influence, no doubt. If Alex could be swayed so easily by Josie, was gullible enough not to realise her motives, then he wasn't the man she wanted to spend the rest of her life with – and the feeling that she didn't care resurfaced.

Was she looking for a way out of their relationship?

Freshly showered and feeling more relaxed in mind and body, she was about to select what to wear at dinner, when she heard the telephone ringing in the hall, followed by Ellie's muffled voice responding to the caller. 'It's for you!' Ellie shouted up to Katherine.

'It's for you – England!' she repeated from the foot of the stairs.

'I'll take it here,' Katherine called out. Walking quickly across the room, she sat down on the bed and picked up the receiver.

'Katherine?' Alex's voice was firm and clear; he could have been in the next room.

Her eyes narrowed. 'You've got a nerve,' she said, trying to keep her cool.

There was silence for a few seconds. 'You okay?' he asked warily.

'No, I'm not okay. *Why* are you using a piece about me this week? Didn't we agree that *nothing* would go into print until I got back?' she retorted angrily.

'*This* week we generate some interest for the follow-up story next week – when you're back with the full picture! And I hope you're taking pics, to back it up?'

Katherine's hand tightened on the receiver. She visualized Josie somewhere in the background, hanging on to Alex's every word.

'Katherine – you still there?' Alex said impatiently.

She spoke slowly and deliberately. 'Dependent upon the situation I found here, Alex, there could have been every reason to kill the story.'

'Could have? Then I take it there *are* no reasons to hold off.

Everything coming up roses,' he laughed. 'So – what's your gripe?'

Katherine fought off tears of dismay and exasperation.

'My *gripe* is that you've gone ahead against my expressed wishes and our agreement on this. Was it *Josie* that talked you into running the story?'

There was silence again.

'*Was* it Josie's idea?' she persisted.

'Well…' Alex faltered.

'I'm right, aren't I? She's out to cause trouble between us, Alex, but *you* can't see further than her fluttering eyelashes,' she challenged, feeling cross that she'd allowed herself to stoop to making girlish jibes.

'You're being unreasonable, Katherine,' Alex said coldly.

'You think so? Then, I'll live up to your opinion of me. You can tell Josie there won't be any follow-up story for the Women's Page or any page if you run the story now, because I won't be coming back to the *Argus*, Alex – I resign!'

Alex laughed halfheartedly. 'Come on – you're *not* serious. The printers have everything set up.'

'Then, in the best tradition of newspaper movies, you'll be able tell them to hold the front page!' she said, and slammed the receiver down with pounding heart.

Had she really meant to resign?

She lay back on the bed, expecting Alex to phone back. He didn't.

Would it be such a bad move to leave the *Argus*? She turned the prospect over in her mind. She hadn't been wholly happy of late and she'd always nurtured the desire to go freelance; do her own thing, be her own boss. She had good contacts and good all-round journalistic experience. She could move into her mother's cottage and work from there.

She experienced a surge of excitement. She *could* do it – she *would* do it.

She'd call Aunt Evelyn later. There was a lot to tell her, and her aunt knew her well enough to know that once she'd made up her mind about something, she would see it through.

Throughout a somewhat strained dinner, Katherine's mind kept turning to her decision to quit the *Argus*. What would her father think of her acting so impulsively? And how would they *all* feel when they discovered they were scheduled to feature in the columns of the *Argus*? She'd intended, before going back home, to raise the question of writing the story. But only with their approval.

Toying with the fresh salmon on her plate, she glanced around the table. Ellie seemed preoccupied with her own thoughts; Meredith was regaling her father and Patrick with details of their shopping trip and lunch at Yolande's.

'And they *all* just loved Aunt Katherine,' she said, coming to the end of her tale and beaming a smile at Katherine.

Michael gave Katherine a knowing wink.

'And how did *you* like *them*, Katherine?' Patrick's eyes met hers across the table and lingered.

'I was made very welcome,' she replied. Averting her eyes from his gaze, she took a sip of wine.

'Katherine had a telephone call today, Patrick – from her fiancé!' Ellie said pointedly.

'He must be missing you. He's an okay guy in my book to let you come see us,' Michael said.

Patrick looked steadfastly at Katherine again. 'He could have come with you?'

'I *think* they had a bust-up… When they were on the phone!' Meredith chipped in.

'*Meredith!*' Patrick scolded.

'Well, I could hear it from my room. I wasn't *listening*, Aunt Katherine. Honest, I wasn't.' Meredith's lip trembled. She looked about to burst into tears.

Katherine got up and put her arm around her shoulders.

'Don't worry about it,' she whispered, giving her a squeeze. 'I got a bit carried away – and when that happens, my voice gets louder and louder,' she said, teasing a smile from Meredith's unhappy countenance.

'I don't want to butt in or anything, Katherine. But long-distance quarrels can be mighty difficult to resolve – if we can help in any way… ?' Michael said with concern.

Ellie snorted. 'It is not our place to interfere in the affairs of virtual *strangers*, Michael.'

All eyes swivelled to Katherine. She felt in imminent danger of bursting into tears herself.

'It is something I have to sort out myself,' she said, wanting to run from the room. She stood up and looked appealingly at her father. 'If you don't mind, I'd like some fresh air. I'll take a walk down to the beach. Clear my head.'

Patrick slid his chair back and stood up. 'I'm coming with you,' he told her.

'Me, too?' Meredith said eagerly.

'No, Meredith,' Patrick said firmly.

Ellie's eyes were blazing. 'It's nearly dark, Patrick!'

He ignored his mother and turned to Katherine.

'We'll get our coats – it'll be chilly out there.' Patrick took Katherine's arm, ushered her away from the table and out of the dining room.

It *was* chilly. There was a sharp breeze coming off the sea and Katherine found herself shivering as they sat on the wooden bench that ran the length of the seaward side of the diner. In the half-light, the ocean looked black and menacing. Against the heavy swell that was crashing onto the shoreline, Katherine could just make out a solitary figure, and a dog bounding excitedly in and out of the waves.

There'd been little conversation on the way to the beach. Katherine had felt choked; unsure of what to say to Patrick. Unsure of her feelings, positivity about resigning from the *Argus* beginning to wane.

She shivered again; the strain of the last few hours perhaps… The close proximity of Patrick? Turning up the collar of her coat, she sank her chin into it.

'We'd better not hang out here for too long – don't want you taking a cold back to the U.K.' Patrick slid an arm around her shoulders. 'You're shivering, Katherine,' he said, hugging her to him.

He smelled good. She felt his warm breath on her cheek. She tensed, then relaxed and laid her head on his shoulder. A feeling of contentment washed over her.

'I'll be fine… Let's stay a little longer,' she murmured, thinking she could happily sit there forever.

'You want to tell me about it?' Patrick said softly. 'I'd like to help. I sure don't want you to be unhappy while you're here with us.'

He turned and faced her. In the dim glow from the amber light fixed to the wooden fascia of the diner, Katherine saw the look of concern in Patrick's eyes.

'I've resigned from the *Argus*,' she said flatly. 'I told Alex I wouldn't be going back to the paper.'

'Resigned? Why would you *do* that? Your career…your fiancé?' Patrick sounded genuinely shocked. 'Is it because of Pop – because of your visit?'

'In a way, yes… But not *just* that.'

'Then *tell* me – I'm *family*! I'm here for you, Katherine.' Patrick nuzzled his mouth in her hair.

Trembling, she pulled away from him and gazed disconsolately at the now deserted beach. How to continue?

As calmly as she could, she explained about Alex running her story without her permission – and of Josie's involvement.

Patrick took her by the shoulders and twisted her round to face him.

'Is this guy Alex a nut? What's with this ... this Josie? You're a beautiful person, Katherine. If I wasn't ...' He let go of her shoulders and turned away. 'Well, I sure as hell wouldn't be looking in the direction of another woman.'

Stunned, Katherine's heart began to pound. 'That's a real boost to my morale right now, Patrick – thank you,' was all she could manage in response.

Not trusting herself to be at his side any longer, she stood up. But he caught hold of her arm and pulled her back onto the bench.

'What are you intending to do – about your job?'

'I have several options ... But I really *don't* feel up to discussing them now,' she pleaded.

Patrick persisted. 'Could one of those options possibly be that you'll look for employment over here? Pop would be cock-a-hoop if you did.'

Katherine grimaced. 'And your mother?'

'I guess not ... but it wouldn't have to be in Asbury Park. There must be opportunities for your talents in New York,' he said enthusiastically.

Her head began to spin. Move to America? That option hadn't crossed her mind. But New York *would* be an exciting new challenge – and she would only be an hour or so from her father – and Patrick.

She was grateful that, in the dim light, Patrick could not see the flush of excitement that rose to her cheeks.

What had she to lose? Her relationship with Alex had soured – not just on account of Josie, but on several levels. His reluctance to make a commitment; his lack of encouragement in tracing her father. And Aunt Evelyn? She may have prevented her mother from making a new life in America so, Katherine reasoned, she'd be unlikely, now, to stand in the way of her niece's happiness.

'New York?' she mused. 'Now *that* could be an option,' she said, with a smile.

As they walked arm in arm away from the diner toward the twinkling streetlights, Katherine felt a strong sense of her mother's presence. Instinctively she knew that, if she did make the decision to leave Cheshire – and all that was in her past – her mother would always be with her.

When they reached the house, Ellie was waiting on the porch. 'I was coming to get you. Your *fiancé* has been on the phone – twice! He's calling back in half an hour. I do so like a happy outcome to lovers' quarrels,' she added. The last thing she wanted was for Katherine to cut her ties with England – who knows what the outcome would be if *that* happened?

Katherine reassured her father and Meredith that she was fine, before hurrying up to her room. Hanging up her coat, she kicked off her shoes and lay down on top of the bed to await Alex's call.

The room was in darkness, apart from a beam of moonlight

that gave a silvery glow to the oil painting of an angry sea hanging above the mock Georgian fireplace.

The hall phone rang.

'It's your fiancé,' Ellie called up to her.

Katherine picked up the receiver and heard Alex's heavy breathing. She waited.

'I've pulled the story,' he said grudgingly. 'Until you get back. Josie's none too pleased – but she's managed to fill the space with a piece about…'

'I couldn't give a damn *how* Josie's managed to fill the page,' Katherine interrupted.

Alex sighed. 'Oh dear. I thought you'd be pleased – *grateful* even,' he said tetchily.

'Grateful?' Katherine retorted, incensed. 'I'd have been *grateful* if you'd stuck to our original agreement and not given *Josie* free rein.'

'Katherine, *please!*' Alex implored.

'Now I suppose you're going to tell me I'm blowing this up out of all proportion?'

'What do you *want* me to say?'

'"Sorry" would have been a good place to start. But if you don't understand what you've done… well, we'll talk about it when I get back,' she said wearily, unsure in her head what her next move would be.

'You *are* coming back then – to the *Argus?*'

'We'll *talk* when I get home! Goodnight, Alex,' she said with finality.

Replacing the receiver, she eased herself off the bed and paced around the bedroom, her legs like jelly. As she contemplated going down and rejoining the family, there was a light tap on the door.

'Aunt Katherine – you okay?' The voice sounded anxious.

Katherine opened the door and looked down at Meredith, smiling tentatively up at her.

'Gramps asked me to check on you,' she said, taking hold of Katherine's hand.

Katherine gave her a reassuring smile. 'I'm just fine, truly,' she said, as Meredith tugged her out onto the landing.

'Don't forget we're going to the cinema to see Elvis tomorrow, Aunt Katherine,' she told her excitedly, as they descended the sweeping staircase.

'Would I forget *that*!' she laughed, the tension of her conversation with Alex subsiding. Tomorrow she would be sitting in the intimacy of the cinema with Patrick.

Looking at Meredith's eager, smiling face, she felt a sense of unease about the inexplicable feelings she had for Patrick. Was it filial love? Maybe if she and Patrick had grown up together as brother and sister…? But there was definitely sexual chemistry between them – it was so bewildering!

Suddenly, the prospect of moving to New York lost some of its initial appeal. Katherine had to come down off cloud nine and give serious thought to the consequences of such a move – for *everyone* involved.

CHAPTER 9

ONLY TWO DAYS LEFT in Asbury Park before Katherine returned to England. She felt despondent as she made her way down to breakfast. The week had flown by far too quickly for her – and for her father. Patrick did not sit beside her in the cinema; Meredith and Cassie had insisted they sit either side of her. Were the tears she shed for Elvis or for herself?

Over the weekend, as the weather had turned warm and sunny, Katherine had decided not to go on a sightseeing tour of the county, promising to do so on her next visit. With the exception of Ellie, instead they'd all gone down to the beach, lunched at local restaurants, and taken another trip to the cinema, this time to see *Star Wars*.

Katherine was regretting her decision not to stay longer than a week – a decision based on the premise that if her initial visit proved problematic, then one week would be more tolerable for all concerned.

She was greeted warmly in the dining room by her father, Patrick and Meredith. Ellie was, as usual, clattering around in the kitchen. Kissing her father on the cheek, she took her place between him and Meredith. Patrick smiled broadly across the table and handed her the crystal jug of freshly squeezed orange juice.

'I squeezed the oranges,' Meredith said, as Katherine poured the juice into her glass. 'And Pop did the scrambled eggs for you,' she added, pointing to the tureen sitting on a heat tray in the middle of the table.

Patrick laughed. 'Don't build up your hopes, Katherine, I probably should have waited until you were at the table. Could be somewhat rubbery by now.' He took a plate from the hot tray, spooned out the scrambled eggs and handed it over to Katherine.

'The plate's not too hot,' he said, as their fingers touched and their eyes met. Katherine's stomach lurched. Putting the plate down, she picked up her fork and took a mouthful. 'Just perfect,' she said, avoiding Patrick's gaze.

Her father echoed her thoughts on the shortness of her visit and expressed his regret that he was not well enough to be with her in New York. Because her flight from Kennedy Airport was early morning, necessitating an overnight stay, he told her he'd asked Patrick to accompany her, allowing time, the day before the flight, to show her the sights of the town and maybe take in a Broadway show.

'I didn't need asking twice!' Patrick grinned.

Katherine felt a rush of excitement.

Meredith pulled a face. 'They won't let *me* come with you to New York.'

'Merry,' Michael responded, 'you and Patrick have seen more of Katherine than I have this week – you've been to lunch and the movies,' he said good humouredly. 'But I'm not griping. The way I feel these days, the comfort of my armchair and the T.V. have their compensations. But, I *do* intend to spend the whole of tomorrow with my daughter... just the two of us,' he said, stroking Katherine's hand. 'Ellie has her hair and beauty sessions; Patrick is taking Meredith for her swimming and dancing lessons. We'll have a leisurely breakfast and, if the weather's fine, we could go down to the diner again or – better still – we could have breakfast at the diner. What do you say, Katherine?'

Katherine felt choked looking at her father's tender expression. He was obviously feeling a growing sense of despair, as was she, that their parting was imminent.

'I say we go down to the diner and do justice to your maple syrup pancakes – and discuss my *next* visit to Asbury, which I hope will be very soon,' she replied.

'Yippee! She's coming back! Isn't that swell, Pop?' Meredith said excitedly.

'Great news.' Patrick beamed a smile at Katherine as Meredith rose from the table and rushed off to the kitchen.

'I'll tell Gram,' she said happily.

Katherine raised her eyebrows at her father.

'Don't worry about Ellie,' he said. 'But, tell me. Have you come to any decision about your work, Katherine – about leaving the paper?'

Katherine swallowed a mouthful of scrambled egg and dabbed her mouth with her napkin. 'Do you mind if we talk about it tomorrow?' she replied, wanting to be certain of her decision, but feeling more certain now that her future lay in America.

Katherine awoke the next morning to the distant pounding of an angry sea. Another stormy day. She stretched leisurely and surveyed the net drapes at the open window fluttering in the strong breeze.

Climbing out of bed, the chill air hit her body. Shivering, she picked up the fluffy bathrobe from the chair, put it on, pulled the belt tight around her waist and padded over to the window. She closed it, and sat on the window seat to look out over the garden. The trees were bending and swaying in the gale and dark, menacing clouds threatened more rain. Unless there was a dramatic change in the weather there was no way she and her father would be going down to the diner. She bit her lip, feeling close to tears as thoughts of leaving him rose to the fore. He'd looked *so* weary... so ill for a man still in the prime of life.

She heard the muted sounds of Patrick, Meredith and Ellie talking in the hall on their way out; the door closing, followed by the sound of the car starting and being driven away.

After showering, Katherine dressed quickly, not wanting to miss a moment of her last day with her father, and hurried down the stairs.

The house was silent apart from the wind whistling eerily around it. Her father looked up as she entered the dining room, a strained expression on his face. There was no smile to greet her as he patted the seat beside him.

'Good morning, Katherine. Looks like breakfast at the diner is off,' he said flatly. 'But we have the house to ourselves for a few hours. There's eggs, mushrooms and hash browns keeping warm for you on the heat tray – courtesy of Patrick.'

Katherine assumed his dejected demeanour was because they would soon be parted.

'How was Ellie… about the prospect of me returning to Asbury Park?' she asked as she went over to the sideboard, picked up a plate and helped herself to a small portion of breakfast, her appetite suddenly waning.

Michael was silent as she put the plate on the table and sat down.

Then, 'Katherine, you have to stop worrying about what Ellie thinks,' he told her firmly. 'We're not going to kid ourselves that you and she will end up buddies, are we? Ellie knows that, for once, she's outnumbered in this house – right? She has to realise that it's important for me to make up for our lost years; she may not like that – but tough!' he said vehemently, and thumped his hand down onto the table, rattling the crockery.

Katherine's eyes widened in alarm at his outburst. 'I take no pleasure from Ellie having to make compromises,' she told him.

'I know you don't, and I thank you and love you the more for it. You have your mother's amiable nature, Katherine,' he said wearily. 'I'm worried that I'm being selfish to even relish the prospect of you giving up everything in England to come live here.'

'Don't be! Ever since I was a little girl, I've felt incomplete. In my heart I was *always* certain that you were alive – always,' she said emphatically, and told him about the photograph she'd cut from the magazine and kept at the bottom of her toy box – her surrogate father; their imaginary walks through the fields and the bedtime stories she pretended he was reading to her.

As the tears rolled down his pale cheeks, she jumped to her feet and threw her arms around him. 'Now that I've found you, there's no way on earth you can get rid of me!' she said through her own anguished tears.

Michael hugged her tightly. 'I wish to God that your mother was here, Katherine. It's... oh, so...' He faltered, searching for the right words.

She kissed his forehead. 'She *is* here,' she told him. 'I felt her presence with me on the plane – and down at the ocean last night... I'm sure that now we are together she will rest contented.'

'I'd give my life to know that was true, Katherine, I...'

She placed a finger to his lips. 'You and I must be contented too – and move on,' she said, standing upright.

Michael seemed to sink lower down into his chair.

'Move on?' His face paled again, his expression more

strained. He held Katherine's anxious gaze for several seconds. 'I'm afraid it's not so simple… Before I can do that, Katherine – before either of us can move on – there's something *very* important I need to tell you. Something I thought I could keep from you. But now that you are definitely planning to move over here… well…' He shook his head sadly. 'I figure there have to be *no* more secrets in our lives. No more, Katherine. You deserve to know the truth before you make a decision to leave England.'

Katherine's heart quickened. Was her father about to reveal some unwelcome fact about his relationship with her mother? She was alarmed by his serious expression as he held her quizzical gaze.

'But I need you to promise me that you will *never, never* divulge to anyone what I'm about to tell you.' He grasped her hand and squeezed it tightly. His hands were clammy and beads of perspiration rose on his forehead as he continued. 'Or *ever* speak of it again!'

'It's… about Mother?' Katherine said, her heart thumping fit to burst.

'No, no! Nothing at all to do with Nancy. It's about Patrick.'

'Patrick?' Katherine gasped. '*What…?*'

'Ellie told me… She *informed* me last night that Patrick is not *my* son. *Not* my son!' he repeated, his voice barely audible.

Katherine felt as though she couldn't breathe. She opened her mouth but couldn't form any words as she stared blankly into her father's dispirited eyes.

'But, how? Why...?' she eventually managed to stutter, as the significance of her father's words struck home. Patrick, who'd stirred so many uncomfortable emotions in her from the moment they'd met at the airport, was *not* her brother? Her father was telling her she was not his sister! Through the turmoil in her head, she became aware of his words of explanation.

'The week before I was shipped back home from Europe, Ellie went up to town with Yolande for the weekend. Apparently they met a group of sailors. Ellie said she'd had too much to drink and Patrick was the outcome! She *says* she has no idea who the guy was, other than his name was Artie. And she wasn't even certain he'd given her his real name as he was wearing a wedding ring!'

Michael studied Katherine's expression of incredulity and continued.

'I'd been stupid enough to swallow hook, line and sinker her story that Patrick's birth was premature. Huh... some fool me,' he said scornfully. 'With hindsight, Patrick doesn't look anything like me – or his mother for that matter. And, looking back to when your mother's letter caught up with me to tell me *she* was expecting *you*, I recall being surprised by the matter-of-fact way Ellie took the news. Obviously she had no redress... Like me, she'd taken solace under the strain of wartime separation when emotions were intensified. But *my* solace was based on a deep love for Nancy. Ellie's? Well... A one-night stand, knowing I'd been wounded – and was on my way home...'

Katherine strived to take in her father's words, but could only concentrate on the fact that she and Patrick were not blood related!

Michael looked at her with anxious eyes, awaiting her reaction.

Wiping away her tears with her fingers, she faced him. 'But for Ellie to give you this shattering news after all these years, why now? With what motive?' she stammered. 'It's so... *cruel*! Why would she do that to you?'

'Her motive? Her insane jealousy! After you'd gone up to bed last night, Patrick spoke about you considering a job in New York. Ellie was enraged by the news – I won't burden you with what she said. But when Patrick retired to his room, she just came out with her demoralizing confession. Patrick is her life and the thought of you being over here permanently – and she's noted just how fond he is of you – well, it tipped her over the edge! Maybe, in her warped mind, she imagined that if she told me Patrick is not my son, *I* would then decide to go to England to be with you – leaving the field clear for her and Patrick. That is the only rational explanation I've been able to come up with, Katherine. The truth is, I just don't know. But what I *do* know is that I'm devoted to Patrick... I've loved him from the day he was born; changed his diapers, worried about him all his life. He will *always* be my son and her malicious confession won't change that. And can you imagine how devastated Patrick would be if he ever discovered I'm not his father? It didn't take much, once Ellie had calmed down, to convince her that Patrick must *never* know the truth. Not when she realised his attitude toward *her* would undoubtedly be sullied… to say the least. And there's Meredith? The implications for her are horrendous… My concern, Katherine, is Ellie's reaction toward you if you do decide to move to the States. I can't predict what she would do; how far she would go in retaliation. Much as I want – *need* – to have you near to me, I felt it only fair, my duty, that you should know of this dreadful turn of events before deciding to turn your life around. But I must emphasise that it is vital Ellie never finds out that you know her secret. All I want, Katherine…' Michael's voice tailed off.

Katherine couldn't bear the look of anguish on her father's face. 'It's all *my* fault,' she told him, fighting back the tears. 'I should have given more consideration to the effect on you and the family before making contact!'

Michael pulled her to him.

'No! Don't ever think that, Katherine. It's *not* your fault! You and Patrick are the innocent casualties. You have nothing to reproach yourself for… nothing! We'll get through this goddamn mess,' he said ardently, and kissed her wet cheek. 'I *want* you over here, Katherine. I know this has been an enormous shock to discover Patrick isn't your brother. But I hope it won't change your relationship with him – and Meredith. It's obvious they both hold you in high regard. We have to try, as difficult as it will be, to carry on as normal. But, it's such a relief to share this with you, Katherine. I just hope that you can cope with it,' he added, his voice breaking.

Katherine hugged him. 'I have to cope, there's no alternative! I'm not going to desert you, and I promise to support your decision not to tell Patrick,' she added, fully aware that making the promise meant she could never reveal her feelings for Patrick; feelings she felt would be reciprocated.

As they regarded each other sorrowfully, lost for words, the front door opened. Ellie, Patrick and Meredith had returned.

Katherine listened as they shook out their wet coats and hung them in the hall closet.

Ellie entered the dining room first, pulling off the pink chiffon scarf protecting her newly coiffeured bouffant hair from the gale still raging outside. Seeing them together, her eyes narrowed and she looked warily at Michael.

'Didn't manage your outing to the diner, then?' she said, moving quickly through to the kitchen without waiting for a reply.

Katherine looked apprehensively at her father's stern expression, and was relieved to see it soften when Meredith and Patrick strode into the room.

'Too bad to hang out at the diner, Pop? You enjoy your tete-a-tete here?' Patrick asked, smiling at Katherine.

Afraid to meet his eyes, she focused her attention on Meredith, who'd rushed to her side, her hair straggly and damp from the swimming pool.

'You *should* have come with us, Aunt Katherine. You should have. We had a great time, didn't we, Pop?'

Katherine heard a voice in her head saying: 'But I'm *not* your aunt – I'm *not* your aunt…' Feeling stressed and confused, and certain her unease would be apparent, she found herself saying, 'I'm really hopeless in the water. I never did get the hang of it… I was pushed into the swimming pool by an unruly boy when I was very young. It terrified me; floundering to get to the surface. I've never been able to get my head under water as a result – pathetic as it is!'

'I bet you look swell in a bathing suit though – when you're at the beach,' Meredith giggled.

'Even if it never gets wet,' Patrick laughed.

Katherine felt panic rising. Still unable to look at him, and feeling the need to absent herself from his presence, she threw an imploring glance at her father, who quickly responded.

'Katherine isn't feeling too well, Patrick. She… she was just about to go and lie down for a while when you came back. She…'

'Just a slight headache, absolutely nothing to worry about,' Katherine said, throwing her father a look of gratitude. 'But if you don't mind, I think I *will* go and lie down for a while. Then I must think about packing.'

Meredith's lip quivered. 'Do you *have* to go back to England, Aunt Katherine? You can stay as long as you like. Can't she, Gramps?' she implored.

Katherine pulled Meredith to her and kissed her upturned face. 'I'm afraid I *do* have to leave tomorrow,' she whispered, before hurrying from the room.

Standing at the bedroom window looking out over the garden, Katherine listened to the distant waves pounding the shoreline. The howling wind rustled through the trees, the autumn leaves clinging grimly to their creaking branches. It had been no excuse that she had a headache. Her head throbbed; she felt nauseous; overwhelmed by the enormity of her father's revelation, compounded by the fact that he was completely unaware of its full impact with regard to her deepening feelings for Patrick.

Alone in the sanctity of the bedroom, Katherine felt able to immerse herself fully in the consequences of what her father had told her, the validity of her decision to move to America no longer clear: her father's concerns about Ellie's reaction; the need to keep the unbearable secret that Patrick was *not* her brother. If he knew there was no blood tie between them, feminine intuition told her there would be a future for them. But *she* could never be the one to tell Patrick the truth about his parentage, and withholding the truth would make the prospect of living in close proximity to him unbearable. The room began to spin and as she stumbled toward the bed, Alex's words came back to her.

'Think carefully before opening an unknown chapter of your life – it could result in a lot of heartache.'

She hadn't valued those words at the time, unsure whether self interest was the motive for expressing his doubts. But had Alex been right all along?

Dropping down heavily onto the bed, Katherine laid her aching head on the pillow. She longed to feel her mother's arms around her; for her mother to help make sense of her dilemma. Her thoughts drifted to the cold, empty cottage that had held so many happy memories for her only a few months ago; she thought of Aunt Evelyn, mourning her sister all alone. She felt a sudden need to get back to familiar surroundings where she could view her position dispassionately and, hopefully, make the right decision for her future. Until then, she had to brace herself to face the rest of the day – her last day with her father. And, despite her world being turned upside down by the secret her father had entrusted to her, she had to appear *normal*!

With a heavy heart, she rose from the bed, took her suitcase from the walk-in wardrobe and began to pack.

Somehow she managed to get through the day, thankful that Patrick had gone to the gallery; her father had retired to his bedroom and Ellie to her refuge – the kitchen.

Katherine sat curled up on the sofa in the sitting room with Meredith, watching Disney cartoons, but neither of them was in the mood for hilarity, the weight of her departure heavy on both their minds.

They were allowed to eat lunch – sandwiches that Katherine had offered to make but Ellie had refused – sitting before the television. Ellie had silently delivered them – salmon and cucumber – daintily arranged on individual white china plates set on ornate, lacquered trays.

When they had eaten, Meredith braved the elements to visit her friend, and Katherine, after taking their plates into the kitchen and offering to wash them but being rejected, returned to the silent sitting room. Should she wait and see if her father might join her? Surmising that, with Ellie around, conversation would be strained, she decided to return to her room and try to relax before the ordeal of dining with the family for the last time; the sadness of the occasion further weighed down by the strain she and her father were under to retain a semblance of normality.

The evening was as daunting as Katherine had foreseen. Her father's demeanour was strained, as was her own, which she hoped would be misconstrued as sadness due to her imminent departure.

Behind Ellie's implacable expression, Katherine thought she saw a hint of fear in her eyes, an uncertainty as to whether her father would reveal her secret. But as the meal proceeded, Ellie visibly relaxed, to the point where she made some effort to talk to Katherine, handing over her plate, pronouncing that she had especially purchased the fresh salmon just for her.

Katherine ventured a quick glance at Patrick as she helped herself to the vegetables from the sectioned silver tureens; he was gazing at her ardently. Her heart sank. She turned to look at her father, who managed a fleeting smile as he lifted the bottle of champagne from the ice bucket and filled her glass.

'Patrick's treat,' he said.

'In celebration of your visit.' Patrick rose from his chair, filled his father's and Ellie's glasses – allowing Meredith the tiniest measure – and raised his glass high.

'To joining the Donnelly family. And to your early return to Asbury Park!'

Katherine forced a smile, not daring to look at her father.

Meredith giggled as the bubbles tickled her nose.

Ellie did not drink from her glass.

As was usual at every mealtime, the tension was lightened by Meredith regaling them with the events of her day and posing many questions, mainly on life in England.

Tonight her questions focused on Katherine's departure. Was she happy to be going home? Would she miss them? And when *would* she come back to them?

Katherine was relieved when her father declared his intention to have an early night, and suggested Katherine do the same, in preparation for her sightseeing in New York prior to her long flight home.

Patrick endorsed the suggestion and quelled Meredith's protestations. As Katherine passed his chair he grasped her hand.

'We're going to have a swell day tomorrow – a day for my sister to remember!'

Katherine saw the affection in his eyes and felt as though her breath had been sucked from her lungs, preventing her from responding. She nodded in acknowledgement, slid her hand from his grasp and left the room, before the welling tears burst forth.

It wasn't until the early hours of the morning that Katherine's runaway thoughts abated and she was able to snatch a few hours' sleep.

CHAPTER 10

THE DAY OF KATHERINE'S DEPARTURE dawned bright and sunny; the gale that had kept her company during her wakeful hours had blown itself out.

Patrick had reserved seats on the train to New York and booked rooms at the Ameritania Hotel where, he'd told her, Frank Sinatra and the Rat Pack had hung out in their heyday. Situated on the corner of 54th Street and Broadway, the hotel was, he said, within easy walking distance of Central Park and the theatres, and he'd booked seats at the Broadway Theatre to see Yul Brynner in *The King and I*.

Despite the strain of everything that had happened, and the prospect of spending so much time alone with Patrick, Katherine decided that, however challenging it would be, she should make the most of her last hours in America – uncertain when, or if, she would return.

Breakfast, like dinner, had been a sombre affair, lightened only by Meredith repeating the questions she'd posed the night before: when would Katherine be coming back to Asbury

Park? When could *she* go to England to see where Gramps was in the war? And could she *please* go to London to see Buckingham Palace and the changing of the guards?

Michael, looking dejected and red-eyed, hardly touched his food. Ellie couldn't resist a parting shot, stating that Patrick was deserting the gallery by making an unnecessary journey to New York when Katherine was perfectly capable of taking care of herself.

Although exhilarated to be spending her last evening in New York alone with Patrick, Katherine hadn't fully quelled her nagging fear of how she would handle the situation.

After breakfast, she hurried upstairs to finish last minute packing. Stowing her passport, make-up and reading matter into her hand luggage, she opened the window and took a deep breath of crisp, sea air. Turning, she gazed around the room to fix it in her memory and, slipping on her jacket, gathered up her bag and walked out onto the landing.

Patrick was standing in the hall beside her suitcase. Meredith was gripping the handles of her father's wheelchair. There was no sign of Ellie.

Choking back the tears, Katherine descended the stairs.

Her father looked broken. Kneeling beside his chair, she threw her arms around him. For several seconds they looked at each other without speaking, before giving free rein to their emotions.

Meredith reached out and stroked Katherine's hair, and she too began to weep.

Patrick cleared his throat. 'Better get on down to the station,' he said softly.

'You're gonna miss the train!' Ellie said, coming in from the dining room.

Katherine kissed her father on the cheek. 'Thanks for everything. I love you. And I'll miss you,' she whispered.

Michael brushed a strand of hair from her eyes. 'I love you too, Katherine – very much,' he said loudly. '*Please* come back to us – *promise?*'

Katherine stood up and took her father's hand. She couldn't tell him she had reservations about returning. 'I will… I promise!' she assured him, and prayed it wouldn't turn out to be a lie.

Katherine and Patrick spoke little on the one and a half-hour journey from Asbury Park to New York, each seemingly lost in their own thoughts. Katherine gazed through the window with unseeing eyes as the train raced toward the city, conscious that every passing mile was taking her further away from her father.

But Patrick did press Katherine on the possibility of her returning to work in New York.

'You don't seem as enthusiastic as you were?' he queried.

She detected the note of disappointment in his voice – he *wanted* her to come back! If only she could tell him the reason for her indecision.

'I… I have a lot to think about back home, I…'

'Alex?' Patrick interrupted. 'He sure will want to make you change your mind – certainly would if I were in his shoes.'

'I can be very strong minded, if I'm convinced I'm in the right!' Katherine told him. 'But I really don't think Alex will care one way or the other.'

'Then he's a *fool*!' Patrick said brusquely, and turned away.

Katherine touched his arm and he faced her again.

'No offence, but can we not talk about this anymore? I really want to make the most my last night in the Big Apple. Please... let's enjoy ourselves for what little time I have left here?'

'Paint the town red?' Patrick responded kindly.

'Something like that,' Katherine laughed.

'Then I'll see what I can do, but – one last word about you coming back, if I may?'

'Patrick!' Katherine scolded.

'I don't want to influence you, but for Pop's sake, and also for mine and Meredith's, I'd hoped that...'

'*Please*...' Katherine implored.

For the rest of the journey she feigned sleep, her thoughts constantly circling around Patrick, more and more certain that his feelings went beyond sibling affection. But would there ever come a time when their feelings could be openly declared?

As the train pulled into Penn Station, Patrick shook Katherine gently. 'Come on, sleepy head. The Big Apple awaits you.'

He helped her down to the platform, and a lump rose in

Katherine's throat. Was it only a week ago that she'd boarded the train for Asbury Park? A dramatic week that had changed her life forever.

'We'll take a cab to the Ameritania, check in and get something to eat. There'll be time for a little sight-seeing before we go to the theatre this evening.' Patrick looked down at Katherine's feet, clad in smart, three-inch heels. 'Can I suggest we go get you some sneakers before we hit the sidewalks?' he said, with a wry smile.

The young, rotund clerk behind the desk of the Ameritania's small reception area greeted them with a convivial smile.

'Just the one night?' he enquired, handing Patrick their room keys.

'I'd love to stay longer but, unfortunately, I'm flying back to England tomorrow,' Katherine responded.

'So,' Patrick said, stepping in, anxious to hit the town, 'we have to get out there for a quick-fire tour of everything the lady wishes to see!'

'I guess I *will* have to come back to see *everything* I want to see,' Katherine said.

'Then we'd be pleased to welcome you back to the Ameritania, ma'am… and may I suggest you start your sightseeing at Central Park, just a few blocks away. You could take a carriage ride through it. Very romantic our guests tell me. Haven't tried it myself. Waiting for the right lady to come along!'

Katherine and Patrick exchanged amused glances as they headed toward the elevator.

Their rooms faced each other across the long corridor. Patrick inserted the key in Katherine's lock, and pushed open the heavy door. Ushering her in, he followed and laid her suitcase on the bench at the foot of the double bed.

'Ten minutes' freshen up, then we'll go get a light snack in the restaurant. We don't want a heavy meal before we hit the sight-seeing trail. We can eat again after the show. And we must get you into those sneakers,' Patrick added before the door clicked behind him.

Katherine looked around the room. Her first impression was that it was dark; intimate. The bedspread and walls were a deep plum colour, as were the curtains, which she drew back, and sunlight filtered in through the white voile nets.

Opening the window, she gazed down to the street far below. The room overlooked 54th Street, but on turning her head to look right, she could see and hear the heavy traffic flow along Broadway. The noise was deafening and she doubted she would get much sleep – but hadn't Frank Sinatra sung about the 'city that never sleeps'! Was he referring to the traffic or the glitzy nightlife, she mused, wishing she'd been a fly on the wall when the Rat Pack were having a soirée!

For several minutes she viewed the scene below. Here she was, with Patrick, in the frenzy that was New York, and tomorrow she would be back in tranquil, leafy Cheshire. With Alex … ?

So much had changed between her and Alex over the past week. She had no idea if he would be at the airport to meet her – but she hoped not. She wasn't ready for a showdown about Josie, not being ready to admit to herself that Josie wasn't the *real* reason why she would end her relationship with him.

Closing the window against the noise, she went into the bathroom. Quickly removing her make up, she splashed her face with the tepid water.

The pale face that stared back at her from the mirror looked tired; older than a week ago. Her red hair seemed to have lost its lustre. She shivered. It was like looking at the face of her mother. As she applied fresh make-up and was adding a touch of colour to her cheeks, the telephone rang.

She went over to the bedside and picked up the receiver.

'You ready, Katherine?' Patrick's voice was buoyant, full of anticipation.

'Ready!' she replied, her heart quickening.

After a substantial sandwich, a refreshing glass of freshly squeezed lemonade, and purchasing a comfortable pair of shoes, they took the desk clerk's advice and sauntered slowly down the packed Broadway pavements toward Central Park.

Looking across a busy junction, Katherine could see the trees outlining the park, and to the left, Patrick pointed out Fifth Avenue and the famous Plaza Hotel that featured in her favourite film *Plaza Suite*.

Patrick took hold of Katherine's hand as they dodged the

traffic, made their way past the horse-drawn carriages lined up at the edge of the park, and went in.

'I'm afraid we won't have the time for a carriage ride,' Patrick told her. 'We'll have a quick look around here and take a cab to Battery Park, where you'll be able to get a good view of the Statue of Liberty. Sorry, no time, either, to take a boat trip around her.'

'As long as I see the Statue, I'll be happy,' Katherine said, feeling thrilled at the prospect of viewing New York's iconic landmark.

'Fine! But we should have time to take the express lift to the top of one of the World Trade Centre towers – there's a breathtaking view of Manhattan from the 110th floor.'

'Sounds good. No time for a shopping trip to Macy's or Tiffany's, I suppose?' Katherine grimaced.

'Nope. Not unless you want to scrub seeing Yul Brynner – and you'd need a whole fistful of dollars to shop at Tiffany's.'

'Audrey Hepburn managed a small purchase,' Katherine laughed. 'But... I think Yul Brynner live on stage has the edge on a shopping spree.'

The paths through the park, as far as they ventured in the time available, were packed with cyclists, roller bladers, joggers and runners, who all expertly dodged the walkers. Katherine loved the park, nestled in the midst of the hectic traffic flow that encircled it; framed by the towering skyscrapers – a green oasis in the heart of the city.

In the cab to Battery Park, Patrick took Katherine's hand. 'The last time I made this journey was with Barbara... when she was really ill. She wanted to have a last look at the Lady Liberty, sail around her again... because I proposed to her on the boat trip.'

Patrick was lost in his thoughts for a few moments, then smiled absently. 'I remember making a joke; something along the lines of sacrificing *my* liberty when I was a married man with responsibilities.'

Katherine squeezed his hand supportively. 'I understand your reluctance to take the boat trip,' she said. 'But I...'

'No, no, Katherine. That isn't the reason, it really is only the time factor. Not sentimentality. You learn, in time, to live with the heartache of being in the places and doing the things you once did together. Initially, after Barbara's death, I wanted to shy away from the places that had meant so much to us. But if you took the grieving to extremes – and it's mighty hard not to – you'd never leave the house. You have to carry on... doing your job... raising your child. Meredith, too, had to cope without her mom. In many ways she was more of a comfort to me than the other way round.'

'Meredith spoke to me about Barbara. When we were shopping in the mall,' Katherine said softly.

Patrick's face lit up. 'It's swell she's talking to you about it, Katherine! I *want* her to keep her mom's memory alive – whatever happens in our lives.'

'Do you think you'll every re-marry?' Katherine asked tentatively. 'You're still young and Meredith, I'm sure, would enjoy... would benefit from having someone she could talk over girlie problems with as she gets older.'

'Other than her grandmother?' Patrick said ironically.

'I meant someone with a younger outlook on teenage problems. I don't know how I'd have coped without my mother at Meredith's age.'

'I guess a mom's an all-important figure in a girl's life. But marriage isn't in the master-plan – Vietnam taught me not to think too far ahead. I believe in the hand of fate. If it's meant to be etcetera.'

'Kismet?'

'Something like that.' He looked into Katherine's eyes then turned away.

'Battery Park.' The cab driver's gruff Brooklyn accent cut into her thoughts.

From the quay they watched the pleasure boats, full of tourists of every nationality, bobbing their way through the choppy waters toward Lady Liberty.

Back at the hotel, resting on the bed after the whirlwind dash around Manhattan – having abandoned a trip to the top of the World Trade Centre as the queue for the lift was too lengthy – Katherine fought to keep her eyes open. She couldn't allow herself to fall asleep with only a short time to shower and dress for the theatre.

Hauling herself from the bed, she headed for the bathroom. The hours were ticking by far too quickly, and she knew it would be challenging to relish, wholeheartedly, the few that remained before her departure.

At the theatre, she was swept away by Yul Brynner's performance as the King of Siam. She'd seen him in the film with Deborah Kerr, but had never heard of Constance Towers, who took the part of Anna. And in the ambience of the theatre, seated in close proximity to the stage, the chemistry of the constrained admiration between their characters seemed to mirror her rapport with Patrick.

Later, discussing the show over a meal back in Charlie's Steakhouse, Katherine felt a glow of pleasure when Patrick likened the songs to *her* circumstances in journeying from her homeland to America.

'For instance, Anna's rendition of, "Whenever you feel afraid",' he said laughingly.

'"I hold my head up high",' Katherine responded.

'And, "Getting to know you",' Patrick sang out loudly, to the amusement of the diners around them.

'"Getting to know all about *me*",' Katherine joined in, before dissolving into a fit of giggles.

'I think we'd better leave it at that before we get thrown out – and no more wine,' Patrick grinned. 'But we definitely chose the right show, didn't we?' he added, touching her hand.

'Ab-so-lutely,' Katherine agreed, feeling somewhat tipsy and lightheaded. 'Apart from the v-e-r-y sad ending,' she said, wagging a finger at Patrick, before taking another slurp of wine.

'Well… we'll just have to hope that your story has a *happier* ending than Anna's, Katherine,' Patrick said, untwining her fingers from her glass and placing it on the table. 'And, I think

I should get you back to the hotel. We have a very early start for the airport tomorrow, and you'll need a clear head.'

Katherine regarded the remnants of her meal and sighed heavily. 'I've been trying hard to forget about tomorrow.'

'So have I,' Patrick said.

They jostled their way through the evening revellers the short distance to the Ameritania. The smiling night clerk handed over their keys and bade them goodnight, after a brief enquiry about their theatre trip. They were silent as the lift ascended to their floor, neither certain that – at the end of a perfect day – it would ever be repeated.

Stepping out of the lift, they walked down the dimly lit corridor. Outside her door Katherine felt an icy chill sweep through her body. She shivered, and faced Patrick.

'You okay?' he said.

'I…' she faltered. 'Look, please don't take this the wrong way, Patrick, but I'd rather you didn't come to the airport. No point in us both getting up at the crack of dawn – and I hate goodbyes,' she lied. In truth, she couldn't bear any longer the burden of deceit that prevented her from telling Patrick they were not brother and sister. 'If you could arrange for a cab for five o'clock – I'll be fine,' she said softly.

Patrick's face registered disappointment. 'Sure – if that's how you want it, Katherine. Quite certain you can manage without the assistance of your big brother?'

Her stomach lurched. Averting her eyes, she turned her door key over in her trembling fingers, desperately wanting to shout: *'But you're not my brother!'*

Taking a deep breath she faced him. 'I'm a big girl, Patrick. I'm used to fending for myself in the male dominated world of journalism,' she said, with false jollity.

'Okay, "*big*" girl,' he laughed. 'But I have something for you in my room – to remind you of the Donnelly clan when you're back home. You'll be rushed in the morning… May I bring it to your room? A quick coffee maybe?'

'To sober me up?' Katherine managed a weak smile.

Patrick laughed. 'I'll give you a few minutes.'

In the bathroom, as Katherine splashed cold water onto her face to enliven herself, she heard Patrick tap gently on her door.

'Come in, it's open,' she shouted, grabbing a towel and patting her face dry. She heard the door open, and Patrick crossing the room to the window.

'I'll close the drapes – deadens the traffic noise somewhat – and fix the coffee,' he called to her.

'Thanks… Make mine strong and black,' she heard herself saying, excitement mounting, and the alarm bells ringing in her head to no avail!

When she felt calm enough to leave the bathroom, she found Patrick sitting in the tub chair beside the bedside table. The room was in darkness apart from the table lamp that threw a rosy glow onto his face. Across his knees lay a flat package wrapped in silver and grey striped paper, tied with purple ribbon. Photographs of the family, perhaps, Katherine surmised.

'That looks rather large for my suitcase,' she said teasingly, sitting down on the edge of the bed, facing him.

'You can't squash it into your baggage,' he said, handing the package over to her. 'It's much too precious and delicate to risk being damaged. Afraid you'll have to take it on board as hand baggage.'

She fingered the ribbon with the intention of unwrapping the parcel.

'No, no.' Patrick reached out and grabbed her hand, sending a tingle down her spine as he held on to her wrist. 'You mustn't open it now,' he said earnestly. 'It's wrapped securely beneath the fancy paper – to prevent it getting damaged.'

She tugged her hand from his grasp. 'Am I allowed to know what's inside, then?'

He gave her a wide smile. 'A painting… An Andrew Wyeth.'

Katherine's eyes widened with delight. 'Not "Wind from the Sea"?'

Patrick nodded. 'Spot on! I knew you'd fallen in love with it when you almost fainted at the gallery,' he laughed.

In her mind's eye, Katherine was back in that moment when her senses had been taken over by the powerful impact of the painting, and the unsettling feelings that Patrick's close proximity had aroused within her.

'I… I *thought* you'd be pleased?' Patrick said, puzzled by her silence.

'Oh, I am! I'm more than pleased, Patrick. You can't begin to imagine how much this painting means to me,' she said softly. 'When I look at it, I'll be reminded so much of…' she faltered. 'Of Asbury Park – of all of you!'

Patrick looked relieved. 'So you're not disappointed then – expecting ancestral photos of the Donnelly family? But I do intend getting prints from the family album to send along with the photos I've taken this week.' Delving into his jacket pocket, he took out an envelope and placed it on the bedside table beside the two cups of steaming coffee.

'This,' he said, tapping the envelope, 'is to appease airport Customs' officials. A receipt for the painting and a note stating it's a gift. Hopefully you won't have to pay duty and, more importantly, they won't insist on unwrapping it,' Patrick added, picking up one of the cups of coffee and handing it to Katherine.

She waved her hand. 'No, thanks – sorry. I think, if you don't mind, what I really need right now is my bed… Try to get some sleep,' she lied, feeling a need to back away from their nearness in the intimacy of the darkened room.

Patrick's face dropped, clearly disappointed. 'I guess you're right. Can't put off the evil hour forever,' he said graciously. Rising from the chair he held on to her gaze for a few seconds before turning his back, walking toward the door and opening it.

Katherine felt a sense of panic. This was it then! In less then a minute Patrick would be the other side of the door. She may never see him again. She couldn't let him walk out of her life – she *couldn't*!

As he opened the door she called his name. Turning, he looked at her, his face ashen.

With pounding heart she ran to him; reached across him and clicked the door shut – with no thought of what she was going to say or do.

For several seconds they stood in silence. Patrick gazed into her eyes expectantly.

'Before you go… I… I haven't thanked you for everything you've done… to help get me through this week. It's not been easy for any of us, has it?' Katherine said with trembling voice, desperate to delay Patrick's departure.

Looking into his eyes, she sensed his understanding of the situation, and flinging his arms around her shoulders he pulled her to him. Quivering, she buried her face in his chest, aware that his heart was thumping in tandem with hers. Bending his head, his lips brushed against her hair and then her forehead.

'*Please* come back to us, Katherine,' he murmured.

Powerless to pull away, she remained locked in his arms.

At last, his lips found hers and he kissed her gently. She could feel him trembling, and closing her eyes returned his kiss with uncontrollable passion. Then her eyes flicked open, and seeing the bewilderment in his, she closed them again as he pulled her tighter into his body. He kissed her eyes, her nose and found her lips again in a frenzy of desire, then, suddenly, he pushed her away.

'I'm sorry, so sorry,' he said, distraught. 'I don't know what came… Oh, forgive me, Katherine, *please* forgive me! It's been so long since I've held a woman in my arms.'

Katherine put a finger to his lips. 'I'm sorry too,' she said tearfully.

'But you have to forgive me,' he implored her miserably. 'I mustn't *ever* put you in this position again, Katherine. Please… please don't let what's just happened affect your decision to come see Pop again. I'll arrange to be away… I'll make some excuse not to be around. A buying trip… anything! But please don't let this affect you and Pop – you have to promise me that.'

Katherine looked at his drawn expression; she was not able to console him, she couldn't console herself – their situation was hopeless! She lowered her eyes, unable to bear his sadness any longer.

Turning from her, he opened the door.

'Goodbye, Katherine,' he said, his voice breaking. And he was gone, the door clanging shut behind him.

She leant against it and sobbed uncontrollably. She wanted to fling it open and run after him. Tell him there was no need to feel repentant; no need for guilt because she *wasn't* his sister.

When her tears finally subsided, she walked across to the window, pulled back the curtain and looked out at the bright, flashing lights of Broadway. An overpowering feeling of isolation washed over her. Her American dream had turned into a nightmare!

Too emotionally drained to think about the morning or worry about the reception she would receive when she got back home, she picked up the painting, lay on top of the bed, hugged it to her and wept again.

CHAPTER 11

KATHERINE'S PLANE TOUCHED DOWN at Manchester Airport on a grey, miserable day that reflected her mood. She'd found the flight unbearable – every hour taking her further away from her father – and Patrick. She'd felt too distraught to make small talk with the two young women sitting alongside her, full of the excitement of their New York shopping spree. She feigned sleep, but couldn't sleep. Alex and Aunt Evelyn both knew of her arrival time, but who, she wondered, would be waiting for her? She fervently hoped it would *not* be Alex.

Grabbing her case from the carousel, she cleared Customs, grateful that she wasn't asked to unwrap her precious Wyeth painting.

As she pushed her trolley out into Arrivals, she spotted her aunt among the crowd, waving and smiling broadly. They embraced, and Katherine glanced around – no sign of Alex.

'I'm *so* relieved you're back home, Kathy,' Evelyn said, her cheeks flushed with excitement. 'I can't *wait* to hear all about it. Michael and the family. Oh, before I forget…' Katherine smiled, not able to get a word in edgeways as her aunt babbled on. '... Alex phoned me to say he couldn't make it to the airport, some big story breaking – but *not* about you and Michael. He told me categorically that the *Argus* wasn't going to print it. What a relief. Come on, dear, let's get you home and have a nice cup of tea. I bet you've missed a good cuppa. They do say Americans don't know how to make a decent cup. I don't think they make sure the water is boiling,' she added, as they made their way out to the car park.

'I'll hang on to this,' Katherine said, when Evelyn attempted to take the painting from her and put it into the boot.

'A present from the Donnelly family?' Evelyn queried.

Katherine hesitated. 'It's a painting... One that I admired at Father's gallery.'

'Michael's shop?' Evelyn asked, as they got into the car.

'Yes, but he's not well enough to make much of an input into the business these days. Patrick' – her stomach turned over at the mention of his name – 'seems to be in sole charge.'

Evelyn started the car, clenched the steering wheel and looked steadfastly through the windscreen as she drove slowly out of the car park. When she was on the straight road home, she glanced at Katherine. 'He... Michael... he's forgiven me, has he?' she ventured.

Katherine touched her arm lightly. 'He's forgiven you, Aunt. He placed a lot of the blame on himself... It's complicated with Ellie... and everything,' she said, noting her aunt's face visibly relax.

'That's generous of Michael. I can't wait to hear *everything* you've been up to. I expect it's been very exciting – once you got over the sticky bit with his wife?'

Katherine was silent. If only she could tell her the truth about Ellie's role in keeping her father and her mother apart, but, in order to keep Michael's secret it was not possible.

The soothing, hypnotic swish of the windscreen wipers gradually closed Katherine's eyes.

Evelyn glanced at her niece again. 'You'll have to get over your jet lag before you spill the beans – no muddled thinking. I don't want you to miss *anything* out,' she laughed.

In the comfort of her aunt's cosy sitting room, Katherine began to relax. After two cups of tea and a delicious homemade cherry scone with jam and cream, she felt totally revived. Evelyn begged her to stay the night, but Katherine felt the need for solitude – she wanted time to think clearly. She arranged to go to Didsbury by taxi, and promised her aunt she would return the next day. She couldn't put off seeing Alex indefinitely, but she intended, if at all possible, to postpone their meeting for a few days until she was certain in her mind what she intended to do about leaving the *Argus*.

Back in her flat, there were two messages on the answer-phone: Alex apologizing for not being at the airport, and her father, hoping she'd had a good flight – no mention of Patrick.

Feeling much too tired to unpack her case, Katherine climbed the stairs to her bedroom, threw off her leather jacket, kicked off her shoes and stretched out on top of the bed. Surveying the room, she compared it to the luxury of the guest bedroom in Asbury Park. Her functional cedar furniture looked austere. She closed her eyes and listened to the traffic rumbling down Barlow Moor Road. Yesterday it was frenetic New York and yellow cabs – today Manchester and black cabs. Air travel necessitated a quick adjustment to get back into one's routine. Her thoughts strayed to the words of her old editor who'd championed sea travel: 'Give me an ocean liner any day,' he was fond of telling everyone. 'Time to relax and arrive refreshed, with a real sense of putting time and distance between home and foreign parts!'

Katherine wished she'd had the luxury of returning by sea. Five whole days to wrestle with, and hopefully come up with a solution to the problems facing her – on both sides of the Atlantic.

The ding-dong of the doorbell broke into her thoughts. She groaned, inclined to ignore whoever it was. When she heard the downstairs door open, she knew it could only be Alex – damn!

'Katherine?' he called as he entered the hall.

Lacking enthusiasm, she eased herself off the bed and slipped her feet into her shoes. Feeling agitated, she went down the stairs and entered the lounge. Alex, flopped on the green draylon sofa, cigarette in hand, had not discarded his short, navy overcoat. He looked at her impassively, lips tight, eyebrows raised questioningly.

'You didn't phone,' he said sullenly. 'Still mad at me, then?'

Katherine surveyed his handsome face but felt nothing. Without replying, heart pounding, she sat down in the armchair facing him.

'It's like that then, is it?' he sighed heavily. 'I've had a hell of a day, Katherine. I'm really not up for fun and games.'

Katherine glared across at him and found her voice. 'And *I'm* really not up for a confrontation right now. I've had a pretty stressful *week*.'

'Well, I warned you not to open the can of worms,' he said, stubbing his cigarette in the chrome ashtray on the coffee table. 'Your wicked stepmother sounded like Mrs. Danvers in *Rebecca* when I phoned to speak to you,' he said, managing a shadow of a smile.

'Can we *not* do this now, Alex, I'm exhausted.'

The smile disappeared and Alex's expression hardened.

'And you know what, Katherine? *I'm* tired of your childish behaviour,' he responded, swinging his legs off the sofa and standing up.

'And you think that riding roughshod over my request to hold the story until I came home isn't childish? Living up to the public perception that journalists would sell their grannies for a good story?' she said harshly.

'Now you're being ridiculous… I killed the story, Katherine.'

She looked up at him towering over her. 'And that makes it okay?' she said wearily.

Alex sighed again. 'When I said you were being childish, I wasn't referring to *the story*, I was referring to your attitude toward Josie.'

Katherine's eyes flashed. 'Well… there's *another* story. Just how far *was* she prepared to go to get her hands on the Women's Page?' she said, annoyed with herself that she felt close to tears.

'I'm going,' Alex said bluntly. 'I'll see you at the office tomorrow.'

'*Don't* count on it!' Katherine yelled as he slammed the door behind him.

And *don't* cry, she told herself sternly. She could sort it – she had to. She'd have a long soak in the bath and, hopefully, a decent night's sleep. She *wouldn't* go into the *Argus* tomorrow; she'd visit Aunt Evelyn as promised, questioning if she should tell her what had happened with Patrick, knowing she was incapable of keeping the unhappy predicament from her for long. Maybe better sooner than later, she decided, though she couldn't hazard a guess as to what her aunt's reaction would be.

Katherine managed a deep, dreamless sleep, and awoke feeling totally refreshed. The sunlight slanting through the venetian blind promised a reasonably warm day for October, lifting her spirits. She had a quick breakfast of cereal and orange juice and, pushing aside her smart office outfits, selected jeans and sweater from the wardrobe.

Driving her red Mini – her thirtieth birthday present from

her mother and Aunt Evelyn – Katherine left behind the built-up areas of Didsbury, Handforth and Wilmslow, turned onto the Knutsford road, and meandered through the lanes to Lower Peover. She never tired of the run – the distant view of the hills above Macclesfield. If she did decide to relocate to New York, she would undoubtedly miss the wild ruggedness of the Peak District – especially Buxton and the Goyt Valley, a great retreat for ramblers from the working environment of Manchester. What could New York offer by comparison, she asked herself? Central Park!

As she drove along the narrow lanes, her wheels crunching through the leaves that had drifted over the grass verge onto the road, she had to pass her mother's cottage, just a quarter of a mile away from Evelyn's. Arriving at the gate, she pulled up and switched off the engine, reluctant to go in and relive the moment she'd found her father's letter. She looked wistfully at the white-washed, picture postcard cottage that had been home for most of her life. It was no longer a home without the person you loved, just bricks and mortar without a soul, full of an aching emptiness that she would find difficult to adjust to. But, if she did resign from the *Argus*, she would have to live here. She would have to give up the flat to save on the mortgage.

She accepted that it was still early days after her mother's death; her mourning eclipsed by the emotional search for her father, and the unforeseen outcome of that search.

Fighting back the tears, she looked at the apple tree that gave the cottage its name; the tree she used to climb in her tom-boy days, its branches nearly bare of leaves, the last of the windfalls rotting on the lawn. She managed a smile recalling the enormous slice of apple pie she'd tackled at Charlie's Steak House, and she was there again, amid the fast track of New York life – a life she could be part of if she so chose.

Switching on the engine again, she drove off down the lane and turned into the gravel drive of Rose Cottage, where she parked behind her aunt's Austin and clambered out.

Evelyn, already standing at the open door, greeted her with a crushing hug and a waft of 'Tweed', her favourite perfume that Katherine had purchased from the Duty Free trolley on the plane.

'You look like your old self today, Kathy, after a good night's sleep,' she said happily. 'You'll stay for lunch, I hope? I've made your favourite mushroom paté, and baked a nice, crusty wholemeal loaf… You look very smart,' she babbled on.

Katherine smiled affectionately at her aunt's ability to make her feel like a treasured child again.

'I've missed being spoiled,' she said generously, as she freed herself from her aunt's embrace.

Evelyn shooed Katherine to the settee and dropped down heavily beside her. 'Well?' Her cheeks glowed. 'Did you have a really exciting time in America?'

'Up to a point. Michael's wife, as you rightly predicted, did her best to put a dampener on things. But … it was so *wonderful* to be with Father and, fortunately, we did manage to have some time alone… We talked a lot about Mother and …'

Evelyn grabbed Katherine's hand.

'You *were* telling me the truth yesterday… Michael *has* forgiven me?'

'Yes! He said he's going to write to you. He still has very *fond* memories of you and Uncle Ted,' she added, noting the relief in her aunt's eyes.

'And do you think he'll come back to Peover?'

Katherine shook her head. 'I doubt it. He's really not a fit man… He has to use a wheelchair… It's so sad.'

'Well, if he can't come over here, I suppose you'll be going off to see him again? You'll have a proper jet-set lifestyle!' She started to laugh, but stopped abruptly, puzzled by Katherine's dejected expression.

'What's wrong?' she said softly.

'I… I don't think I *can* go back,' Katherine replied, and before she knew it, she'd poured out the whole unhappy dilemma: her father's disclosure that Patrick was not his son; her feelings for Patrick that she couldn't declare – and how that restraint impacted on a move to America. And, finally, the problems she'd encountered in her absence from the *Argus*.

Evelyn, sitting in stunned silence, looked shocked and saddened by what she was hearing.

'Poor, poor Michael,' she said at last. 'To find out after all these years that Patrick isn't his son.'

'And it's all my fault,' Katherine said tearfully. 'If I hadn't contacted him Ellie never would have told him about Patrick, I'm certain of it. I believe her confession was brought about by her jealousy of me ... moving into her territory!'

Evelyn put her arms around her. 'It's *not* your fault – it's that spiteful Ellie's fault. Think about it. If Michael had known what Ellie had done at the time he received Nancy's letter, well – I'm pretty sure everything would have worked out for him and Nancy. They were *so* in love.' She sighed. 'Love! Such a commonplace word that has such massive consequences on people's lives.' She fell silent, then looked earnestly at her niece. 'If you're asking for my advice, Kathy – about *you* and Patrick – well, I have to be honest, dear, it is all a bit sudden, isn't it? You say you fell in love with Patrick in a week – even when you thought that he was your half-brother?'

Katherine shook her head. 'I've always consigned the idea of love-at-first-sight to Mills and Boon, magazine stories and letter pages. But what other explanation is there?'

Evelyn sighed. 'Well, I've known you long enough to know you haven't gone into past relationships lightly. But I agree that you can't tell Patrick he's not your brother and risk destroying his relationship with Michael. Anyway, you promised Michael you'd keep the secret, didn't you? And I agree that it would certainly be difficult to be in close proximity to Patrick if you went to work in New York. Other than that, I really don't know what ...'

'I have to work through this myself,' Katherine interrupted and, taking a tissue from the embroidered box on the sofa table, blew her nose hard.

'Well, all your life you've managed to come up with the

right course of action, and if you do try for a job in New York, I certainly won't pressure you to consider me. I owe it to Nancy to be happy for *you* – whatever your decision.'

Katherine leaned toward her aunt and kissed her flushed cheek.

'Thanks, Aunt Evelyn. And I apologise. I've given you a lot to take in, haven't I? But it's been a relief to talk about it. I'll have to put Patrick on hold until I've tackled Alex. If I do leave the *Argus* but stay here, I've enough contacts to make a reasonable living freelancing. I could move into Mother's cottage and sell the flat, which will relieve me of the mortgage and free up more cash. I'll be fine moving there,' she added, with more conviction than she was feeling.

'Well, you know you can always come to me if you get into financial difficulties. *Never* be afraid to ask, Kathy. Ted left me pretty comfortable.'

Katherine looked at her aunt's concerned expression and kissed her again. 'Thank you. You and Uncle Ted have already done so much for me … and Mother. I know I can rely on you if things go pear-shaped. Now – lead me to that paté and crusty bread, I'm starving!'

Back at the flat, Katherine decided the first thing she should do was ring her father. It would be noon in Asbury Park. Dialling the number, she fervently hoped it wouldn't be Ellie that picked up the telephone, equally apprehensive at the thought that it might be Patrick.

'Hello, Donnelly house,' Meredith said, in a very grown-up manner.

Katherine gave a sigh of relief.

'Hello, Meredith! How…'

'Aunt Katherine! It's Aunt Katherine!' Meredith interrupted excitedly. 'Gee, it's real swell to talk to you in *England*, Aunt Katherine.'

'And it's good to talk to you, Meredith – even though it's only been a day since we last spoke,' she laughed.

'But I'm missing you already. When are you coming back? You really… Oh, please! I haven't *finished*, Gram!' Meredith's voice rose in agitation.

Ellie's voice was harsh in Katherine's ear.

'Michael's taking a nap, and I don't…'

'But he'd *want* to talk to her!' Katherine heard Meredith's plea in the background. The line became muffled. She couldn't make out what was being said and guessed Ellie had covered the mouthpiece.

'I'll let Michael know you called,' Ellie said icily.

Katherine knew she would do no such thing – but also knew for certain that Meredith would inform her grandfather of her call. Although it was comforting to know that in Meredith she had an ally, she felt angry and concerned at the thought of the misery Ellie's jealousy might inflict upon her granddaughter.

'Just tell Father I'm returning *his* call to me, Ellie. He left a message on the answer phone,' she said as politely as she could.

'I'll ring again,' she added, and put the phone down with some satisfaction. If she *was* going to transplant herself to New York, then she'd have to make a stand against Ellie's jealous, domineering ways.

She went into the small galley kitchen, made herself a cup of tea and took it over to the window. It was already dark and raining heavily. The headlights of the rush-hour traffic and the illuminated shop signs reflected in the puddles on the high street. She watched the shoppers hurrying in and out of the little supermarket opposite – buying food for a welcoming evening meal for their loved ones, she speculated sadly. She turned away and returned to the lounge. It looked cold and uninviting – the stripped wooden floor, the harsh, white fluorescent ceiling light – part of the fixtures and fittings she'd inherited when she'd bought the flat, intending to replace it but never getting around to it. Switching it off, she turned on the table lamp that gave out a yellow glow beneath the gold silk shade. As she sat down beside the mock coal electric fire, she visualized the open hearth and *real* coal fire in her mother's cottage. She smiled wistfully, remembering the times she and her mother had sat together, toasting thick slices of bread on the long, brass-handled toasting fork. Her reservations about the move back to the cottage began to slip away, assured she'd be surrounded by so many loving memories.

The telephone rang, interrupting her reminiscing. Picking up the receiver, she hoped it wasn't Alex.

The soft American drawl reassured her.

'Katherine?' her father queried.

'Hello… Dad!' She hadn't called him that before; it just slipped out naturally. She was pleased when she heard him laugh.

'Dad? I guess that's a very English word – but I *like* it.'

Katherine chuckled. 'It's great to hear your voice again… How are you feeling? Ellie told me you were resting and didn't want to be disturbed when I rang.'

'*You* can disturb me any time you want, Katherine, you know that. Please ignore Ellie,' he said firmly. 'Meredith told me you'd called so – here I am! Did you have a good flight home? Got over your jet lag?'

'Pretty much.'

'You're not at the *Argus* today?'

'No. I've been over to see Aunt Evelyn.'

'How is she? Pleased she's gotten you back home, I guess? How did she take the news that you may leave the old country for the U.S. of A.?'

'She was absolutely fine about it. I think she feels she can't put up any objection – seeing as she was partly responsible for keeping you and Mother apart.'

'Poor Evelyn. I guess she's never gonna get that off her conscience,' Michael said, without a trace of bitterness.

'I guess not… But as regards coming over… I haven't had much time to think it through properly. And I need to make the right decision – for everybody,' Katherine said, not able to tell him that that decision rested solely on her dilemma over her unresolved relationship with Patrick.

'Sure, sure, honey. I understand,' Michael assured her. 'You take all the time you need. Have you seen Alex yet? You know he's gonna try to dissuade you? And I can't blame him. But I'm going to be selfish here and tell you that we'd all be so happy to have you come over – well, three of us, anyhow. You know, Katherine, I have to tell you that Meredith blubbed for an hour after you and Patrick left for the train, she…'

'How is Patrick?' Katherine jumped in quickly, taking the opportunity to talk about him.

'Sombre… Only word for it. Sombre. He sure is missing his sister!' There was silence on the line for several seconds. 'I feel real bad that I'm deceiving him on that score, Katherine… Real bad. He'd be mighty upset to find out he isn't your brother.' Michael's voice was choked with emotion.

'Me too,' Katherine said and, afraid she might burst into tears at any minute, resorted to a white lie. 'I have to go, Dad – there's someone at the door. Sorry.'

'Maybe Alex hot on your trail? I'll call you tomorrow, see how things have gone… I *love* you, Katherine.'

'And *I* love you. Say hello to Patrick for me… Talk to you tomorrow.'

CHAPTER 12

KATHERINE ENTERED the revolving door that spilled you out into the Small Ads section of the *Argus*'s Advertising Department. Behind the long, polished wooden counter, Jenny, a glamorous brunette, glanced up from the customer she was dealing with.

'Hi, Kathy – great to see you back,' she said enthusiastically. 'Catch up with you in the canteen over a cuppa. She's just back from *America*,' she informed the suitably impressed young man in skin-tight jeans, who turned and gave Katherine a cheeky smile as she entered the lift.

Pressing the button for the first floor, Katherine braced herself as the doors opened. The unmistakable aroma of printer's ink pervaded the air as she stepped out into the corridor.

To her right, she could hear the clack clack of the teleprinters further down next to the sub-editor's room.

As she approached the door to the Reporters' Room, Randolph, the editor, came out of his office beyond, clutching a sheaf of galley proofs. He looked his usual rumpled self – tousled grey hair, tie awry.

'Ah … the wanderer returns,' he said, smiling broadly as he walked toward her. 'Those yanks didn't try to purloin my best girl then – though I *can* visualize you in the glitzy ivory tower that is the *New York Times*,' he laughed. Then, in an instant, his smile disappeared. He looked at her sternly and his voice took on an edge. 'Wasn't too happy with Alex holding back on the Yanky-doodle story though.'

Katherine's mouth tightened and her eyes flashed. 'I presume by "Yanky-doodle story" you are referring to the very *emotive* meeting I had with my father,' she said coolly.

Randolph fixed her with a look of indifference.

'Alex was lucky I got out of bed the right side. He's *not* editor yet,' he said stonily, as he walked away.

Katherine shook her head. Fired up now for confrontation with Alex, she pushed open the door to the Reporters' Room and walked in.

She was met by the clatter of typewriter keys and the disjointed babble of one-sided telephone conversations emanating from the desks of the half dozen or so reporters. They acknowledged her with a wave and various murmured greetings. The large, square room, dominated by two floor-to-ceiling windows, had been her home from home for so many years. Could she really leave it and the comradeship behind, she asked herself? Momentarily her resolve wavered. Her legs felt weak. Then Alex emerged from the copy typists' cubbyhole, closely followed by Josie.

They stood side by side, gazing at her; Alex uncomfortably, Josie, in her figure-hugging red sweater, challengingly. The clattering typewriters ceased. The telephone conversations subsided to whispers. Irrationally, the shoot-out scene from *High Noon* flashed into Katherine's mind. Her eyes narrowed. I intend to win *this* face-off, she told herself confidently.

'Katherine!' Alex walked over to her and kissed her on the cheek. All eyes swivelled toward Josie, who'd turned on her heel and was needlessly shuffling papers on her desk.

'Good to get you back,' Alex said brightly.

Katherine gave him a long, hard look. 'Can we go somewhere with more privacy?'

Alex looked visibly taken aback. 'Sure, sure… Corner Cupboard?'

Katherine nodded her assent.

Neither of them spoke as they went down the back stairs to the little pub – a watering hole for thirsty journalists and printers, tucked away in the back street behind the *Argus*.

Katherine settled herself on the well-worn, red leather bench seating that ran around the walls of the 'snug'. Dull brass and copper plaques hung on the walls, yellowed by smoke, and a collection of dusty pewter tankards and ceramic toby-jugs sat on the wooden picture rail encircling the room. The snug was empty apart from Inky, the old black cat, curled up on the hearthrug in front of the dying embers of a coal fire in the soot-blackened, Claygate red brick fireplace.

'Usual?' Alex asked, standing over Katherine. His face bore

an expression of uncertainty, unrelated to the question he'd put to her.

'No, thanks – I'll have a bitter lemon.' She needed a clear head for what she was about to say to him and, at this moment, she wasn't at all certain just *what* she intended to say.

Alex left to get the drinks from the bar and Katherine looked around the room that held so many happy memories. Unwinding with colleagues, discussing the events of the day; having a laugh. The intimate cosiness of the snug was unlike anything she'd encountered in America. Her brow furrowed. There was so much she would miss if…

Alex returned and placed her glass on the beaten, copper-topped, cast iron table.

'Can't wallow down here too long,' he said, the tone of his voice slightly agitated.

As Katherine looked up at him as he stood, tumbler of whisky in hand, his handsome face suddenly took on the expression of little-boy-lost. The image of Josie kissing his full, sensual lips swam before her eyes and she felt a momentary pang of jealousy.

'I wouldn't want to take up *too* much of your time, Alex – not over something as unimportant as our *future*,' she said, picking up her glass and taking a sip.

Alex sat down beside her and reached out to put his arm around her. He sighed heavily as she pushed him away. 'I thought… now that you're off cloud nine and have had time to think rationally… maybe, just maybe, there was a chance we could get back to something bordering normality. Life as we knew it before you went globe trotting.'

Katherine laughed. 'Back to normality? Me and Josie the butt of sniggers and snide remarks in the Reporters' Room? Do me a favour,' she replied hotly.

Alex tried to take hold of her hand, but she brushed him away again.

'Josie means *nothing* to me, nothing at all – you know that. I was jealous... You over there... not knowing...'

'Are you admitting you *slept* with her?' Katherine interrupted, her voice full of the fury she'd bottled up for a week.

Alex's confident composure finally snapped.

'What is it you want to tell me?' he said curtly.

Katherine heard herself say it: 'I'm leaving the paper. Immediately. I don't intend to work out my notice, so you can tell Accounts to stop my pay as from today.'

Alex's face paled. His eyes widened in astonishment, then softened, and he smiled laconically. 'Really? Immediately? You know it's not that simple, Katherine.'

His smile only served to further infuriate Katherine. 'I *am* serious!' she yelled at him.

'And *what* do you propose to live on? Or have you already got yourself a job on a New Jersey rag?' he said sourly.

'No. I may go freelance,' Katherine said calmly. 'I have Mother's cottage. I can operate from there.'

'Oh... Then you're not deserting me for your new found

family. That's something, at least.' The silence hung between them. Alex twisted his glass in his hands. 'Look,' he said softly, 'I know I've disappointed you, Katherine. I've been an idiot, I admit it… The Josie thing… I'd had too much to drink. Nothing serious. We can work through this, can't we? You and I are good together.'

'Past tense… *Were* good together. At the start. But now, Josie aside, we're just rubbing along like an old married couple. You know that, Alex. The passion's somewhat spent.' She looked away remembering the passion in Patrick's kiss. 'Maybe you'll find it again – with Josie,' she said wearily.

'For God's sake. How many times do I have to tell you…?' Alex stopped suddenly and gazed at her quizzically. 'Is there someone *else*? You've met someone over there. That's it… isn't it?'

Katherine's heart began to thud. 'In a week? Of course not,' she said, hoping her denial sounded convincing.

For the first time, Katherine was aware of Alex's vulnerability. With the realisation that she *was* deadly serious about leaving the *Argus*, the shell he'd built around himself after the failure of his marriage cracked before her eyes; his remorse touchingly obvious.

She reached out and touched his hand. 'I am sorry, Alex. Truly,' she said softly.

'*Please* don't tell me it's all for the best,' he replied, reverting to his bluff manner. He stood up. 'This would *never* have happened to us if you hadn't found that damn letter from your father. I knew... I just felt it was...' He didn't finish the sentence. For once, lost for words, he raised his arms in a gesture of resignation and walked out of the snug, banging the door behind him.

Was he walking out of her life? Katherine felt numb but incapable of running after him. *She* felt no remorse; only huge relief that she'd been able to end their relationship without overwhelming histrionics.

She sat deep in thought gripping her glass, staring blankly at Inky who was purring contentedly, oblivious of the drama that had been played out. Loud banter and guffaws emanating from the bar masked the sound of the snug door re-opening.

'Mind if I join you?' Josie's confident voice startled Katherine. She edged away as Josie sat down alongside her, her expensive perfume overriding the smell of stale beer and the smoky atmosphere.

'What do *you* think?' Katherine replied dispassionately. 'If Alex has sent you, I...'

'He doesn't know I'm here.'

'Then why *are* you here? I've nothing to say to you, Josie.'

'Well, *I've* got something to say to *you*... Alex told me, briefly, that you're set on leaving the *Argus*. You're being *very* immature about this, Katherine. Have you given any thought to how it will impact on Alex's position on the paper?'

Katherine laughed as she turned and looked into Josie's earnest eyes peering through the curtain of her blonde fringe.

'What's so funny?'

'I don't intend to spell it out for you,' Katherine said, rising to leave.

Josie clutched the sleeve of Katherine's jacket. 'Look… I know you and I have never been the best of friends – but you've got it all wrong if you think *I* want Alex. I…'

'You jumped pretty quickly into my shoes – or should I say bed – as soon as my back was turned,' Katherine said contemptuously.

'We were both drunk,' Josie replied, matter-of-factly.

'And that excuses you both, does it?' Katherine said wearily. 'You've openly flirted with Alex since the day you arrived, Josie. Well… front page exclusive for you – Alex and the Women's Page are all yours! *You* deal with any repercussions!'

Katherine shook her head and with a certain amount of satisfaction – and a lasting impression of Josie sitting open-mouthed and speechless – moved away from the table. 'But you may need a lucky black cat or two,' she said, bending down and stroking Inky before taking her leave.

When she got back to the flat, two messages awaited her on the answer phone: one from the editor of the *Argus*, and one from Luke, the court reporter and father of the NUJ chapel – both requesting she return their call.

She decided to see what Luke had to say before what she assumed would be the more formidable conversation with Randolph.

Luke's voice, amid the background noise of the Reporters' Room, was full of genuine concern.

'You're joking… right? Doing a runner because of Alex and Josie? Come on, Katherine,' he said, pushing his spectacles up his nose and doodling a noose on his notebook.

'I'm touched by your concern, Luke, but give me some credit – I wouldn't leave the *Argus* over that,' she responded. 'You must know about Alex running the story about my father before…'

'He pulled it. You know he pulled it?' Luke interrupted, and stubbed his cigarette out to join the other butts on the chipped canteen saucer.

'At the last minute, only *after* he realised how incensed I was… I trusted him, Luke!'

Luke sighed. 'You know that *madam* was behind that?'

'I guessed as much – and *that's* what makes his insensitive behaviour so unacceptable. Meeting my father and his family was one of the most difficult things I've had to face in life… and with little support from Alex, I might add!' She pushed her hair back, and suddenly feeling exhausted, lifted up the phone, carried it to the settee and sank down. 'I appreciate you calling, Luke – but I really *have* made my mind up,' she said firmly.

'Then there's no chance – if I call a chapel meeting – that we can dissuade you from this… this drastic action, Katherine?'

'No chance. But thank you, Luke,' Katherine replied, feeling more certain now that she'd made the right decision – and more confident about confronting the editor.

'Right… Well, we can't let you just ride off into the sunset. I'll arrange a get-together with the clan – minus two!' he added. 'If you have any difficulty about your decision not to work the statutory month's notice, I'll see what I can do union-wise. Compassionate grounds maybe? But I don't think the powers-that-be will be happy! Keep me informed, Katherine… You know we're all going to miss you and your calming influence around the place… I hear you're considering freelancing?'

'I may give it a go,' Katherine responded, wondering just how far up the grapevine this news had travelled.

'I think you'd miss the Reporters' Room. Freelancing can be very solitary – and unpredictable.'

'I realise that. But I've got the contacts and I'm prepared to give it a try. If it doesn't work out, I could try for one of the nationals.'

'Or an American rag, maybe?' Luke queried.

'Who knows?' Katherine said, experiencing a sudden tingle of excitement.

After replacing the receiver, Katherine's eyes were drawn to the open-shelved bookcase, above which hung the framed *Argus* front-page mock-up of her thirtieth birthday. She gazed wistfully at the smiling faces of her colleagues. She would definitely miss the camaraderie of the Reporters' Room. Doubts rose as her hand hovered over the telephone. Don't weaken, she told herself firmly. Taking a deep breath, she dialled the *Argus* again.

Peggy, the switchboard operator, answered.

'Hi, Kathy! You're back then… Have a good time in the States?' Her pencilled eyebrows arched, and she licked the biscuit crumbs from her scarlet lips.

'I had a wonderful time thanks, Peggy.'

'And… you got on all right with your father and his family?' Peggy queried.

'Yes – really well.'

'Then I expect you'll be popping over to see them quite regularly – lucky you. I've always wanted to go to America – New York, San Francisco… and especially New Orleans – and all that jazz!' she laughed. 'You'll have to tell me all about your trip when you've got time.'

'I'm pretty tied up at the minute… Would you put me through to Randolph, Peggy,' she said, anxious to put the expected showdown with her editor behind her.

'Sure,' Peggy said, picking up on Katherine's anxiety. 'Nothing wrong is there?'

'I'll talk to you later, Peggy – okay?'

Katherine leaned back on the settee and waited.

Aileen, the editor's secretary came on the line.

'Oh dear,' she said, sounding flustered. 'You're in for a bumpy ride, Katherine. Brace yourself!'

Katherine pictured Aileen, prim in her proverbial grey suit, sitting behind her desk in the room adjacent to Randolph's. Her stomach lurched.

'Is it *that* bad, Aileen?'

'What do *you* think?' Aileen said. 'I'll put you through.'

Randolph – who could roar like a lion when the situation demanded – sounded remarkably calm, in contradiction to Aileen's summary of his demeanour.

'Katherine, Katherine,' he said soothingly. 'What's all this nonsense I'm hearing from Alex? You want to *leave* us? Why, why, why for God's sake?'

Katherine took a deep breath. 'I presume Alex has *told* you why, Randolph. I really don't want to go over it again.'

'Look, Katherine.' Randolph's voice hardened. 'Josie? Come on, she'll be back page news next week. Alex needs stability. He needs you, not a social butterfly.'

'Is that a back-handed compliment, Randolph? Well, maybe I'm tired of being stable – anyway, there's more to this than Josie, as you well know,' she said bitterly. 'Try lack of trust… Reneging on our agreement not to run my story until I came home.'

Randolph sighed. 'Then I take it your mind's made up?'

'Firmly,' Katherine replied, with more confidence than she was feeling.

There was a heavy silence and Katherine visualized Randolph lounging back in his red leather swivel armchair, the imperious portraits and photographs of past editors of the *Argus* looking down on him from their lofty positions on the oak-panelled walls.

'Right… Then you must go,' he said coldly.

'I… I intend to go now – not serve my notice. I'm prepared to…'

'Leave it with me. I'll see if can charm the powers that be in your favour.' His voice softened again. 'Look, I appreciate you've had a pretty rough time of it recently, Katherine – losing your mother so suddenly...You don't think you should, maybe, give yourself more time. It's a major life-changing decision.'

Katherine felt a wave of sadness. 'But I feel I'm doing the right thing... You know how much I've enjoyed working for you.' Her voice broke. 'I... I hope we can keep this amicable?'

'Sure, sure...' Randolph cleared his throat. 'We'll get together soon... and it goes without saying that I'll see you get a first class reference. We'll all miss you, Katherine.'

'I'll miss you too,' was all she managed to say, before putting the receiver down and bursting into tears.

After several cups of tea, followed by a hot bath and a meal of Aunt Evelyn's crusty bread and paté (that her aunt had packed her off with, along with two carrier bags of food to stock up her fridge), Katherine felt the tension of the past few hours ebbing away. She'd expected far worse from Randolph; expected him to insist she stick to the letter of her contract to work out her month's notice. Now that things were more settled, she felt able to think seriously about her future. First step – sell the flat; move back into the cottage; and then give serious consideration as to whether or not to set up as a freelance or – take up the more challenging option of relocating to America.

CHAPTER 13

THE FOLLOWING DAYS were hectic. Katherine received lots of phone calls from colleagues – none from Alex – and a surprise call from Angela, the General Manager's secretary, who wanted the option to purchase her flat.

At twenty-two, Angela had decided it was time she flew her parents' nest and, as Katherine's flat was within walking distance of them, she reasoned leaving home would be less traumatic if she were close by.

Within weeks, Katherine had moved back to Lower Peover. She'd decided, for the time being, to keep all her mother's furniture, leaving her own furniture in the flat for Angela.

Mid December saw Katherine comfortably settled into Apple Tree Cottage. Everything had moved so fast, and with so much to do, she put her concerns about Patrick and what her next move should be on hold. With the money raised from the sale of the flat, and an unexpected, large amount left to her by her mother, she was under no immediate pressure to find another source of income.

She had several conversations with her father and Meredith, but Patrick never seemed to be around when she telephoned. It became obvious that he was avoiding speaking to her.

With all her energy taken up with the move, Katherine had pushed the thought of Christmas – which she was dreading – to the back of her mind. But now that it was two weeks away, sitting in the warmth of Evelyn's kitchen with a glass of sherry and a homemade mince pie, they both faced up to the heart-wrenching reality of Christmas Day without Nancy. A day that, hitherto, had been filled with much joy and laughter. This year neither of them had had the heart to decorate their respective cottages.

Evelyn took her niece's hand across the cedar kitchen table and rubbed it affectionately.

'*I've* had Christmas on my mind for weeks, Kathy. I may have been out of order, but I thought a complete break from our usual routine of alternating dinner at your place or mine, so… I've tentatively reserved a table for us at the Bells. They get fully booked pretty early but they managed to squeeze us in… They'd have no trouble filling our places if you don't fancy the idea?' Evelyn looked apprehensively at Katherine, and took a sip of sherry.

Katherine's hand tightened around the stem of her glass and her eyes filled with tears. *Wherever* they were, they were going to feel extremely sad. She understood her aunt's reasoning to get away from what they'd done every Christmas since she was born. But since moving back to where her mother had died – far from experiencing any unease, she'd felt her mother's presence and knew that on Christmas Day she would be with them in spirit.

She surveyed her aunt's anxious expression, awaiting her response. 'I did the wrong thing, didn't I? I just thought…'

'No, no!' Katherine exclaimed. 'One of us had to think ahead, and I've been so busy.' She met her aunt's eyes. 'No… That's not the truth of the matter. I *didn't* want to think about Christmas. But… would you mind if we stayed at home? I'd like to have a go at cooking the meal – but you'll have to clear out the turkey giblets,' she chuckled, lightening the moment.

So it was settled, and Evelyn agreed to stay at Apple Tree Cottage over the festive period.

Christmas Day dawned crisp and sunny. With a heavy heart, Katherine threw the red cotton tablecloth her mother had made over the oak dining table. The night before, she'd washed the seasonal dinner service that only saw the light of day over the Christmas period. She laid the prized white, gilt-edged china plates, bordered with green holly and red berries, on the dark green table mats, remembering her mother's pleasure every year as she stood back to admire the total effect with the red candles in their silver candlesticks.

She stood, tears rolling down her cheeks, wondering how she would get through the day. The dining room door opened and Evelyn came in from the kitchen, having prepared the vegetables for lunch, and stood alongside her, putting her arms around her.

'We'll get through it,' she said softly, and kissed Katherine's wet cheek.

After breakfast in the kitchen, reminiscing over Christmases past, Katherine checked the turkey cooking slowly in the oven, and they exchanged gifts before getting ready to go to church.

They donned their boots and thick winter coats. Katherine put on the matching brown faux fur hat and cravat, a present from her aunt and, after scraping the frost from the Mini's windows, they set off slowly down the lane for the short drive to St. Oswald's. Katherine's heart was heavy at the prospect of returning to the church where, only a few months ago, she'd attended her mother's funeral. She glanced at her aunt's sombre face. Why was she putting herself through this anguish? But she had to carry on as normal, doing all the things she and her mother had done together, and the Christmas Day observance had been important to both of them.

The hoar frost glistened on the hedgerows as they bumped down the cobbled lane leading to the backwater where the small, thirteenth century, black and white half timbered church nestled alongside the Bells of Peover Inn and the village school.

Katherine was fortunate to find a parking space near to the lych-gate and, carrying the wreath that Evelyn had lovingly assembled with the holly and mistletoe from her garden, took her aunt's arm.

In the churchyard, they trod gingerly down the path that had been sprinkled with cinders to where her mother was buried.

Huddled together in silence beside the grave, unable to

control their tears, Katherine broke away from her aunt and knelt down on the frozen ground, the cold striking her knees through her black velvet cord trousers. As she propped the wreath against the newly erected headstone, the bells began to peel. Pulling off her gloves, Katherine put a hand to her mouth, kissed the tips of her fingers and touched the gold lettering on the grey granite that spelled out her mother's name. 'God bless – I miss you,' she whispered and, taking hold of her aunt's outstretched arm to steady herself, she rose to her feet.

They stood for a while to compose themselves, turned away and walked back to the church for the service.

There were many sympathetic words and glances from those in the congregation who remembered Nancy and the wonderful floral wedding arrangements she'd bedecked the church with over many years. Fighting to keep control of her emotions, Katherine focused her eyes on the twinkling lights on the tall Christmas tree that reached up to the dark oak beams, not wanting to look directly at the chancel where her mother's coffin had rested. Despite the lump in her throat, she managed to join in some of the carols. But her mind drifted away to times she'd sat with her mother, Aunt Evelyn and Uncle Ted in the boxed-pews where, if you failed to latch the door at the end of the pew and leant on it, it would swing open and deposit you in a heap in the aisle. Katherine smiled, recalling such an event when, as a young child, her mother had scooped her up, dried her tears and sat her back in the pew.

After the service as they were leaving the church, the vicar, his family and many of the parishioners known personally to them, offered words of comfort and reiterated the invitations they'd extended at Nancy's funeral – to call on them whenever they felt the need.

Katherine found their concern heartwarming – and it was also a relief that no one mentioned her visit to America, despite the fact, so her aunt had told her, that it was common knowledge in the village that she had gone there to meet her father.

Back at the cottage, after their Christmas lunch – turkey with all the trimmings that Katherine had proudly presented, followed by Evelyn's homemade plum pudding and brandy sauce – they drank a toast of white wine to Nancy and Ted, and shed more tears before settling down on the settee to listen to the Queen's speech on television – a tradition Katherine had grown up with.

She glanced at the telephone, willing her father to ring, apprehensive of making the call herself in case Ellie – or Patrick – answered. She nestled her head back into the settee's feathered cushion and closed her eyes, feeling sleepy as a result of all the food she'd consumed.

'How about we crack the bottle of Advocaat? Nancy would have had it open long ago,' Evelyn laughed. 'Do you remember when you were little, we used to let you have a taste? You really liked it.'

Katherine opened her eyes. 'I do remember sticking my finger in the dregs at the bottom of the glass and licking them

off and, if I was lucky, I'd get the cherry on the cocktail stick …
Allowing me to do that gave me a lifelong taste for Advocaat.
It's still my favourite liqueur.'

As Evelyn made to rise from the settee, Katherine put a
restraining hand on her knee. 'I'll get the bottle.'

'I put it in the left-hand cupboard in the Welsh dresser…
Sorry I forgot to get the cherries. Let's use your mother's sherry
glasses; they hold more than the liqueur ones,' she giggled,
feeling slightly tipsy after the two glasses of wine.

Katherine poured a goodly amount of Advocaat into the
sherry glasses, and they sat quietly, lost in their own thoughts.
The ticking clock and glowing log fire induced a somnolence
that soon closed Evelyn's eyes. Katherine gently prized her half-
full glass from her fingers, and placed it alongside the wooden
bowl of nuts and the tangerines on the oak side-table.

She looked at her watch. Three-thirty – ten-thirty in Asbury
Park. Dare she risk making a call?

Rising carefully from the settee in order not to disturb her
aunt, she walked over to the Welsh dresser where the
telephone sat among an array of Christmas cards. But before
she could pick it up, it rang, making her jump. Grabbing the
receiver she put it to her ear.

'Merry Christmas, Katherine!'

Her heart sank. It wasn't her father – it was Alex.

'Katherine?' he said tentatively.

'Hello, Alex,' she said flatly, not inclined to add, 'Happy
Christmas to you too.'

'I thought… today… Well, I know how difficult it must be for you without Nancy.'

Katherine could hear voices and laughter in the background.

'I'm in the Bells,' he explained. 'On my own… Excellent lunch!'

Katherine sighed inwardly, thinking how fortunate it was that Evelyn had cancelled their table at the Bells. Alex was the last person she would want to share the day with. She wondered why he wasn't with Josie and, picturing him sitting all alone eating Christmas lunch, annoyingly she felt a moment of pity.

'I thought,' Alex went on, 'seeing I'm so close, I could…'

'No!' Katherine interrupted, pre-empting his request to come to the cottage. 'I appreciate the thought… It has been a difficult day, but Aunt Evelyn is with me… Today is not the time to visit.'

'Are you saying there's *going* to be a time to visit, then? I'm really missing you, Katherine.'

She swallowed hard, picturing Alex's handsome face – a face that for so long she had adored. But although she'd been lonely these past weeks, it was Patrick not Alex she was missing.

'No. That's not what I'm saying,' she told him firmly. 'It's best for both of us if we leave things as they are.'

'Right!' he said tersely. 'Then I'll bid you adieu,' and he slammed the phone down. Pursing his lips, he picked up the receiver again immediately and dialled. 'Happy Christmas, Josie! Just thought I'd check to see how *your* day's panning out?' he said jovially.

'I gather that was Alex?' Evelyn said, roused from her slumber by the call.

'It was – and he put the phone down on me. Would you believe he's in the Bells? He wanted to come round!'

'And you said "no". Probably for the best. I'd have given him a piece of my mind. Who was he with?'

'He said he was on his own – but let's *not* start feeling sorry for him,' Katherine added, in response to her aunt's, 'Oh dear'. 'I bet Josie will feature somewhere in his Christmas jollifications… I really don't know why he bothered to ring.'

Evelyn picked up her Advocaat from the table. 'Men aren't good at accepting rejection, Kathy. Not without putting up a fight. I daresay he'll keep pestering you for a while… No hope you'll get back together, then?' she queried, wondering if life wouldn't be easier for everyone if things got back to how they had been before Katherine discovered her father's letter.

'Not a chance… *Don't* feel sorry for him,' Katherine reiterated. 'He won't be alone for long I can assure you.' She poured herself another glass of Advocaat. 'I think I'll call Dad… Would *you* like to say hello?'

Evelyn shifted uncomfortably on the settee, put down her glass, picked up one of the hand-embroidered cushions and punched it back into shape. 'I… er…' she said, somewhat flustered.

'Don't worry – if you don't feel up to it yet,' Katherine said kindly, noting the rosy glow rise from her aunt's neck to her cheeks.

Evelyn lumbered up from the settee and straightened out the pleats of the new skirt she'd bought in an attempt to cheer herself up. She looked with sadness at her beautiful niece; her tumbling red hair, creamy complexion, and green eyes enhanced by the emerald polo-neck cashmere sweater. She was so like Nancy, it was heartbreaking.

'I think today is for you and Michael,' she said softly. 'But do give him my regards. I *will* speak to him… but not today, Kathy. I'll leave you to it. When you've finished, I'll make us a nice cup of tea… and I'll cut the Christmas cake,' she said, as she bustled out of the room.

To Katherine's surprise and pleasure, it was Patrick who answered the telephone.

'I was hoping you'd call, Katherine.' His voice was strained.

She felt her legs weaken, and in imminent danger of them giving way, sank down onto the cane chair that stood beside her by the Welsh dresser.

'I didn't… couldn't bring myself to phone *you*, Katherine… not knowing how you feel about…' His voice tailed off.

Katherine felt a surge of excitement.

'It's fine… really. Happy Christmas, Patrick,' she said, her heart thudding madly.

'Happy Christmas to you too, Katherine,' he replied, with obvious relief. 'But I guess it's been a difficult one for you without your mom?'

'Yes... but Aunt Evelyn's here with me. We're managing. We kept up the family tradition and went to church this morning. I put a holly wreath on Mother's grave.'

'That must have been hard. Merry and I will be going to Barbara's grave. I wish you weren't so far away from us, Katherine.'

Her eyes misted. 'So do I,' she said softly. 'How... how is Dad? Can I speak to him?'

There was silence for a while and Katherine felt alarmed by the delay in Patrick's reply.

'He's not feeling too well right now, that's why he hasn't phoned – didn't want to worry you. But I thought I should call you. He...'

'What's wrong? Tell me, please,' Katherine interrupted.

'He's had a fall... this morning. He tumbled out of bed. It shook him up quite a bit, so I got him to lie down. I'll get him to speak to you from the bedside phone. Hang on.'

Katherine heard Meredith's voice in the background.

Patrick came back on the line. 'Someone else anxious to speak with you, Katherine. Can't hold her off any longer.'

'Merry Christmas, Aunt Katherine,' Meredith gushed excitedly.

'Merry Christmas to you too,' Katherine said, visualizing Meredith's radiant, happy face. 'Have you had many presents?'

'There's lots under the Christmas tree, Aunt Katherine – your parcel is there. But Gram says I'm not allowed to open *any* presents until we've eaten.'

'Well, you'll have to contain your curiosity for a while longer,' Katherine laughed.

'I have *squeezed* the parcels when no one was around,' Meredith confided.

Katherine smiled. 'I remember doing that when I was a girl.'

'Books are easy-peasy to guess, aren't they? But if stuff is in a box...' and Meredith lowered her voice, '... then you have to shake the parcel. Yours is in a box – and it rattles! Can you give me a teeny clue, Aunt Katherine?'

Katherine laughed. 'Now, that would be spoiling the grand opening, Meredith – but I'm certain you'll like what's in there.'

It had taken Katherine a shopping trip to London to purchase a model of Buckingham Palace, and other souvenirs of the city that Meredith had expressed an interest in.

She'd caught the train from Crewe and made a sentimental visit to Harrods, where she and her mother had lunched on a previous shopping trip in the spring. It brought back many happy memories of the day's outing, but never in her wildest dreams could she have foreseen that within the year, her mother would be dead and she would be back shopping for presents for her father and his family!

She'd finally settled on an expensive Arran sweater for her father, and a small Celtic brooch for Ellie, knowing that she would be impressed by the Harrods monogrammed presentation box. For Patrick, she'd decided on a blue Macclesfield silk tie and matching handkerchief set.

Her father's voice talking to Meredith jolted her back.

'Say goodbye to Katherine,' he was telling Meredith kindly.

'Bye, Aunt Katherine,' Meredith said. 'Have a swell day – and please, please come and see me soon. Promise?'

Katherine frowned. She desperately wanted to be back in Asbury Park but didn't want to delude Meredith.

'Well … I still have a lot of sorting out to do here. But when I get back on track I'll give it my full attention, Meredith.'

'Promise?' Meredith persisted.

'Promise!' Katherine replied.

'That's good to hear,' she heard Michael say. 'Now, will you please clear the line, Merry. Go see if you can help your grandmother.'

'Bye!' Meredith threw in a parting shot.

'She's been pestering to speak to you since she got up – *very early*. Then I stupidly toppled out of bed – not the best start I've had to Christmas Day,' her father told her.

'But you're all right now?'

'Sure am, honey,' he said lightheartedly, disguising the fact that his bruised ribs were painful and he still felt a little light-headed. 'I'm looking forward to lunch and the grand gift opening. Have to make the best of it for Meredith … I hope it was okay to send you the dollars to buy something you really want?'

'Dollars are most acceptable – you were *very* generous, Dad. I shall exchange them for sterling in the New Year. There are quite a few kitchen items I need. Who knows, my New Year resolution could be to start baking bread and cakes.'

'Following in Evelyn's footsteps? I don't remember your mom being too domesticated,' Michael laughed.

'Well, she had to learn pretty fast when I came along.' Katherine screwed up her face, immediately sorry that she'd made the insensitive remark without thinking. She heard her father sigh.

'I guess so, Katherine... Difficult for you today, huh?'

'Aunt Evelyn and I managed – somehow – to get to the point where the debris of the dinner is now waiting to be cleared away. She's making a pot of tea, then we'll get stuck in to the excellent Christmas cake, laced with plenty of brandy, that she's always baked for Mother and me...' Katherine's voice tailed off.

'I wish I was there with you.' Michael's voice dropped to a whisper. 'I wish we could be together, Katherine. Have you given any more thought to coming over here to work?'

Katherine looked around the cosy living room. Every nook and cranny reflected her mother's input. Could she *really* leave this behind and start afresh... Could she? But to be near to her father – and Patrick? Her heart missed a beat.

'I *do* like the idea of working for a magazine in New York.'

'And I'm sure you'd fit in just great,' Michael said enthusiastically. 'You prepared for the fast lane? I remember Manchester was quite a busy city – but New York? As much as I love the place, after a couple of days in town for the shows, I'm sure glad to get back to Asbury.'

Katherine's heart quickened at the thought of Broadway;

the shows, the museums, picnic lunches in Central Park – or Charlie's Steak House. It was very appealing.

'I'm sure I'd love it – and if I didn't, I could maybe try for a provincial paper.'

'We have a good one right here in Asbury, Katherine!'

'But don't you think it wise to put some distance between me and Ellie? There's an awful lot to consider, isn't there? It's not going to be easy.'

'I guess you're right, Katherine,' Michael conceded.

'Is Ellie within earshot?' Katherine said tentatively.

'Nope. She's cooking up lunch.'

'How *are* things between you since she told you about Patrick?'

Michael lowered his voice as Meredith hovered in the background. 'We go on as normal – I have my precious Merry. She's right here beside me,' he said, making the point that it was difficult for him to elaborate further.

Katherine could hear Meredith chuckling in the background. She'd been surprised, and delighted, by the bond they'd formed in so short a time, helped in no small measure by Meredith's endearing response to *her* from the moment they'd met.

'I admire your fortitude, Dad. What a tangled web! Still, I'm sure we aren't the only family with skeletons in the cupboard… I appreciate how difficult it is for you, but stick with it. I *will* give serious thought to making the move,' she added with conviction, suddenly feeling they ought not waste any more time apart. *He* needed her support – *they* needed each other.

'So… 1978 could be *our* year?' Michael said happily.

'Let's hope so… I'll keep you in the picture. We *will* get through this, you know.'

'Together?'

'Together!' Katherine echoed. 'Enjoy the day. Next year we could be enjoying Christmas lunch together,' she said positively. 'Give Meredith a kiss and a hug for me and – give my love to Patrick. I'll see you all sometime next year.'

A lump rose in her throat as she replaced the receiver and became aware that her aunt was back in the room.

A pot of tea and the Christmas china cups and saucers were laid out on the coffee table, alongside two generous slices of Christmas cake.

'I guess – from that – you've made a decision about your future?' Evelyn smiled at her from the comfort of the armchair beside the crackling fire.

'I guess I have,' Katherine replied, thankful, from her aunt's expression, that she appeared to have her blessing.

CHAPTER 14

SPECULATION OVER the feasibility of a move to America gathered momentum between Christmas and New Year. Katherine knew of a prestigious weekly magazine – the *New York* – that, apart from news, covered a wide variety of topics, including fashion, lifestyle and entertainment, all of which she had experience of.

She drafted several letters to the editor setting out her qualifications and the reason for the move from England, before finally coming up with a C.V. she was satisfied with. Nurturing the same feelings of trepidation and optimism she'd felt when posting her first letter to her father, she went to the post office, got the letter weighed, and watched as the counter clerk applied the stamp and airmail sticker, then dropped it into the mail bag. Once again she was back to the waiting game!

She decided to be confident and, in the firm belief that everything would work out right, she set about sorting out possessions for the move – essentials and sentimental items that could realistically be shipped out to America.

Initially, she planned to lease a small apartment in New York, and knew, in that respect, that she could rely on Patrick's help, pushing to the back of her mind the problem of how their relationship might develop. At this stage, she had to concentrate on the issues involved in relocating.

When she received a telephone call from Angela, with a query about the central heating system in the flat, Angela asked her how she was getting on away from the *Argus*. Katherine told her of her plans to move to New York, and was heartened by Angela's response.

'New York! I hope you get the job!' she said enthusiastically. 'It has to be more interesting than the *Argus*.' She went on to volunteer the information that everyone in the Reporters' Room thought Alex was in *very* low spirits – which was his own fault for being stupid enough to dally with Josie.

Katherine had had no intention of enquiring about the current situation between Alex and Josie, but Angela went on eagerly to inform her that there was a distinct 'frostiness' between the two of them and, she perceived, whatever their relationship *had* been, it was now at an end.

'He's been a fool to lose you, Kathy,' was her parting shot.

Katherine took no satisfaction from the news that things were not going well between Alex and Josie. It didn't matter to her anymore. Nothing mattered now apart from getting to America as soon as possible.

Two days after her conversation with Angela, sitting at the dining table sorting through the photographs, letters, and greetings cards that she'd squirreled away over the years, she received a telephone call from Alex. She braced herself.

'Hi,' he said breezily, as though nothing had changed between them. 'Thought I'd see how you're getting on out in the sticks.'

There was silence as Alex awaited Katherine's response.

She remained silent.

'I've got some interesting info for you,' he continued, undeterred. 'Heard on the grapevine there's a job coming up on the *Congleton Herald* – suit you down to the ground. Just the ticket! If I were you, I'd get on the blower to Reggie and …'

Katherine's face tightened. 'Angela's told you, hasn't she?' she snapped angrily.

'Did you tell her *not* to tell anyone that you've got some crazy notion of working in New York?' Alex snorted. 'And …' he faltered. 'There's something else you should consider… Josie's talking about leaving the *Argus* … moving to London. And I'm not discouraging her, Katherine.'

'And you think I'll come trotting back when, or if, she leaves? It's *over*, Alex,' she said softly. 'I'm going to America to be near to my father – whether or not I get a job on the *New York*.'

There was silence again for several seconds before Alex responded.

'In that case I can only wish you bon voyage!' he retorted truculently.

Katherine replaced the receiver. Would she ever see Alex again? She shivered. Ending any relationship was complex. She made herself a mug of coffee and returned to the task at the dining table. She selected photographs of Alex and put them to one side.

The following week, Katherine received a promising letter from the editor of the *New York* inviting her to drop in and see him on her next trip to the States. Overjoyed, she telephoned her father and gave him the good news – her enthusiasm undeterred by Ellie's indifference as she handed the phone over to Michael.

'That's wonderful news, Katherine,' her father said and, lowering his voice, told her he would phone at a more appropriate time – which Katherine took to mean when Ellie was not around.

Full of excitement and renewed energy, she set about sorting out the kitchen. It was impractical and not essential to transport all the fine china her mother had collected over the years; she couldn't bear the thought of parting with any of the delicate tea and coffee cups and saucers. But she had to be realistic. She decided to select the Wedgwood dinner service and her mother's favourite – the Christmas holly berries.

Within an hour of speaking to her father, she received a call from Patrick. Her legs weakened at the sound of his voice.

'Pop's given me the good news, Katherine,' he said, with obvious pleasure. Her heart began to race. 'I… I don't want you to think I'm acting out of hand here, but if you do land a job on the *New York*, I have a business acquaintance in Manhattan who has a vacant apartment above his antique shop. I could speak with him … if you wish?'

'Thank you … That would be great,' Katherine managed to respond.

'Then … you don't mind … You don't have any reservations?'

'No reservations, Patrick … We have to put the past aside and get on with life, don't we?' she said, wondering just *how* or *if* that was possible.

'Good!' The relief in Patrick's voice was palpable. 'Then I'll make some enquiries.'

'And I'll get things moving this end – possibly a flight over next week to have a look at the set up on the *New York*,' she said, bursting with happiness.

'Shall I meet you – show you the apartment?' Patrick asked.

Katherine hesitated. 'Thanks for the offer, but I think I ought to go it alone for a few days – independent girl-about-town,' she laughed. 'If the prospects look favourable on the magazine, I'll give you a call and you can come up to town and I can have a look at the apartment – or I could go to view it on my own?'

'Wouldn't dream of letting you do that – independent girl-about-town or not!' Patrick responded. 'You'll book in at the Ameritania?'

'Definitely.'

'Then I'll see you Stateside … Good luck, Katherine.'

'I feel my luck *is* running good – but it's completely out of my hands.'

'Kismet?'

'Kismet… Karma? Call it what you will. I have strong vibes that I'm doing the right thing, Patrick – and that everything is going to work out for me.'

'And for Pop!'

'For all of us… Fingers crossed for your mother!'

'I'm sure Pop and I can smooth that path for you.'

A sudden sense of foreboding curbed Katherine's elation.

'I hope so,' she said, wishing she could share his conviction – and wishing too that she was not party to the duplicity she shared with her father about his paternity.

'What's happened to Kismet, Katherine? Keep your eye on the ball – don't weaken at first base,' he laughed. 'Afraid I have to go now. Have to get back to the gallery. Meredith sends her love – she misses you… I'll see you very soon – I hope. Goodbye, Katherine. Take care – and *don't worry.*'

Katherine stood for a while hugging the phone to her chest. Was it too good to be true? Was it really going to be so simple?

Fifteen minutes later, as she was tugging on her black leather boots to trudge through the grey slush to Aunt Evelyn's – having decided not to risk the car – to acquaint her of the latest development, the telephone rang. Could it be her father again? She rushed over to the phone and picked up the receiver.

Ellie's brittle voice assaulted her ear.

'*So* – you intend to muscle in on my family?' she snapped.

Katherine stood transfixed and took a deep breath.

'I beg your pardon?' she managed to say calmly – ready to move off first base.

'Patrick tells me you intend to make your home over here – in New York?'

'That's correct. If things work out and I manage to get a job on the...'

Ellie cut her short. 'You're making a *big* mistake... leaving your country... your family.' Ellie's angry words tumbled out.

Katherine pictured her distorted, flushed face.

'The *only* family I have here is my aunt – and I have her blessing,' she replied.

In the silence that followed, Katherine wondered if Ellie had put the phone down on her, but she hadn't heard any click.

'Well... consider this.' Ellie's voice was shaky. 'Before you make any such move, you should be aware that Michael's heart is in a pretty precarious state – he wanted to spare you that information... Any... *any* added stress in his life – and he's had quite enough already when *you* turned up... I'm sure you can figure out the consequences for yourself.'

Katherine held her breath, wondering what Ellie's next ploy would be.

'And furthermore,' she continued icily, 'you should be made aware that *when* your father passes over, you won't *have* a family in Asbury Park to be a part of!'

Katherine gasped involuntarily, now certain of what Ellie was going to say.

'You should be made aware that Patrick is *not* your brother… half-brother… whatever… And *Meredith*, therefore, is *not* your niece.' Ellie spoke with undisguised triumph in her voice. 'Your mother wasn't the *only* woman to find solace in the arms of a lonely serviceman. I'll leave you to figure it out! You needed to be told the truth to stop you making a big mistake… And I rely on your integrity *not* to reveal this conversation to Patrick or Michael and destroy *my* family.'

Katherine heard a click on the line as Ellie abruptly ended the call, pre-empting Katherine's dilemma as to whether to tell her she already knew about Patrick and that it made *no* difference to her plans.

Sitting down, she put her face in her hands and began to cry. When her tears were spent, she calmly evaluated Ellie's call. It was obvious Ellie didn't know that her father had already told her of her confession. Nothing had changed from her perspective, and it seemed unlikely, after her warning, that Ellie herself would reveal the truth to Patrick – and certainly her father wished it to remain secret.

But as she trudged down the lane to Rose Cottage, the doubts began to creep in. She felt unsure, on reflection, of just how far Ellie *would* go in order to prevent her move to America.

Evelyn opened the door of the cottage as Katherine lifted the latch of the wrought iron garden gate and slithered up the winding path.

'I ran out of salt to sprinkle on the patches of ice that are left. Do be careful,' Evelyn called to her.

Ushering her into the hall, Evelyn's brow creased as she registered Katherine's dejected expression. She took her niece's coat and boots from her, and put them in the cupboard beneath the stairs.

'Problems?' she ventured, as they crossed the hall to the sitting room.

Katherine pulled a face. 'Big problems – *very* big,' she said, and they settled on the sofa.

'Tea first or after?' Evelyn asked.

'After. But I'll need something stronger,' Katherine said, managing a weak smile as Evelyn headed toward the kitchen.

She returned with a quarter-full bottle of Advocaat and two sherry glasses. 'May as well polish this off,' she laughed, setting the glasses down on the coffee table and pouring a good measure into them.

Evelyn listened intently as Katherine related Ellie's telephone call, and outlined the predicament she now faced. How *would* Ellie react if she went ahead with her plan to move to New York? Would she go as far as to actually tell Patrick that Michael was not his father? That she was not his sister? 'And there's Meredith to consider… Can I really take that risk, Aunt Evelyn?' she said miserably, and sank her head into her hands.

Evelyn put her arms around her. 'I don't think Ellie would take the risk of losing her son by giving him the devastating news that Michael isn't his father,' she said reassuringly. 'Surely she can't be that vindictive. Call her bluff, Kathy. *Tell* her that Michael has already told you! If she *is* jealous and unhinged enough to tell Patrick, then it wouldn't be your fault, would it?' She looked at her niece's grief-stricken face; brushed the hair from her eyes and kissed her on the cheek. 'What *matters*, Kathy,' she said tenderly, 'is that you and Michael should be together – and as soon as possible if he is as ill as Ellie makes out. Isn't that what you and Michael want more than anything else?'

'Yes… but…' Katherine wiped the tears from her cheek with the back of her hand.

'No buts – don't weaken, Kathy. If you are offered a job in New York, then for goodness' sake, *take it*. You mustn't hesitate!'

Katherine took her aunt's hand. 'Thank you… That's made me feel much better.'

She smiled. 'I can always rely on good advice from you.'

Evelyn squeezed Katherine's hand. 'I'm only giving you the advice Nancy would have given to you, Kathy.'

Back home, after turning everything over and over until her head felt ready to burst, Katherine went to bed. But tossing and turning, sleep evaded her. Her aunt had made the solution sound so simple. She wished with all her heart she could be as confident. Switching on the bedside lamp, the illuminated hands of the alarm clock were at two twenty. She gazed lovingly at the photographs of her mother and father that she'd put in a dual silver frame and placed on the bedside table beside Meredith's Statue of Liberty.

Meredith? Poor Meredith. She'd had enough hurt in her young life losing her mother. *Her* welfare should be paramount. Could she, *should* she take the risk of Ellie keeping the lid on the can of worms?

Giving up on sleep, she snuggled down under the duvet listening to the distant hum of traffic on the M6. Her mind in turmoil, she contemplated getting in the car and driving – *anywhere* to get away from everything!

Then the phone rang. At this hour, it had to be a call from Asbury Park.

Jumping out of bed, she dashed barefoot down the stairs – bemoaning the fact that she hadn't got around to putting a phone extension in the bedroom – and picked up the receiver.

'Hello?' she said breathlessly.

'Katherine!' Her father's voice was barely audible. 'I…'

'What is it? What's the matter?' she cried in alarm.

'Patrick… It's Patrick. He…'

Katherine felt her chest tighten. He'd had an accident – or worse. She couldn't speak.

'He knows, Katherine… He knows *everything*,' her father said angrily.

'Ellie *told* him?' Katherine gasped, horrified.

'No, not Ellie. It's much worse, Katherine. It was Merry… She overheard Ellie's call to you… Ellie thought Merry was in her bedroom watching T.V. She…' Michael began to sob.

'Oh God!' Katherine searched for words but her mind was numb. She stood, in shock, shivering in the dark, chilly room.

'Katherine?' Michael appealed sadly.

She tried to clear her head.

'I'm here. How is she?... How is Patrick?... Where are they?' she stumbled on, incoherently.

'They're both in Merry's room.' Michael began to sob again. 'She was hysterical, Katherine... And Patrick? Well... I guess he's trying to stay calm for *her*. We haven't had an opportunity to talk yet,' he said, his voice breaking.

'And Ellie?' Katherine said stonily.

'To be fair, I have to say... she was devastated! She's left the house. Probably gone to Yolande's who, I suspect, has known all along about Patrick.' Michael cleared his throat. 'She'll be back. We have to sort out this mess... At the moment I don't know how it's going to play out. I've been wondering how I can help Patrick and Merry get through this. I think it would be good for them to get away from the house for a while – as soon as possible. We are all in shock right now, Katherine. But I wondered... Merry has been so keen to see England. What say you if I suggest to Patrick they come visit you? And perhaps you could all come back to Asbury? What do *you* think?'

Katherine couldn't think. She felt physically sick. Everything was moving so fast.

'Katherine?' Her father's anxious voice sounded a million miles away. 'If Patrick agrees, and you feel up to it, I'll go ahead and book them a flight to Manchester... Are you okay with this?'

Standing rigid in the darkened room, Katherine looked across to her mother's chair, illuminated by the shaft of moonlight shining through the window. An overwhelming feeling of warmth swept through her. Her taut body began to relax.

'Of course it's all right... More so than you could *ever* imagine,' she replied through her tears.

The following day Patrick telephoned. His voice was flat and he struggled for words.

'I need to know how you really feel about this arrangement of Pop's?'

Katherine gazed round the sitting room and pictured Patrick and Meredith sitting before the log fire she'd lit. Not in her wildest dreams had she envisaged such a scene possible.

'It's the least I can do, Patrick,' she replied, her voice breaking. 'And... I feel that I'm responsible. If I hadn't contacted Father, none of this would have happened.'

Patrick interrupted, his voice stronger. 'Don't even go there. This had to come out – it would have, in time, I'm sure. You and I... we are the innocent ones here. Remember that. Don't beat yourself up, Katherine. Please.'

'It'll be difficult,' Katherine said tearfully.

'Kismet, Katherine,' Patrick said tenderly. 'Hold on to *that* thought. Merry and I will be with you soon.'

CHAPTER 15

TWO DAYS LATER, at Manchester airport, Katherine felt excited and apprehensive in equal measure at the prospect of seeing Patrick again. Every second seemed like a minute; every minute an hour.

Having risen early after a restless night, unable to sit at home any longer, she'd reached the airport well ahead of the scheduled arrival of the connecting shuttle service from Heathrow. She'd watched the bobble-hatted passengers arriving from Switzerland, skis over their shoulders; and the sun-tanned, summer-clad passengers returning from Australia. At last, the information board confirmed the Heathrow flight had landed.

She scanned the first trickle of travellers filtering through the door, walking on or pausing to greet friends and family at the barriers.

Then she saw him. Patrick was trundling a large suitcase, Meredith walked alongside looking anxiously into the crowd. Spotting Katherine, her face lit up. She waved furiously, ran ahead of her father and flung herself at her, tightening her arms around her waist, burying her head in Katherine's coat. Before she relaxed her grip, she looked up.

'I don't care if you're *not* my real aunt … I love you … and Gramps,' she said passionately. 'He'll always be my Gramps,' she added, and pressed her face into Katherine's coat again.

Katherine felt heartbroken. She smoothed Meredith's rumpled hair, lifted her chin and kissed her. Over the top of her head, she was relieved to see the love and affection in Patrick's eyes. Shaking his head sadly, he moved toward them and kissed Katherine on the cheek. Words were superfluous.

Later, at Apple Tree Cottage, after a supper of Cheshire cheese sandwiches, pork pie and pickles – suggested by Evelyn because it had been a favourite of Michael and his buddies – an exhausted, but happy, Meredith was tucked up and soon fast asleep in one of the twin beds in the spare room.

Alone at last, Patrick and Katherine sat in contented silence either side of the crackling log fire; Katherine on the settee, Patrick facing in her mother's armchair. They held crystal tumblers half-filled with the bourbon that Patrick had bought from Duty Free, the ice cubes in Katherine's clinking as she unconsciously twirled it around between her fingers.

'Think you could get used to bourbon on the rocks?' Patrick grinned.

'I'll try – but Advocaat is my tipple.' Her eyes met his. They were warm, inviting. She ran her forefinger around the rim of her glass wanting, but unsure how, to open up the inevitable dialogue and discuss the traumatic events that had brought Patrick to Cheshire. She gazed at him quizzically.

As though reading her thoughts, he placed his glass on the coffee table between them and edged forward on the chair. 'I guess we have a lot of talking to do, Katherine? While Meredith is out of the way! The point of coming over here is to help her through all of this and the least we speak about it...' His voice trailed off. 'But you and I need to go through this, don't we?' he said softly.

Katherine clutched her glass tighter. Her head began to throb, unsure of her part in the unravelling story of deception. Had her father informed Patrick that he'd told her of Ellie's confession before she'd flown home? Had Patrick realised she knew he wasn't her brother when she'd allowed him to kiss her so passionately in the Ameritania Hotel? Her hands began to tremble and she put her glass down.

'If you're ready,' she said weakly. 'But you don't need to if...'

'I *do* need to talk, Katherine,' Patrick interrupted, brushing a hand through his hair. 'I have to get through this... this nightmare... with your help. Nothing will ever change between me and Pop because of what's happened. He's always been a wonderful father – always will be. I love him,' Patrick said emphatically.

'And Meredith?'

'She's gotten over the initial shock to some extent. Right now... she's mighty cross, mixed up about her relationship with Mom. But there's been no change in her relationship with her gramps. She'll bounce back ... given time. It's helped both of us enormously coming over to visit with you, Katherine. I'm grateful.' He leaned toward her. 'But what about you? It must have been an enormous shock finding out you're not a big part of the Donnelly family.'

Katherine eased herself back on the sofa, wondering just how much her father had told him, and how much she should reveal? Her head ached with the uncertainty she'd been wrestling with before and since Patrick's arrival.

Patrick picked up the bottle, poured a good measure of bourbon into his glass and took a big gulp.

'You *knew*, Katherine!' he said tenderly. 'You knew before we went to New York of Mom's confession! I ... I don't know how on earth you managed to cope with that knowledge.' He frowned. 'And I'm not sure Pop did the right thing putting you under that pressure when you were leaving us.'

The tension drained from Katherine's mind and body. Patrick *knew*! The relief overwhelmed her and, for a few seconds, she was incapable of speaking.

'Father reasoned I *should* have the facts before making any move to uproot my life to join him. Because, he said, as a result of Ellie's confession, there was no longer an extended family for me to be part of – a point you've just made. He was aware how fond I'd become of you and Meredith ... and didn't want me to make a decision to leave Cheshire without knowing the truth.' She closed her eyes. 'The hardest part for me was not being able to tell *you* – I gave Father my word that I'd keep the secret.' Picking up her glass with a shaky hand, she took a sip and met Patrick's eyes. 'And I never *would* have told you, Patrick, but… I can't begin to understand how *you* must be feeling knowing Michael is not your father.'

'I was totally distraught, for Pop as much as myself… I tried to reassure him that he would always be my father. And my feelings for Mom?… That's gonna take time. But it was the *after* shock that hit me; the realisation that you and I are not related in any way – and what effect that must have had on you, Katherine. I tell you, I was real mad! But, out of all this, I guess Mom's revelation has backfired on her – because it changes things for you and me… Changes them for the better…'

Katherine's heart raced. She looked into Patrick's searching eyes and could find no words in reply.

'Mom's been scuppered by her insane jealousy,' Patrick said angrily.

Katherine held her breath as Patrick rose from his chair, deftly skirted the coffee table and sat down beside her.

'You know… in the short time we've gotten to know each other… I've grown very close to you. And I'm hoping that these feelings are mutual?'

Katherine put her glass down, took his from his hand and placed it beside hers.

'They *are*,' she said faintly.

Patrick leant forward and she kissed him gently on the lips. His face visibly relaxed. Smiling broadly, he pulled her into his arms. 'It's pretty mind-blowing what's happened between us,' he said, pushing her hair back from her eyes and touching her cheek. 'Out of the blue I have a gorgeous sister come into my life who, from the very first moment we met, I fancied like crazy. Inconceivable scenario to wrestle with. And then – *wow!* It's the stuff movies are made of!'

He cupped her face between his smooth, sensitive hands. His lips found hers and he kissed her passionately. Trembling, they clung to each other.

'Kismet?' she whispered, running her fingers through his hair. 'From the moment I met you I was perturbed by feelings. Was it sibling affection, I asked myself? I was *so* confused. Struggling with the emotion of meeting Father for the first time – trying to deal reasonably with Ellie's antagonism toward me.' Katherine sighed contentedly and snuggled her head into Patrick's chest. 'Experiencing love and hate all in one week? *I* couldn't have written it as a believable story – a dark plot worthy of Shakespeare!' she added, freeing herself from Patrick's arms. 'But the trauma for you all with Ellie's confession!' she said dejectedly.

'It's all right… It's going to be all right, Katherine.' Patrick pulled her to him again.

Seeing the tears in his eyes, she took his hand. 'Father was adamant that nothing *had*, or ever *would* change for him. You'll *always* be his son… You and Meredith are his whole world – were his whole world before all of this happened!' She paused for a few seconds then asked, tentatively, 'And what of your biological father? Would you … have you considered looking for him – as I did?'

'Not a chance,' Patrick said firmly. 'It was different for you, Katherine. *You* had a deep longing. A need to know – to search for the father you believed existed. I *have* mine – and I don't need to search for a stranger who doesn't even know I exist. *No one* could ever take Pop's place – I've told him so!'

'And the future … Ellie? Father told me she'd left the house, possibly to stay with Yolande?'

'I didn't go looking for her – guessed she would be with Yolande. She came back the next day, very remorseful. But the atmosphere at home is pretty strained – limited conversation. We're all skirting round each other. Meredith refuses point blank to speak to Mom. And I'm letting her ride it out her own way. If things don't get straightened out between Pop and Mom, we could possibly convert the space above the gallery for her. Keep the two of them at arm's length. But … she is my mom!' Patrick shook his head sadly. 'I dealt with the situation of Pop and your mother, Katherine. I guess, given time, I can deal with this. But what bugs me is the thought that Mom never loved Pop and only married him to save being disgraced! And I guess Pop has come to that conclusion. I know that he's tried his damnedest to make the marriage work – well, he would, wouldn't he? With his sense of guilt, under the assumption – wrongly as it's turned out – that he was the only guilty party! Maybe … just maybe the trauma caused will serve to soften Mom when she realises what she has to lose.' Patrick hugged Katherine tightly. 'And she has to realise that, despite her best efforts, you *are* and will stay a member of the Donnelly family. Let's hope she will be truly contrite and change her attitude. So, from now on I say we try to put this behind us and start enjoying life. As from tomorrow… I'd like you to show me the Stars and Stripes in the little church that Pop told me about… and the lane with the bridge over the stream where he courted your mom. Meredith is desperate to go to London and, we have to go see Aunt Evelyn,' Patrick said enthusiastically.

Katherine studied his relaxed, elated expression, and wondered if her father had told him of her aunt's implication in this family saga of Shakespearian proportions? She hoped not. She preferred to deal with that particular scene at a less sensitive time.

Patrick took a gulp of his bourbon and smiled broadly. 'And after this week's vacation, Katherine, we have to deal with our plans for the future.' He kissed her tenderly on the lips. 'Right now though, forgive me, m'am, but I need to turn in. Jet lag and bourbon have gotten a firm hold of me,' he grinned.

Katherine returned his kiss. 'Try not to wake Meredith, Patrick – the floorboards creak and groan in these old cottages.'

Patrick rose from the settee somewhat unsteadily.

'Once Meredith's head touches the pillow, be assured she's away with the fairies. A stampede of buffalo on the floorboards wouldn't wake her,' he laughed, raised his glass and took a final sip. 'To tomorrow, Katherine. We'll start the day by calling Pop to tell him not to worry. Everything's going just swell.'

'Perhaps we should wait until after lunch – unless you want to wake him up in the middle of the night?' Katherine said, giving Patrick a contented smile.

That night, lying in bed listening to the rain pattering on the window panes, Katherine felt overwhelmingly happy. The two people she'd grown to love in so short a time were only a few feet away. She was too excited to sleep. Her thoughts drifted to her mother, wondering what she would have made of the extraordinary situation that had arisen from her wartime encounter with her father. It was agonizingly sad that she was not able to tell her of Michael's declaration of undying love for her, and she let her imagination run away with a scenario that if her mother had not died, then – as a result of Ellie's confession – she and Michael could have been reunited. She sighed, aware that she was posing a hypothetical question – but she could dream, couldn't she?

The light from the landing, left on so that Patrick and Meredith could find their way to the bathroom, shone through the fanlight over the bedroom door. It illuminated the wardrobe, where Katherine had found the box containing the letter that had so dramatically altered the course of her life. She told herself firmly that she had to look forward from now on. The past could not be altered, but would forever remain the epicentre of her life to come. Pulling the patchwork quilt that her mother had worked at for many a month, tight under her chin, she snuggled down, closed her eyes and slept the deep sleep of the contented – a state that had eluded her since first opening the new chapter of her life.

The week that followed was one of the most hectic, but happiest, of Katherine's life. Sharing Meredith's pleasure and wonderment as she experienced her 'English' adventure; cosseted and cuddled by Aunt Evelyn; playing Pooh Sticks from the bridge over the stream where Michael and Nancy had once stood as lovers.

They made a poignant visit to St. Lawrence Church, Over Peover, where Michael and his comrades had worshipped alongside General Patton. Patrick photographed the Stars and Stripes hanging on the wall, and other places Evelyn told him had been special to his father and Nancy during their all too brief courtship.

Patrick, at Michael's request, asked to visit Nancy's grave at Over Peover. Leaving Meredith with Evelyn, happily helping her make scones for tea, they went to the florist where Patrick bought two long-stemmed red roses. They stood together before the grave, the chill wind sweeping across the exposed churchyard from the fields beyond, blowing Katherine's hair into a tangle across her face. Shivering, she gazed at the headstone, the holly wreath still in position. Patrick pulled her to him, and brushed the strands of hair from her eyes, before bending down and placing one rose through the wreath. Standing up, he handed the other to Katherine and gave her a long, lingering kiss.

'From Pop,' he said, and kissed her again more passionately. 'That was from me,' he murmured into her hair. 'I love you, and I want us to be together, Katherine.' She looked up and met his eyes, full of tenderness and yearning. She stroked his cheek. 'We will be… I promise,' she murmured.

They went back to Evelyn's and warmed up beside a roaring fire in the sitting room, while she and Meredith fussed around handing out warm cherry scones, topped with homemade strawberry jam, that Meredith had helped bake.

'Aunt Evelyn's written down the recipe for me – I'm going to make some for Gramps when I get home,' she told them proudly. 'But I'll have to take a pot of English strawberry jam back with me, won't I?' she said happily.

Early evening, Evelyn cooked traditional roast beef, Yorkshire pudding, roast potatoes and all the trimmings. A meal, she told them, much requested by Michael and his friends during their short stay in Cheshire.

Everything fell naturally into place. Sensitive to Meredith's feelings – and aware of just how easy it was for children to pick up on 'vibes' between adults – Katherine and Patrick held back from outward shows of affection, and contented themselves with cuddling up on the sofa in the evening, resisting the temptation of a bedroom tryst once Meredith was soundly asleep.

Katherine tried to pack in as much sightseeing for them as was possible in the time available.

They'd taken the train to Chester, which proved a big

success. Meredith and Patrick were captivated by the black and white Tudor architecture and the Roman history, and enjoyed walking high up on the city walls. They ended the day with a sail down the River Dee and a fish and chip supper, a must that Michael had insisted Patrick and Meredith had to experience for themselves – stressing not to forget the mushy peas!

It was arranged that the sightseeing trip to London should be at the end of their visit, before flying home from Heathrow Airport. Katherine decided against accepting Patrick's proposal that she fly back with them. He was obviously disappointed but agreed, on reflection, that whilst Ellie was still living in the house, and there was still much to be resolved, Katherine should take time arriving at a decision for her long-term future; whether or not to seek employment in New York or, based upon the situation with Ellie, consider looking for a local paper in the vicinity of Asbury Park. Katherine had several conversations with her father who, although stressing *he* did not wish to pressure her in any way, told her he would be overjoyed if she chose to make the move to be with him.

After taking an early morning train to Euston and depositing the suitcase in left luggage, they embarked on a whirlwind sight-seeing bus tour, taking in the Tower, Houses of Parliament, Westminster Abbey, Hyde Park, and Buckingham Palace – Meredith's specific request.

Returning to Euston to pick up the luggage, they took a black cab to Heathrow Airport. Meredith, snuggled up between her father and Katherine in the back of the cab, hugged a toy bear dressed as a Beefeater, chattering enthusiastically about the day and pleading for a return visit in order to see the Crown jewels and the changing of the guard at the Palace.

Over the top of Meredith's head, Patrick gave Katherine a long, loving look.

At the airport, after the tearful farewell before Patrick and Meredith went through to Departures, Katherine waited to see their plane take off in the sleet and disappear into the grey clouds. With a heavy heart, she made her way to the Domestic Terminal and boarded the shuttle to Manchester, but the sadness she felt slowly evaporated as she focused on her future – a future resting entirely on her father, Patrick and Ellie sorting out and coming to terms with their relationships. When the plane touched down at Manchester, she'd already accepted the fact that she had to take a back seat; curb her desire to be with her father and Patrick without delay, and join them only when the time was right – which she hoped would be sooner than later.

Patrick telephoned to let her know they were back in Asbury Park and that, during his absence, Ellie had agreed to move out of the house and into the apartment above the gallery after the proposed renovations. She would visit the house, but a daily woman would take over her household duties and help with the care of Michael.

Over the weeks, Katherine and her father had frequent

conversations, updating progress on the apartment, and Katherine began packing with confidence. The initial plan was for her to live with the family in Asbury Park, before making any decision to take up employment in New York, or on a regional newspaper.

It was also decided that, when the time came, Aunt Evelyn should fly out with Katherine for a holiday – which would enable her to make her peace with Michael.

Katherine received phone calls from her colleagues on the *Argus* – including one from the editor – but Alex did not get in touch.

Luke, father of the chapel, despite Katherine's protestations, arranged a belated leaving party at The George, Knutsford.

The night of the party she arrived, unaware of who would be there, with a mixture of apprehension and sadness. The *Argus* had been her life, and a final goodbye would require supreme control of her emotions.

The oak panelled room was already crowded when she walked into the smoky atmosphere, thankful it wasn't the room where she'd celebrated her mother's fiftieth birthday. Propping the bar were the editor, Luke and several sub-editors. Her colleagues from the newsroom were seated at tables with representatives from the photographic, advertising and accounts departments. Faces turned toward her as Luke shouted laughingly above the babble: 'Here she is – here's the defector!' Setting his pint mug on the bar, he wove his way between the tables toward Katherine. Glancing round the room, she was relieved to see no sign of Alex – or Josie.

As though reading her thoughts, Luke took her hand. 'Relax, they ain't here, Kathy.' He planted a kiss on her cheek. 'But if I were Alex, I'd move heaven and earth to keep you here,' he said, wrinkling his nose and pushing his gold-rimmed specs up from the tip. 'He's been a fool – and that's a unanimous opinion … But we are all here to drown our sorrows over your impulsive departure, and Randolph has a bottle – nay, several bottles – of respectable champers on ice. He's got a soft spot for you, you know. Doesn't turn up at all the leaving parties, as you well know. He's very selective!'

'I'm honoured,' Katherine laughed, and relaxing, looked across at Randolph grinning at her, holding a bottle of champagne above his head. With an ache in the pit of her stomach, she made her way toward him, delayed en route to receive the kisses, good wishes and expressions of regret from her ex-colleagues.

'Here's my girl,' Randolph said, putting his arm around Katherine's shoulders and handing her an overflowing flute of champagne. His steely-grey eyes softened as he kissed the tip of her nose – to a chorus of 'whoas' and wolf whistles, and the flashing of cameras. 'It'll cost you to keep *that* off the front page!' one of the photographers called jokingly from his table.

'I don't make a habit of kissing my staff – male or female. Unlike some I could mention,' Randolph said, pulling a face and relaxing his grip on Katherine's shoulders. 'Let's find a quiet corner so we can talk,' he whispered, picking up his glass and the champagne bottle.

Randolph found a table in the ante-room and, seated across from Katherine, fixed her with an enigmatic smile. 'Do you want the good news first?' he questioned.

'Leave it till last – I'll go out on a high,' she replied, raising her eyebrows.

'Right.' Randolph topped up her glass.

'You've noticed the two of them are not in attendance?'

'Not unless they're upstairs in the four poster!' Katherine said sardonically.

'Cynical… but I can't blame you for that.' Randolph toyed with the stem of his glass. 'I suppose you heard on the grapevine that Josie was looking to move on to Fleet Street?'

Katherine nodded.

'They're *both* going – got to get jobs first, of course. But that's plan B… It's not news to you that she wanted me to elevate her to Women's Page editor. When I said no to her plan A – didn't like her style – she decided to move on, and when Alex couldn't sway the issue in her favour… well! He has many contacts on Fleet Street – but you remember he came to us because he was disenchanted there? Maybe it will work out for the two of them, who knows? But the speed with which they welded – I have serious doubts.'

Katherine had listened in silence, surprised that she felt not a flutter of resentment, or jealousy, toward either of them.

'I'm sure they'll slot in well,' she said. 'I was well aware that Josie had designs on Alex. Can't speak for him. Never saw any signs – but who knows?'

'Not bothered then?'

'Not at all,' she confirmed, picking up her glass. 'Let's raise a glass to them, shall we?'

Randolph laughed loudly. 'This means, of course, that when the two of them hit the high road, you could come back … I *don't* want to lose you, Kathy,' he said seriously.

Katherine smiled and touched his hand. 'I'm grateful for that, Randolph, but it's not just Alex and Josie – I *have* to be with my father. I'm sure you understand – finding him after all these years? He's a sick man. There's no knowing how many years he has left,' she said forlornly.

Randolph smiled sympathetically. 'Well, I had to try, and I do wish you well.' He put his hand inside his jacket pocket, pulled out an envelope and a slim, cream box and placed them on the table between them.

He tapped the envelope. 'Your *glowing* reference and a cheque – the balance of the cash raised by your colleagues for your leaving present.' Randolph picked up the box and handed it to her. 'Hope it's to your taste, Katherine.'

Katherine lifted the lid, embossed with the name of a local jeweller, and revealed a broad, hinged, silver bangle.

'It's beautiful,' she said, opening the clasp and fitting it onto her wrist.

'Good. The concensus of opinion was that you preferred silver to gold, and silver, I'm reliably informed, is a better metal for engraving purposes. Have a look inside.'

Katherine undid the clasp again, and opened up the bangle.

The fears she'd bottled up of how she would cope with the finality of leaving the *Argus* were uncorked as she read the inscription: '*Your story doesn't end here – good luck from all at the Argus.*' She bit her lip as the unrestrained tears rolled down her flushed cheeks.

'Sorry,' she murmured. 'I have been dreading today!'

Randolph took her hand and put the bangle back on her wrist. 'Our good wishes go with you – you're due some happiness, Kathy. I have a feeling that you won't entirely desert the old country when you cross the pond, and we'll all be pleased to see you back if things don't pan out for you. We'll all miss you around the office!'

Katherine pulled a handkerchief from her jacket pocket and wiped her eyes.

'And for sure I'm going to miss all of you – and I will be back.' She screwed up the damp handkerchief and returned it to her pocket. 'I've decided not to sell the cottage so that I'll have a base in England. I'm exploring the possibility of holiday lets and, if things don't work out in America – but hopefully they will – then I'll have a home to come back to.'

Randolph squeezed her hand. '*Things* will work out for you, I'm sure. Positive thinking!' He released Katherine's hand and picked up the champagne. 'Now, let's get back to the rabble and enjoy ourselves.'

As the day for her departure drew nearer, all ends were tied up with the letting agent, and the boxes of effects she was taking with her had been handed over to the dispatchers, Katherine's worries receded. Her excitement mounted, matched by

Evelyn's who, having rehearsed over and over what she intended to say to Michael, began to relax and look forward to her first flight across the Atlantic.

Excitement was also building up in Asbury Park. Patrick and Meredith were to meet their flight in New York, and had booked them all in at the Ameritania for a few days to show Evelyn the sights. Ellie, now installed in the apartment above the gallery, would be keeping an eye on Michael, but would not be there when they arrived. Relationships, her father had told her, were to be kept amicable in the interests of Meredith.

Once again, Katherine found herself sitting in the Departure Lounge, awaiting a flight to see her father. This time without the apprehension of the unknown, but an overwhelming sadness that her mother was not a part of the euphoria she and Aunt Evelyn were experiencing.

AUGUST 1983

Outside the Bells of Peover Inn, diners sat at tables beneath the striped umbrellas that shaded them from the oppressive heat of the sun.

Little attention was paid to the small group emerging from the church, only yards away. The vicar in his black robes; following close on his heels, a striking woman with an abundance of shoulder-length red hair, dressed in a flowing, white cotton sundress, a sheaf of long-stemmed red roses in one hand. The other hand was tightly clasped by a tall, handsome man in grey slacks, white shirt and slim black tie.

Behind the trio was a portly woman in a floral dress, clutching the hand of a child of about three years of age, wearing a pink and white gingham sundress, her curly red hair tied in two bunches by white ribbons. Holding the child's other hand was a slim teenager in tight black jeans and skimpy yellow sun-top, her long, blonde ponytail held in place by a butterfly clasp.

The solemn group gathered together and stood for a few minutes in discussion, before the teenager and the child left the party and walked gingerly down the narrow, uneven flagged path that led to the Inn. Once they were seated at the only unoccupied table, the vicar, carrying a small wooden box, ushered the remainder of the group toward the path leading to the lower churchyard.

'Where's Pop and Mommie gone? Want to go with Mommie!' the child said petulantly, bouncing up and down on her chair and kicking her legs around.

The teenager lifted the child onto her knee, brushed her hand through her curls and kissed her on the cheek.

'Mommie won't be long, Nancy,' she said tenderly. 'When they get back, then you can have a nice cold Coke. Won't that be swell?' she said soothingly.

'With a straw, Merry – can I have a straw?' the child asked, sliding off her knee.

'I guess so – if you're real good and sit still on your chair!' Meredith replied, raising her eyebrows to the occupants of the adjoining table, who'd looked at them enquiringly on hearing their American accents.

The youngest woman in the party of four smiled broadly.

'You've come a long way from home to see the church. Where in America do you live?' she asked.

Meredith prized an empty wine glass that had been left on the table from Nancy's hand, and placed it out of her reach.

'We're from Asbury Park – New Jersey,' she added, seeing a look of puzzlement cross the woman's face.

'Over on holiday?'

'Sort of,' Meredith replied, flustered, wondering how to respond to the question as she viewed the look of expectancy on the woman's face.

'Don't be so nosey, Virginia!' snapped the rotund man with florid cheeks sitting next to the woman. 'Leave the poor girl alone,' he added, quaffing a long draught from his pewter beer tankard.

Meredith noted the hurt expression on the woman's face.

'It's okay, truly,' she said, giving her a sympathetic smile. 'Mom used to live in the village until five years ago, before she came to live with Pop, Gramps and me.' Her voice dropped and she gazed toward the graveyard, tears filling her pale blue eyes. 'We're here… because Gramps died… We've brought his ashes to put in Mom's mother's grave – so they can be together!'

Meredith turned to Nancy whose eyes had closed and was in imminent danger of toppling off her chair. Reaching out, she hoisted the inert child onto her knee.

'My sister, Nancy, is named after Mom's mother,' she volunteered.

'And she would be… *your* grandmother?' the woman queried.

'No… Nancy's grandmother,' Meredith replied, wishing she hadn't embarked on the conversation, and had had the courage to go with the others to the grave to see her grandfather's final resting place. Seeing the woman's baffled expression, she sighed. 'It's a complicated story,' she said and, raising her face to the sun, closed her eyes to fend off further questions.

Her thoughts drifted to her grandfather – whatever grown-up transgression had occurred in the past, he would always be *her* Gramps! She pictured her grandmother, alone in the apartment above the gallery, and felt a tinge of sympathy for her.

After the 'bust-up', after she'd learned from Ellie's phone call to Katherine that Gramps was not her real grandfather – that her real grandfather was some unknown person – she'd retreated to her bedroom bewildered, experiencing emotions she never knew she had; emotions that had suddenly been thrust upon her. And her world totally fell apart. Grownups! What was it all about? She'd cried and cried into her pillow; pushed her father away when he'd followed her, and lay on top of her bed trying to make sense of what she'd overheard. Later her father had returned to her darkened room, switched on the light and sat beside her on the bed.

She'd opened her eyes and looked into his face. His eyes were red – like hers. She was alarmed to see that he, too, had been crying. She'd only ever seen him cry once before – at her mother's funeral.

She sat up and threw her arms around his neck and they wept together. She understood, without any words, that she, her father and grandfather, had had a very big shock – as a result of her grandmother's unforgiving, harsh words on the telephone to Katherine. She understood that, in an instant, their lives had changed forever. What she couldn't understand was how they were going to move forward from the shock they'd all received that day.

When, at last, they'd left the bedroom and gone down to where Gramps and Ellie were sitting in silence, facing each other in the sitting room, Ellie had run to her, weeping. She'd hugged her and said over and over again how sorry she was – that she wasn't aware Meredith was listening to her conversation with Katherine. But Meredith had freed herself from her grandmother's arms and run sobbing to her grandfather.

Those few days before she and her father had flown to England were still raw in her mind. The house was not the secure, happy home that it had been before the bust-up. Everyone was polite to each other – which Meredith suspected was solely for her benefit. Surprisingly, her grandmother's demeanour had softened. She was less abrasive, her eyes softer – and sorrowful. She raised no objection when Gramps made the suggestion they convert the rooms above the gallery into an apartment for her. And that's how they'd moved on. Until the apartment was completed, Ellie had stayed with Yolande, and in the short time before Katherine came to live with them, Angelina – from the diner – had kept an eye on Gramps. In fact, she was now quite a regular visitor to the house, and Meredith suspected she had a soft spot for him!

And so, they'd lived a comparatively contented life. Katherine had taken a job on the local newspaper; she and Pop had married and along came Nancy...

A buzzing bee around her head brought Meredith back from her reverie. She opened her eyes, loosened an arm from around Nancy's warm body and wafted the bee away. Nancy, undisturbed, slept on.

It was wonderful to see Gramps so happy – at least he'd had a few blissful years before the cruel stroke had taken him from them.

Gazing up at the Stars and Stripes and the Union Jack hanging side by side on the gable end of the Inn, Meredith felt a rush of pride.

Gramps hadn't spoken of his time in the war, and she'd never liked to question him. But when she was studying World War II at school, she'd tentatively asked about his experiences in Europe. He wouldn't elaborate on the battle when he was wounded, or on his time in France, but had spoken with great affection about this small corner of Cheshire where he'd met Nancy, and of the Bells of Peover where his 'boss', General Patton, and General Eisenhower – the Allied Supreme

Commander – had met for strategy meetings before the U.S. Third Army moved south for D Day.

Now, here in this idyllic spot, her history lessons became more meaningful. She pictured her grandfather and Nancy walking hand in hand along the Cheshire lanes; sitting – as she herself was now – on the terrace of the Inn. Falling in love; experiencing that warm glow she felt for her boyfriend, Greg, who was missing her back home. But when Gramps left Nancy, it was not for a week or two – it could have been forever when he was plunged into the horrors of war. Such a small word, 'war' – such colossal consequences.

Meredith had looked up the definition of 'war' in her dictionary: 'armed hostilities between nations'. She understood that Hitler was responsible for Gramps' suffering and that the fanatical Nazi ideology had to be eradicated. But her father's involvement in the Vietnam war? And the present war in Iraq?

They'd discussed and contemplated in class, the fear and heartache of mothers, wives and sisters who, throughout the centuries, had stoically watched their loved ones march away to war. If they'd been given a powerful voice, would the course of history have been so brutal? Maybe it was up to her generation to try to influence the strategy for war – idealistically, try to avoid it at all costs!

Hearing distant voices, she turned and looked toward the church. Her father was carefully guiding Katherine down the uneven path toward them.

Meredith hugged the sleeping Nancy to her and smiled

wistfully. Was it naive to hope that the baby boy Katherine was expecting would never have to face the horrors of warfare like her grandfather and father? Surely not! – she reasoned, with the optimism of youth.

END

ABOUT THE AUTHOR

BORN IN NORTH STAFFORDSHIRE, Shirley worked for several years as a news copy-typist in the Reporters' Room of a provincial newspaper, where she met her husband. Later they went into partnership with friends to produce a free monthly newspaper circulating in Cheshire. She now lives in West Sussex with her daughter and family.

Before concentrating on her first novel, *Solace of War*, Shirley had short stories published in women's magazines and The West Sussex Writers' Club Book – *It's an 'Ology*, had a character study read on BBC Southern Counties Radio and poems published in various anthologies.